THE HEALING WAY
By Fran McNabb

ISBN: 978-1-959788-90-4

To Mary LeDoux: Without your encouragement, this book would not have been written. Thank you for your support, and, of course, for your cherished friendship.

CHAPTER ONE

Independence, Missouri, 1853

Douglas Fletcher slid his hand into his leather satchel on the seat of the stagecoach, wrapped his fingers around his pistol, then eased it out of its holster. He never moved the rest of his body or took his gaze away from the masked man harassing the two female passengers across the tiny aisle from him. Why the bandit turned his back to him, he'd never know, but he would take advantage of the man's amateur mistake.

He blew out a big breath, said a prayer to keep everyone safe, grabbed the man from behind, and stuck a gun to his back.

"Don't move or you'll find out what this gun can do." With two other bandits outside the stagecoach, he kept his voice low.

Slowly, the masked bandit raised his hands. Douglas grabbed the gun from the man's hand and stuck it in his waistband, then glanced toward the open door to make sure the others had not heard the scuffle. Luckily, they were too busy rummaging through the passenger bags on the ground.

As quietly as possible, he spun the bandit around and shoved him onto the seat where he'd been sitting. Douglas pulled the mask off his face and shook his head. The man wasn't much of a man, barely old enough to grow the scraggly hair on his face. Douglas felt sorry for the kid, but there was nothing he could do but treat him like the rest of the bandits.

"You move or make a sound and you'll be sorry."

The boy's eyes were huge. He nodded.

With the gun still aimed at the kid, Douglas patted the boy's body to make sure he didn't have another weapon. "Who are those men?"

"My brothers." The kid swallowed. "Sam and Cory."

"Which one gives the orders?"

"Sam, the one with the red bandana."

Douglas glanced at the ladies sitting across from him. "Ladies, are you okay?"

Two ladies, both well dressed, held onto each other's hands. The younger was beautiful, but the older one, probably her mother, was just as attractive.

"We're okay," they said in unison.

Douglas checked the activity once more outside, then turned his attention back to the ladies. "I need something to stuff into this man's mouth and to tie his hands. You wouldn't have something in your bags, would you? My bag is, or was, on the top with the other luggage."

The younger lady hesitated, then pulled out a dainty white handkerchief from a satchel with beads and embroidery. He thought she had earlier introduced herself as Emma O'Hara, but he wasn't sure. He'd been so tired when he boarded the stagecoach, he'd fallen asleep almost immediately. He'd ask her name later.

"Thank you." He took the handkerchief, hating to use it for what he needed to do, and jammed it into the boy's mouth. "Don't move."

"I have something to tie his hands." The elderly lady, who was still digging through a large, embroidered bag, finally pulled out a belt and handed it to Douglas.

"Perfect." Douglas yanked the boy's arms behind his

back, tied them, then pushed him back on the seat. He pulled the boy's gun out of his waistband and spoke to the younger lady. "Have you ever shot a gun?"

She stared at the gun. "Only once."

"That's enough." He put the handle of the gun in her hand and folded her fingers around it. "Don't hesitate to use it if he tries to get up."

"I'm not sure I can . . ."

"Yes, you can. It's your life or his."

The lady paled, but nodded.

Douglas gave her his sweetest, most reassuring smile then turned to the boy. Before he had time to warn him about doing anything stupid, a shout came from outside the stagecoach.

"Charlie, what's taking you so long?"

Douglas put his hand over his mouth to muffle his voice and hoped it was enough to fool Sam and his brother. "I'm coming, Sam."

He looked at the ladies. "Wish me luck."

"Please, be safe," the older lady said. The younger lady gripped the gun with both her hands but said nothing.

Douglas could tell she was terrified. He hated to leave them with the kid, but he had to turn his attention to the men outside the stagecoach.

"Thank you. I will."

He waited for the right moment. When the two brothers kneeling on the ground turned their backs to the coach once again to rummage through the luggage, Douglas signaled the two stage drivers now standing with their hands in the air. Hoping they understood his meaning, he jumped out the coach and landed next to Sam. At the same time both drivers charged the other man.

Douglas grabbed Sam by his shoulders to slam him to the ground, but before he could, Sam swung his right hand and caught Douglas on the side of his left eye. His hat flew into the grass on the side of the trail. Ignoring the pain that shot through his head, he returned the punch and sent Sam to the ground. Once more Sam swung, but this time Douglas jerked back, and the swing missed.

Douglas grabbed his arm, flipped him over face-down in the dirt, then held his hands close to his back. "Don't try to move. I don't want to hurt you, but I will if you don't cooperate."

Glancing at the two drivers, he nodded. "Good job." Sam's brother lay on the ground held down by the knees of both drivers.

"I've got rope in the coach," one of the drivers shouted.

Douglas flipped Sam over and looked directly into his eyes. "Sam, you're lucky I didn't shoot you and your two brothers. I'm not sure how you thought the three of you could rob this stage. You're about as stupid an outlaw as I've ever heard of."

Sam squinted. "You'll be sorry for this."

"We'll see about that."

The man squirmed to get away, but Douglas pushed him harder in the dirt. When the driver brought the rope, he tied Sam's hands as tightly as he could get the rope. Sam didn't look like anyone to take lightly. He'd run the first chance he'd get.

Neither Sam nor his brother said another word. In a way, Douglas felt sorry for them. Men had to reach their last hope in life to rob innocent passengers, but knowing someone could've been seriously hurt, he pushed his feelings aside and helped the stagecoach drivers tie Cory.

"Good job, guys." He looked at the luggage and ladies' apparel spread across the dirt. "We didn't lose anything, but some of these niceties will need to be scrubbed. As soon I get the other guy from the coach, I'll help you tie these two on their horses."

Douglas climbed back to the coach. The lady still held the gun with both hands pointing at Charlie. He smiled and took the gun from her.

"Good job, Miss."

She grabbed her mother's hand. "I couldn't have shot that man."

"I know." He looked at Charlie, still lying on the seat, then back at Emma. "But, he didn't know that." Douglas lifted the boy from the seat and pushed him toward the door. "Ladies, stay inside. I won't be long."

"We can go out and pick up our things." The younger lady had already started to stand.

"The drivers and I will do it. We can't guarantee those men won't break free. You need to stay inside for your safety."

The older lady nodded and touched her daughter's hand.

Douglas helped the drivers tie the three men to their saddles, then tethered the horses to the back of the stage. One driver climbed on top of the stage, aimed his rifle at the three bandits, and warned them he had no qualms about using the gun if they tried to get away.

The coach driver walked over to Douglas and stuck out his hand. "Thank you. I'm not sure what we would've done had you not been on board." He shook his hand over and over again. "You're hurt. That needs to be looked at."

Douglas smiled and finally pulled his hand away from the driver and touched his face. "I think it's okay. I'm glad no one else was hurt. We're close to Independence. Sheriff Victor Sanchez will take care of those three."

Now that things had calmed down, Douglas realized he was bleeding. He rubbed his face against his shoulder. Blood smeared the fabric. *That wasn't smart.*

Shaking his head, he turned to hunt for his hat. It lay under a bush in not too bad a shape. He brushed dirt from the rim, then jammed it back on his head being careful not to get blood on it. He tried to clean away the blood still oozing down the side of his cheek with no success. He gave up, climbed back into the coach, then threw his body back onto the hard seat.

"That was very brave of you, sir," the younger lady said. "I'm Emma O'Hara, and this is my mother, June O'Hara. We introduced ourselves earlier, but I'm not sure you remember. You went to sleep as soon as you entered the coach."

He squinted. "Yes, ma'am, I was exhausted. My name is Douglas Fletcher."

The older lady joined it. "You're our hero."

"Hero? No, ma'am. I'm just a tired traveler eager to get home to my family." Now that he was back in the coach, his head pounded. He stuck his hand into his small satchel and rummaged through his belongings for something to stop the blood.

Emma leaned across the aisle and placed her hand on his face. "You're hurt."

Startled to have the lady touching him, he pushed himself against the seat.

With her hand still on his face, Emma didn't flinch. "You're going to have a horrible bruise and a black eye, but I don't think the gash will need stitches." She pulled another white handkerchief out of her satchel and pressed it against his wound. "It's still bleeding though, but not too much."

He stared at the beautiful stranger who slid to the edge of her seat closer to him and turned his head with her other hand. Still uncomfortable, he leaned away from her.

"Did I hurt you?"

"No, I'm fine." He placed his hand on the handkerchief. In the process he touched the lady's hand. He jerked his hand away, then grabbed the handkerchief again. "Thank you for your concern, but I'll hold this."

Not sure why he was so uncomfortable being that close to the lady, he turned to check on the outlaws out the back window. They were fine. He knew they'd be but he had to have something to look at besides the beautiful lady across from him. He felt rather than saw her slide back onto her seat.

Still holding the handkerchief against the side of his face, Douglas turned and laid his head against the seat back, closed his eyes, and again thanked God no one else was hurt during the unsuccessful holdup. He'd have a black eye, but things could've been a lot worse. Now if the pounding in his head would stop, he could rest a bit before arriving in Independence, Missouri. He couldn't wait to make his way to his ranch.

Fletcher Ranch lay a few miles out of town. It had been over three years since he'd been home. Getting his veterinarian license had taken his full attention. Now he couldn't wait to get to his beloved ranch where his brother Lucas and his wife Abigail were awaiting the birth of their second child. He hoped Lucas would forgive him for leaving the ranch and all its problems on his back.

Studying in New York had been an eye opener. He always knew he loved living on the ranch away from town, but deep inside he wanted to see the world outside of little Independence. Now that he had, he was ready to return to his old life. Knowing he'd be back home with his family kept him going through the grueling last few years of study. He hadn't had much time to socialize with all the lectures, studies, and working alongside experienced veterinarians, but he had managed to enjoy life and even to meet someone he wanted to spend the rest of his life with—not that it would happen. The beautiful blond in New York had another idea.

As usual, just the thought of Lily squeezed his chest. She was the one he thought he'd bring home to continue the tradition of raising children on land that had been in the family for three generations.

Lily wanted no part of that plan. Big city life with its theaters, opera, thriving business area and high fashion was far more enticing to her than living on a ranch away from a town she said was on the outskirts of civilization. She wanted no part of it. She'd professed her love, but obviously her love wasn't as strong as her need for what the big city offered.

Maybe he was naïve to think any woman would want to live in a beautiful home surrounded by thousands of acres of family land. Maybe he was as stubborn as she was. He couldn't live in a city like New York and give up the life in which he was raised.

Lily and the big city of New York were all behind him now.

He pushed her thought out of his mind and concentrated on being home soon. Since old Doc Richards had died after a horse kicked him, Independence and ranches like Fletcher Ranch had been left without someone to help with their animals. Doc Richards wasn't a true doctor. He simply had a knack with animals and had earned a good reputation. Now Douglas hoped he could fill the void he'd left.

"I'm glad you weren't hurt, Mr. Fletcher." Emma spoke softly to him.

He opened his one good eye and chuckled. He had almost forgotten where he was. "I am, as well. I didn't want to be held up from seeing my family when I'm this close to home."

"So, you live near here?"

"Yes, our family has a ranch outside of Independence. I'm eager to see it again."

"We're both going to Independence. I recently graduated from medical school."

June O'Hara sat us straight. "My Emma is now a doctor. I'm so proud of her."

"I'm sure you are." Douglas looked at the two ladies and saw the resemblance. Mrs. O'Hara was as beautiful as her daughter with her hair pulled up under a small tan hat, but it couldn't hide the deep brown hair with only a sprinkling of grey. Her daughter wore a black hat with a net pushed up with strands of dark brown hair peeking out from the sides. Was the lady a widow? Her last name was the same as her mother's, so it didn't seem she was, but what did he know?

Maybe she took her former name back, or maybe she liked wearing black.

"I wish her dear father was with us to see how she turned out."

"I'm not so sure he'd approve, but thank you, Mother."

Emma smiled at her mother, but not before Douglas caught a glimpse of a frown.

She looked at Douglas. "I've accepted a job in Independence. My mother and I hope to make our home there."

Douglas crossed his arms in front of his body and stared at the lady. He had heard some medical schools were allowing females into their programs, but he never thought he'd actually see one in his hometown.

Emma sat up straight. "You don't approve, sir?"

"I didn't say that."

"You didn't have to. Your face said it all."

Douglas laughed, then stuck the handkerchief back on his head and tried to open the eye that was already swelling shut. "What else did my face tell you besides the fact that I'm bleeding all over your dainty handkerchief?"

"Since you stepped into this stagecoach, you haven't said two words to us. Those actions would say you're rude."

"I'm not a rude person, Miss O'Hara. I'm tired. I have a lot on my mind, and I now have a tremendous headache."

She ignored that comment. "And by your expression, I believe you're still stuck in the last century. We are in the middle of the Nineteenth Century. This is 1853. You need to catch up with the times. Women can be doctors or whatever else they want to be."

"I'm not sure I agree with that entirely, but I'm usually quite a liberal thinker. I've never met a female doctor. I know a little bit about medicine, though. I'm a veterinarian. If you ever need help, call on me."

This time, Emma laughed. "No, thank you. I'm sure I can handle my human patients without the help of a horse doctor."

Her mother placed a hand on her daughter's arm and whispered. "Emma, be nice. You never know when we might need help from this man or from his family."

"I doubt that, Mother." She looked at Douglas. "Good luck to you in your practice. I'm sure I'll see you around town."

Douglas smiled and swallowed another jab he so wanted to throw. "Thank you, Miss O'Hara. I certainly hope your practice goes well." He pulled the handkerchief away from his face, grimaced at the blood on it, and offered it back to Emma.

Emma frowned and shook her head. "You can keep the handkerchief. I'd hate for you to bleed all over that nice shirt you're wearing, even though it could use a decent pressing."

Douglas fisted his hand with the handkerchief inside, then glanced at his shirt. Sure enough the shirt and his trousers he'd pulled on before leaving his hotel room two days ago had wrinkles from the collar to the hemline that now hung out of his belted trousers. Both had dirt on them from rolling around scuffling with Sam. Unconsciously, he rubbed a hand down one side then the other, but seeing it did no good, he chuckled.

"Yep. It's a little hard staying neat on these coaches, especially when you're wrestling stagecoach bandits. As I said earlier, I was exhausted when the time came to board. If I appeared to be rude, I'm sorry." He raised the bloody handkerchief. "Thank you. I'm sure I'll cherish this." At that he tipped his hat to the two ladies, dropped his head against the back of the seat once again, grimaced when it hit, then closed his eyes.

What a shame! Emma O'Hara was a beautiful lady. Too bad she would be someone he'd try to avoid once they settled in Independence. It would be for the best. His life was complicated enough without having another woman in it, especially one who seemed to look down on his profession he'd worked so hard to obtain.

Dealing with animals was a lot easier than understanding women, especially women like this Emma with her bad attitude, and Lily, who led him on unmercifully. He still felt the stabbing heartache when he thought about the way she'd dumped him.

Mrs. O'Hara had called him brave. No way. His brother Lucas was the brave one.

I'm simply the younger brother trying to make a life for myself.

CHAPTER TWO

Emma O'Hara gathered her belongings, then opened the stagecoach door. "Mother, be careful getting out of here. That's a long step down, and I don't see the drivers anywhere."

As soon as the words came out of her mouth, Douglas Fletcher stepped in front of the door and held out his hands to help. "Ma'am, watch your step. Our drivers are making sure the three brothers are still secure." Douglas stood at the bottom of the stagecoach step with a quirky smile on his face waiting to help.

Emma rolled her eyes, but June O'Hara took his hand, blushed a little, then leaning on Douglas, she stepped into the dusty street. "Thank you, sir. You're not only brave, but a gentleman, as well."

Seemingly embarrassed by the compliment, Douglas simply nodded and smiled, then turned his attention to Emma. She gripped her satchel tightly against her body, held onto the door frame with her free hand, but when she looked down, realized there was no way she could step out alone. She looked into Douglas's hazel eyes.

With his hand still extended, he smiled, revealing straight, white teeth.

Emma hated to accept help from him, but she knew her limitations and jumping out of a coach wearing a skirt was not the prudent thing to do today. Now, had she worn the trousers she so dearly loved, she would not have needed help, but, alas, her mother insisted she wear this widow's outfit. "People will be a little more respectful when they see you're in mourning," she'd said. Even though she knew in her heart she was not in mourning of the man who was a dishonest cheat, she went along with her mother's wishes. She understood the dangers of women traveling alone.

Reluctantly, with a forced smile, she extended her gloved hand to Douglas Fletcher.

He held it tightly with one hand, reached up with the other hand and placed it on her waist. She gasped at the touch of his hand on her body, but before she had time to voice her objection, he lifted her effortlessly out of the coach and onto the street. Neither moved for a second, then Douglas dropped his hand quickly and stepped back.

Flustered as she hadn't been since she'd been a young girl in Cambridge, she felt the heat rise to her face. Straightening her shoulders, she got her composure. "Thank you, Mr. Fletcher. I'm glad to see the men in Independence are gentlemen."

Douglas smiled. "Yes, ma'am. We try to be." He nodded with a smile. "Have a good day. The hotel is right down the street. At least I guess it's still there. That's where I'm heading." He looked to the west. "I really want to ride to the ranch, but I have business in town before I head out and daylight is about gone."

"I do appreciate your help, but I was told a small house would be available for mother and me to use until we are able to find something more permanent." Emma looked down the street then back at Douglas. "However, I could use directions to find the sheriff's office. He was supposed to have all the information for me."

"If you'll wait, I'm sure he will be here shortly to take care of these three men."

He nodded, then walked toward the stagecoach and

spoke with one of the drivers checking on the men still tied on their horses.

She looked in the direction of the bandits. Sam and Cory both glared at Douglas. Charlie dropped his head and looked down at the horse's head. In spite of the fact that Charlie had scared her and her mother in the coach, she felt sorry for the young kid. His brothers probably convinced him to join them in the holdup. *What a waste of a life.* She hoped someone would intervene and help him find the right path. Obviously, it would not be his brothers.

June stepped close to Emma. "That young man is certainly nice and so good looking."

"Are you talking about one of the three bandits or Mr. Fletcher?"

"Emma O'Hara, don't get cute with me. You know I'm talking about Dr. Fletcher."

"I'm sorry, Mother, but you're always trying to play matchmaker," she whispered. "I have too much to think about with my new practice. We are perfectly fine without a man."

"There's always room for a nice man in a lady's life."

"Nice men are few and far between. You ought to know that by now since neither of us found one." Emma looked around. "There's a bench in front of that store. We can drag our baggage that little way. I hate to see the condition of our things after those men tore into our bags."

She bent over, grabbed the large chest with one hand, then lifted one of the smaller ones with the other.

"I'll get that big one, ladies." Douglas stepped next to them and reached for the large trunk.

Amazed that the man showed up every time she or her mother needed help, she blinked and watched him lift the trunk.

"Thank you. We appreciate your help." She nodded toward a store with a simple blue print dress in the front window displayed next to an assortment of tools and tin plates. "We plan to wait for the sheriff on the walkway in front of that shop."

"The sheriff shouldn't be long, but you do need to get these bags off the street. It'll be dark soon and if Independence is still the same as when I left it, ladies shouldn't be out alone at night. Some of the ranch hands coming into town for the weekend aren't always gentlemen, and people coming here to join the wagon trains aren't always the most careful or knowledgeable of the animals they buy. I've seen several people run over by uncontrolled oxen. Sometimes I wonder if they've any experience with the oxen they're trying to control. It's amazing some of them actually survive the trek to California."

"I can't imagine going across the country in a covered wagon."

"Believe me, I have no desire to do that either."

She looked down the street. "I thought I'd see covered wagons throughout the city, but we only saw one and that was before we got into town."

"There might not be a wagon train gathering at the moment, but even if one was getting ready to pull out, most of the pioneers camp a few miles outside of this area. You see them come and go getting their supplies. Most of the shops along the town square cater to their needs, but, like I said, one train may have just pulled out."

"I see. Thank you for that information." She thought about the window display. The simple, durable dress and the tools and tin dinnerware would certainly be appropriate for the trail. Of course, what did she know? Her dress of fine linen and silk ribbons didn't hold up well on the coach. She'd mentioned Douglas's wrinkled clothing, but hers didn't fare well either. She'd have to rethink her wardrobe if she planned to fit into this town.

"Let's get you into a safer place." Douglas carried the heavy trunk toward the walkway in front of the general store. "Are these your medical supplies?"

"They are. I would've been devastated had the bandits destroyed them."

His quirky grin told her what he thought about her opening a practice here on the outskirts of the populated cities. Of course, as she glanced at the buildings along the main street and the town square, she realized the town was much more modern than she had anticipated. The brick courthouse with its beautiful steeple was as stately as any building in Boston where she had studied, but the buildings were few and far between. Most of the ones they'd passed coming into town appeared to be as old as the town itself. Built with timber, aged and weathered from years in the winds blowing in from the Missouri River, she wondered how the buildings had not gone up in flames years ago. Thank goodness the modern courthouse would lead the way into the future.

She hoped the fair citizens were just as progressive and could accept her as their new town doctor.

Douglas pushed the trunk against the store wall. "I'm sure I'll see you ladies around town. I need to get going. By the way, the sheriff's name is Victor Sanchez. You'll like him."

He tipped his hat and headed down the sidewalk with one of his bags slung over his should and another one at his side.

"As I said earlier, Emma, Dr. Fletcher is such a nice man."

"Yes, Mother. I agree."

Emma hoped her mother was right about the new veterinarian in town, but then, her mother always found the good in everyone. *I did at one time as well until I learned better. People, especially men, rarely showed their true selves until they got what they wanted.*

She pushed those thoughts aside. This new area of the world would give her and her mother a new start away from the gossips in Cambridge and away from everything that reminded them of their old lives. Independence. Even the name of this little town gave her confidence she could start a new and better life. Maybe her dreams could come true.

Within the hour, Emma and her mother stood in the doorway of a small, stuffy smelling house behind the building that the sheriff pointed out as her office.

"The house is doable, Emma."

"It will have to be, Mother, but it will take some work."

"We know about hard work, don't we? We can make this a really cute place for the two of us. Our trunks with the little furnishings we could pack may not arrive for some time, but this little house will be fine."

"At least it's close to my office." She looked at the worn floors, walls that needed painting, a small table and three mismatched chairs, an old wood burning stove and a table with a basin on it, then walked over to the closest window and pushed. It didn't budge. "Maybe the sheriff will be able to get this window up so we can get some fresh air."

On the side wall, she pushed aside a faded curtain that hung from near the ceiling to the floor to find a tiny bedroom with two small beds. A straight-backed chair and a small table were all the furnishings in the room. She smiled and nodded to her mother. "As you said, Mother, it will do."

"I can already see how cute this can be." June O'Hara walked around touching the sparse furnishings. "We can make it our own little paradise."

Emma stepped near her mother and put an arm around her shoulder. Pulling her into a big hug, she kissed her forehead. "I'm so glad you're here with me. You make life happy."

The sheriff knocked and stuck his head in the front door. "Your trunk is safely inside the office, Dr. O'Hara."

Emma walked into the front room. "Please come in."

Sheriff Victor pulled off his hat and stood by the door. "We will pass the word around that the town now has a full-time doctor. I can't guarantee the townspeople will warm up to you right away, but we have to give it time. You were the only doctor willing to come here."

Emma laughed. "I guess I ought to be offended by that remark, but I'm happy to be here. I look forward to winning over the confidence of the people of Independence."

The sheriff held his hat in front of his body. "I hear we now have a new veterinarian. Douglas Fletcher went back east to study and now he's got his license to practice. For a while the people around here might want to go to him for their medical needs. You and he might have to work out a deal to work together until everyone gets used to having a female doctor."

"I don't think there will be any deals made with Mr. Fletcher."

Sheriff Vic didn't smile. "He's Dr. Fletcher now, just like you."

"Oh, no. Don't. . ."

Mrs. O'Hara had come into the room and cut in. "Sheriff, thank you for helping us get into here." She glared at her daughter.

Realizing what he'd earlier said, she put her hands on her hips. "Do you really think these people would actually go to an animal doctor for their medical needs?

"Why not?" He raised an eyebrow. "Before our last doctor came here, the townspeople used the barber in town."

Emma's shoulders slumped. "Back East I'd heard stories about crude medical personnel, but I never believed it." *I guess I really am in an uncivilized area of the country.*

The sheriff pulled his gaze from Emma and smiled at her mother. "We're glad you decided to come to Independence. We're growing so fast, I can't understand why other doctors didn't answer our call."

June O'Hara took his hand. "We were thrilled to receive the invitation. Thank you for your help and for giving my daughter your confidence."

"And we thank you for coming."

Emma shook his hand as well. "As soon as we get our

things into this house, I'll go over and begin to set up my office. Is there a nurse in town willing to work here?"

He shook his head and chuckled. "No such luck. You and Dr. Fletcher will be the only two medical people around. We had an older doctor, but he passed last winter. You might find a young lady willing to help you and learn from you. If I hear of anyone, I'll pass the word." He turned to go then turned back to her. "You'll like Douglas if you give him a chance. The Fletcher family has been around for a really long time. They're good people."

"I'm sure the Fletchers are upstanding citizens." She glanced at the window. "Before you go, would you try to open a couple of these windows? A little fresh air would be nice."

He nodded and walked over to the nearest window. With one massive push to the outside, the window opened." He picked up a stick from the floor and braced it open. "That ought to do it."

"I see. I guess I assumed it would lift up and not out."

He looked as if he wanted to say more but headed for the door instead. When he stepped outside and the door closed, Emma turned to her mother, now dragging her trunk towards the bedroom. "Mother, I'll get that."

"I'm fine." She stood at the curtain. "I guess we'll leave our things in the trunk. I don't see a dresser or even a box to store them."

"Then the trunk it will be. We'll manage."

For the next thirty minutes, they dug into the trunk, refolded clothes, and laid out some of the better pieces on the beds.

"I have two sets of sheets, but they are much too big for these narrow beds."

Emma looked up. "They'll work. We'll tuck them into the sides."

Her mother pulled out a coverlet that had been bundled up and stuffed back into the trunk after the bandits had rummaged through their things. June spread it on the bed and rubbed her hands along the lace edging to smooth it out. "My mother embroidered this lace when we were planning my wedding to your father." She held the end of it to her chest. "I'm so glad those awful men didn't have the opportunity to take it off with them."

Emma closed her eyes and wondered why her mother felt sentimental toward her father. The man had made her and everyone else in her family miserable. She shook her head.

"That Dr. Fletcher saved the day, didn't he?"

Emma hated to agree, but she nodded. "Yes, Mother, Mr. Fletcher did keep things from getting too horrible on the road."

"I wish your brother could've traveled with us. I would've felt so much safer."

Emma stopped what she was doing. "I'm sure Edward would certainly have kept us safe, but unfortunately, he decided to go off on his own. I was hoping he'd meet us here as he'd said, but I guess he decided to continue to California. I hope he didn't, but I know that was one of his plans. Why he thought he could find his fortune out West, I'll never know. He has no idea how to start a business or how to pan for gold. Who know what he will end up doing."

"I hope he is still in this area. I need to know he's safe." June let out a huge sigh, pulled a chair out, then sat. "Edward has never been a happy young man. Your father never helped him get along in the world. He always found fault with him. I felt so sorry for him at times."

"My father had a way of making all of us feel bad about ourselves, Mother. Even you. He was not a good man."

Her mother crossed her arms in front of her body. "You watch how you speak about the dead."

"I'm simply stating the truth. Your life is much better without him."

"Maybe so, but he did have some good qualities. When I first married him, he was good to me."

"But by the time I was old enough to remember him, he had become a mean man."

June's shoulders slumped. "I guess."

Emma stepped near her and placed a hand on her arm. "Mother, I know you loved him, but it's time for you to enjoy life. I'm so glad you came here with me. I want you to do whatever you want that will make you happy."

Her mother looked up and smiled. "You're a good daughter, Emma. Thank you. Maybe God will answer my prayers and Edward will join us here."

"I know you miss him." She kissed the top of her mother's head, then looked around. "While you go through the trunk, would you mind if I go to my office. I'm eager to get it in shape."

"Certainly. I'll come over when I make some sense of this place."

Emma headed toward her office thinking about the miserable life her mother had with her husband, the unhappy circumstances of her own marriage, and now the misery her brother Edward was causing her mother.

"Are there any good men around?" she mumbled to herself as she carefully stepped through the yard that was mostly sand and weeds. Her mother always had a beautiful yard. Maybe she'd know how to make it look better.

She stopped outside the back door of her office hoping it was in better shape than the house. *God, if it's horrible, please help me know how to make it better.*

At this point in her life, she wasn't sure God ever listened to her prayers, but it didn't hurt to try.

CHAPTER THREE

Douglas rubbed the neck of the horse he'd just bought in town. He was a beautiful palomino, well trained and fast. So far, he'd been a good horse, but he wasn't Major, the horse he'd had for years before he left home. He couldn't wait to be reacquainted with him at Fletcher Ranch.

He patted the horse once more. "We don't have far to go, and I know you'll like the ranch. We treat our horses like royalty."

As he topped the hill not far from the sprawling ranch house, he stopped to take in the view below him. He loved his home where he'd been raised and where his grandparents and parents and now his brother and family lived. He breathed in the fresh April air. Nostalgia filled his soul.

"Come on, boy. Let's go. I can't wait to see everyone." The horse took off in a smooth gallop. Douglas laughed into the wind.

Within minutes he rode along the perfectly maintained fences that lined the acres surrounding the large ranch house. Two workers raised their hands in greeting as he headed under the iron arches holding up the *FR* brand.

Abigail, wife of his brother Lucas, stood on the porch, lifted her watering can, and shaded her eyes from the midmorning sun. He knew exactly when she recognized him.

She put her can on the porch railing, held up her skirt bottom, and waddled down the steps. At this late in her pregnancy waddling was the best she could do.

He flicked the reins. "Hurry, boy, let's not make the lady walk any farther than she has to."

"Douglas! You're home. Oh, my goodness, you're home."

When Douglas got next to her, he jumped off his horse and threw his arms around Abigail. "Look at you. You're as beautiful as ever." He looked down at her. "And how's my little nephew or niece doing?"

"I think our newest addition is ready to meet the family. She's kicking up a storm today."

"So, you think it might be a girl? That would be great."

"I'm not sure why I'm calling it a girl. This pregnancy feels a little different from the other. I think Lucas would be thrilled to give Caroline a sister now that she has a little brother, but it really doesn't matter to us."

"And, speaking of which, where is my nephew? I need to meet the little fellow."

"William is taking a nap, but he'll be up before you know it and raring to go. He's got more energy than I ever thought a three-year old could." She stepped back and looked up. "What happened to your face?"

"It's nothing. We had a little trouble on the stage coming in."

"You're cut, and your eye is swollen and closed."

Douglas rubbed his hand across the lump that now protruded next to his eye. "It's not bad. I'm hoping the swelling will go down so it doesn't look so bad." He looked across the corrals and into the fields that stretched for miles. "I guess my brother is out on the range."

"Yes, we've had some problems lately. He and Mason are checking things out. He'll be thrilled that you're home. He can use the help."

"I hate to hear we're having problems, but I'm not sure

I'll be of any help to him. I've been gone for over three years."

"And you're still the same Douglas that rode off on his own." She stepped back and looked closely at him. "Well, maybe a little taller."

He laughed. "It happens." He looked around. "Is Mother inside?"

"In the kitchen. She still loves to cook."

"I can't tell you how I've dreamed of hers and Carmella's and Bonita's meals." He pulled her next to him for another hug. "I've missed all this."

Together they headed to the house. When they got to the front steps, Abigail kissed him once more on the cheek. "Welcome home. We've missed you so much."

"Not as much as I've missed all of you and this ranch."

He helped her up the steps. "I'll see you in the house. I'm going to the kitchen door to surprise Mother."

He walked his horse to the back of the house where he tied him to the hitching porch. "You stay here, boy. I'll get you in the barn and fed as soon as I find my mother."

He took the steps two at a time. "Mother, where are you?" He called out even though he knew she'd come running out of the kitchen.

"Douglas! Oh, Douglas, you're home." She burst through the door coming from the hallway and threw herself into his outstretched arms. "I've missed you so much."

Douglas heard her sniffle. He pressed her body against him. "I've miss you, too." She felt much smaller than when he left.

She stepped away and brushed her hand across her eyes. "Look at you. You look like such a man."

"Mother, I'm almost thirty. I hope I still don't look like a little boy."

"Of course, you don't. Little boys don't have black eyes." She passed her hand gently over the lump next to his eye. "What happened? Did you see a doctor?"

"It's nothing. I had someone look at it. It really feels better than it looks." He thought about the brown-haired Emma on the coach. He could still feel her soft touch on his face. He cleared his throat. "Three bandits tried to rob the stagecoach. I helped the other men on the coach take them down before they hurt anyone. They're in jail now."

"Good. You've always been the peacemaker." She gave him a quick hug. "Are you hungry? I made a big pot of vegetable and beef soup, and I have cornbread in the oven. I know it's early, but Lucas said he and Mason would be in about now to eat an early lunch. They're meeting with some men about noon today. I'm glad you're here. I know he will want your input."

"Input?"

"We're having problems with some outsiders. We need solutions."

"Abigail mentioned some problems. I'll be glad to give them my two cents, but I've been gone so long, I'm not sure I'll be able to help."

"You are the same Douglas who rode off three years ago. Your opinions about the running of the ranch still are important to us."

"That's the same thing Abigail said, but I'm not sure I'm the same man. I do love the ranch now as much as I always did, so I'll talk to Lucas about all this later. Where are Bonita and Carmella? I've missed those wonderful meals they serve."

"They were here earlier. I gave them the morning off. I felt like cooking, and I wanted the kitchen to myself."

He pulled her to him once again. "You never change."

They both looked up when one of the ranch dogs barked.

Douglas walked to the side door of the large kitchen and stepped out. Lucas and Mason, the ranch supervisor, walked toward one of stables. A tall, young man walked alongside of them. Douglas stared.

"Is that little Matthew?"

Mrs. Fletcher looked out the door. "Yes, but he's not so little anymore. He's such a delightful young man. We're so glad he's still with us. He's definitely part of this family."

"If my memory serves me right, he had his eye on Caroline when I left."

"That he did, and now that she's growing up, I think she's starting to enjoy the attention. When he finishes his chores for Lucas today, I heard he and Caroline were heading to town."

"Hmmm, what does Lucas say about all of that?"

"I think he finally understands Caroline is growing up. She's not his little baby anymore." She smiled. "It's hard. He's been so protective of her since Sarah died. It's hard to let her grow and find her own way in life."

"I'm sure. I don't know about kids, but I can only imagine."

"Speaking of which, when will we see our Douglas settle down?"

"Now, Mother. I just got home. Don't push."

She laughed. "Okay. I'll be patient" She rubbed her hand down the front of his shirt. "I know a sweet wife would never let you go out with such a wrinkled, dirty shirt."

Remembering what Emma said about his shirt, Douglas shook his head and laughed. "You're probably right. I didn't bother to find a clean one this morning. Everything in my bag was as wrinkled as this one."

He looked out the back door once more. Lucas and Mason parted ways, Lucas headed toward the house, and Matthew raced toward the bunkhouse.

Douglas smiled watching the young man. Young love. Would he ever feel that way again? He watched Matthew disappear into the bunkhouse, then he stepped out onto the back stoop.

"Little brother, you're home." Lucas headed toward the house, then smiled big. He took the steps two at a time. As soon as he got near his brother, he gave Douglas a huge hug.

"Man, I missed you."

"I missed you, too." He waved an arm in the air. "I missed all of this. The buildings were closing in on me in New York."

"I'm so sorry we couldn't make your graduation. You know we're proud of you, but with Abigail getting late in her pregnancy, I was scared to leave her, and she certainly couldn't travel to New York."

"You don't have to explain. Believe me, you didn't miss anything. We did have a good speaker though. Dr. D. D. Slade spoke on the newest knowledge of treating horses. You would've enjoyed listening to him."

"I hate I missed that topic. Come on in. Let's get caught up." Lucas looked at Douglas and tilted his head. "You look as though you've been sleeping in those clothes for days."

Again, Douglas looked down at his shirt and pants. "As a matter of fact, I have. It's not easy riding a train and then a stagecoach."

"Not easy coming out of a fight with a black eye either."

Douglas laughed. "Let's go inside and eat some of Mother's soup and cornbread. I'll tell you about all of it."

The day flew by for Douglas. By the time he escorted his mother into the big dining area that evening, he had seen everyone on the ranch, had ridden out with Lucas and Mason to check the fields and the fences, and had played with his new nephew William. The only one he had not seen was Caroline.

"I thought she'd be home by now," Lucas said as he helped Abigail into her chair."I worry about her when she's not on the ranch."

"Matthew rode out with her as soon as he finished his chores," Abigail touched her husband's arm.

"That's what I'm afraid of."

"Lucas, the boy is the best kid around these parts. You can trust him."

"Yeah, I guess. Still, I don't like her being gone all

afternoon, especially if they went into the city."

"They've only been gone since lunch."

Douglas reached for his glass of water. "That town has really grown in the last four years."

"I don't like it."

"Lucas, you didn't like it when it was nothing but a dirt road and a few stores."

"I like being on the ranch."

"I can't blame you, but towns do offer a lot these days."

"You can't convince me of that. Let's say grace." He bowed his head. "Lord, thank you for getting Douglas home to us safely. Please watch over our Caroline as she makes her way home, as well. We thank you for this delicious food and for our wonderful ladies in the kitchen. Amen."

"Proud of you, brother." Douglas stabbed a big piece of ham. "I remember a time you made someone else at our table ask the blessing. You wanted no part of it."

"You have a good memory. I can thank Abigail for helping me in the God department." He smiled at his wife.

Douglas felt their love and wished one day he would find someone to love as his brother had, but then, he thought he had when he'd found Lily. Too bad she wanted something else.

William squirmed in his grandmother's arms. Lucas reached over and took him.

Douglas smiled at his brother. "I've got to tell you, Abigail, I'm so pleased you named that little fellow after our father. I think he'll have light hair like him. I'm sure he's looking down and smiling."

"Lucas suggested the name early in my pregnancy if it was a boy. I was all for it. From what I've heard about the man, we couldn't have found a better person to honor."

"Unless it would've been his handsome Uncle Douglas."

Lucas shook his head. 'I love you, little brother, but not that much."

Douglas laughed, then he and everyone turned when the

dining room door flew open. Caroline and Matthew nearly knocked each other down getting through the door and to the table.

"Glad you two could make it." Lucas glared at Matthew then Caroline.

Douglas could tell his brother wasn't pleased with them. He bit his lip to keep from smiling.

"Daddy, we stopped at Simmons Creek and fished. We were catching so many trout we forgot about the time."

Lucas lost his frown. "Trout? Did you bring them home? We'll have that tomorrow night."

"Sure did, Daddy."

"I haven't had fresh trout in years." Douglas waited for Caroline to realize he was sitting with the family.

"Uncle Douglas!" She ran to him.

He got up and held his niece. "Look at you. You're a grown lady."

"Yes, I am. Would you please tell my father that I am." She glared at Lucas.

Douglas laughed. "I think he knows."

"Please, sit so we can eat." Lucas helped himself to a bowl of mashed potatoes, then passed the bowl to Abigail.

Caroline sat next to Matthew, then looked at Douglas. "Are you going to be the new veterinarian in town? Will you still live at the ranch with us?"

"Yes, to your first question, but probably no to your second."

"Aaaah. I wanted you to live here with us again."

"I'll probably get a place in town, but I'll be here so much you'll get tired of seeing me."

"I doubt that. I'd never get tired of being with you, Uncle Douglas. You're fun to be around."

Lucas cleared his throat. "Which means I must not be."

"Daddy, you know I don't mean that. You're old and you're my father. You're not supposed to be fun."

Douglas chuckled. "Think I'll stay out of this

conversation."

"Good idea." Lucas concentrated on his plate.

Mrs. Fletcher spoke up. "Both my boys are fun when they aren't burdened by problems on the ranch."

"Thank you, Mother." Lucas got serious, gave William a piece of bread to keep him occupied, then looked at Douglas. "Have you heard anything about the water situation while you were in town?"

"I wasn't there very long. It was late when we got in so I rented a room and got up this morning to ride out. I wanted to get back out here as fast as I could. My mouth was watering knowing Bonita and Carmela would probably be cooking tonight."

Abigail spoke up. "They never disappoint. I'm watching them to learn how they cook some of Lucas's favorite dishes."

Lucas looked at his wife and smiled. "God watched out for me when he sent this lady to tutor Caroline."

"You're a lucky man, brother." Douglas raised his glass of water as if in a toast. "Now, tell me about the problems you're having. I can't imagine there being a water problem with all the rivers around us."

"You'd think that would be true, but I can tell you, it isn't. We have a few settlers outside the city who are determined to run some of us out. I hear they want to buy up as much of the land as possible to get the railroad run around the town and straight through their property. I heard they plan to form a town of their own just northwest of here by the river. Having a rail line would make for a quick growing town."

"Do you mean they want to buy Fletcher Ranch?"

"Not all of it. They're only interested in the north acreage beneficial to their plan."

"So just tell them the land isn't for sale."

"Easier said than done. They want to harass us enough until we just give them the land. They're damning the streams from the rivers and cutting off the water to our fields."

Douglas put down his fork a little too hard. "You've got to be kidding. That's insane. It's illegal. It's murderous if our cattle die from lack of water."

"It's all of those things. That's why I'm glad you're home. The other ranchers and I need some new ideas."

"I'm all ears, but you do realize I'm a veterinarian, not a gunslinger."

"You're right, but I remember how you could outshoot all the young men around these parts. Attending all those lectures and classes didn't take that away from you, did it?"

"No, but you know I don't like bloodshed."

"None of us do, but sometimes to protect what belongs to your family, you have to push aside your likes and dislikes and do what's right."

Douglas inhaled. "I guess, but after seeing you almost die on that last cattle drive we did together, I reevaluated how I feel about guns."

"But you still carry one?"

"I do, but it's mostly for show. Like I explained earlier, I did pull it out on the coach coming here. Those three bandits were the most incompetent criminals you've ever heard of. Luckily, I didn't have to shoot one of them."

"Then you understand you sometimes have to push aside your feelings and protect yourself and others around you."

He rubbed his lump. "Yep. That's exactly what happened on the coach."

"Glad that's all you got. We'll talk about the water situation later. This is your first night home. Don't want to ruin it."

Douglas nodded and tasted the huge slice of beef on his plate, but his mind wandered to the stagecoach and the pretty doctor who bantered with him. He fought back a smile as he tried to concentrate on the conversation floating around the table, but instead of seeing the cattle that Lucas talked about, he saw the dark brown hair and the golden eyes on the female doctor who infuriated him. She might look down on his profession, but even now, he had to smile. He'd promised himself he'd avoid her, but he knew that would be almost impossible with both of them being in town.

Maybe they could continue their banter and he could convince her that veterinarians were necessary in this part of the world, and maybe she could prove to him that a female doctor could do as well as any male doctor.

A lively conversation with someone that beautiful could be fun.

He smiled. His future in Independence, Missouri, just might be interesting.

CHAPTER FOUR

The next day Emma stood at the open door of her office. Her shoulders drooped as she eyed the few pieces of dusty furniture, the worn rug on the floor, and the door leading to her examination room that needed a new coat of paint. She held a hand over her nose from the stuffy smell. Obviously, the office had been shut up for months just as the small house had been, but now she was ready to tackle the problem. When she'd looked over the office yesterday, she hurried through, not taking time to do anything. Today, she would put her entire effort into making the office presentable and usable.

Pushing aside a yellowed lace curtain, she pushed the window and found a short stick to hold it out.

She smiled and nodded. "Now, my first accomplishment!"

From the front office, she stepped through the door into a sad-looking examination room. One table with a torn cover sat in the middle of the small room. Several glass-enclosed cabinets lined the walls. She walked over to one and was pleased to see the last doctor had left a few instruments. She opened the first one and examined several scalpels and a leather case of needles used for stitching. "Nice. Old but very well made." She hoped she wouldn't have to use a scalpel too soon. She loved helping patients. Her strong point was diagnosis and delivering and administering to new mothers, but a little more experience in an operating arena would make her feel more confident.

"I certainly won't let out that piece of information," she said as she continued to examine the surgical equipment.

After looking through all the cabinets and boxes of bandages and bottles of medicines shoved around the room, she had a good idea how she would proceed with the office after she helped her mother with the house. Instead of going to the back of the office and the door that led to their small house, she headed to the reception area to check out the desk that was pushed up against the wall. She wiped away the dust on the top, opened all the drawers and decided it was in better shape than it looked.

With another glance, she opened the front door and stepped out onto the small porch to get a breath of fresh air. Wagons filled with travelers and river workers, horses and pedestrians moved about the crowded main street. Several families in covered wagons passed. Even before she'd left Cambridge, she knew Independence was one of the main towns where wagon trains organized before heading out west. Now that she was here, the reality of seeing these people getting ready to travel across the country sank it.

She couldn't imagine traveling across such a wild, undeveloped country to get to the other side of the continent. "Such strong, brave people."

"Hello, Miss O'Hara," a familiar voice made her look down the wooden sidewalk.

"Hello to you, Mr. Fletcher." She walked to the railing and waited.

"I'm sure you meant to say Doctor Fletcher, but I answer to anything."

In spite of herself, she laughed. "I'll remember that in the future."

He walked toward her with a long, determined stride. His

dark brown boots, splattered with mud on one side, appeared to be richly engraved. His dark brown trousers and tan shirt were not perfect, but she could tell they had been fresh and neatly pressed before he started his day. His black bowler pulled low over his brow, couldn't hide the hazel eyes she had noticed in the coach. Even with the black eye, Douglas Fletcher definitely rivaled any of the men she had seen in Independence with his good looks.

She shook that thought out of her head. "Have you found a place to set up your office?"

"I've looked at a couple small buildings this morning, but nothing seems right, I might have to be less picky if I plan to open soon."

"I certainly understand. This office isn't exactly what I imagined for a practice in a city like Independence, but it will have to do. I'm thrilled to be here with my own office."

He placed his foot on the bottom step, leaned on the railing, and inhaled deeply.

Emma swallowed hard and blinked.

"So, do I remember you saying you were going to live near here?"

She found her voice. "Yes, the small house provided by the town is in the back yard behind this office. It will be nice once we get it fixed up and some of our things arrive."

"I'd love to find an office with living accommodations as well. I could even use one of the older homes off the main road. Most of my patients will not be brought to the office. I'll spend a good bit of my time traveling to the different ranches near here to care for horses and cattle. I plan to spend a lot of time at our family ranch."

"Yes, I remember you said your family has lived near here for three generations."

Douglas stood up straight and smiled. "You're a good listener. I'm surprised you remembered anything I said in the coach."

Now it was her time to smile. "Oh, I remember

everything you said, Mr. Fletcher."

"If you can't bring yourself to call me Dr. Fletcher, please call me Douglas."

Emma clasped her hands in front of her body. "Then Douglas it will be."

Douglas threw his head back and laughed out loud. "So I'll wait patiently for the day you can find it in yourself to call me Dr. Fletcher."

"You don't look like the type of man with a lot of patience."

"You know nothing about me, Miss O'Hara."

"Please call me Emma. You're right. I really don't know anything about you except for the fact that you save damsels in distress from stagecoach robbers."

"Not my usual habit, but I was glad to be able to help. Of course, those three bandits were easy to subdue. They had no clue what they were doing."

"Still, they could've done a lot of harm had you not intervened." She leaned nearer to him and touched the side of his face. "Your wound needs cleaning and some ointment. It's red and swollen and could be getting infected."

Douglas leaned away from Emma. "It is still sorer than I thought it would be today."

"Why not follow me to our house in the back. Mother is there. I could clean the wound and at least put something on it."

Douglas thought a moment. "I appreciate your wanting to do that for me, but I'm in a bit of a hurry. I'll be sure to have my mother or my sister-in-law look at it. Thank you for your interest though. I'm sure you're a true professional."

Emma didn't know how to take his remarks. Did he not want her to touch him because she was a female doctor? She stared at him. Was he really in a hurry or did he want to get away from her?

Douglas stepped off the stairs. "I'll probably see you around town now that you're situated here."

"Yes, we are bound to run into each other. And, Douglas, I do hope you find an appropriate place to set up your business."

"Thank you, Miss Emma. I hope I do as well." At that, he nodded and turned away.

He walked down the sidewalk for a short distance before crossing the busy street waving to several men on horseback. One turned his horse around and stopped to talk. Douglas put his hands on his hips and seemed quite interested in what the man was saying. Finally, the man on horseback raised his hand and the men parted. She wondered what the conversation was about, but she knew she'd never know.

She needed to go to the house to help her mother, but it was hard to pull her gaze away from the man. He had a swagger in his walk, one that told her he was confident in himself. She wished she could say the same for herself. Becoming a doctor had always been her dream, but now that she found herself getting ready to open a practice, doubts bombarded her daily. She knew she would be a good doctor, but how would she convince the town that she was.

Blowing out a big breath, she watched Douglas move down the busy street, weaving in and out of buggies and wagons. As he stepped onto the wooden sidewalk and disappeared into an office, Emma walked around the side of the office and through the gate that led to her house.

As she stepped into the door to the house, she found her mother staring out the cloudy window. "Mother, I'm home. Are you okay?" She walked up to her and put a hand on her shoulders.

June O'Hara turned and swiped a hand across her eyes.

"Mother, what's wrong? Are you missing your old house back home?"

"Heavens, no. I was glad to leave that house and all those memories. I'm ready to start a new life here with you."

"I'm glad to hear that, but you looked so sad when I walked in."

June stared at the dirty window. "I keep thinking your brother will come riding up to find us here. I'm so scared something has happened to him."

Emma pulled her mother into a big hug. "We have to think positive about Edward. He'll show up one day and have some wonderful stories to tell us about his adventures." Even as she said the words, she didn't believe them. She, too, worried about her younger brother.

"I hope you're right." June stood up straight, took a deep breath and turned to Emma. "You're back early. Did you get anything accomplished in the office?"

Glad to see her mother had shaken off her outward signs of worry, Emma did the same. She sat at the table and stretched her legs. "Not really. I came back to see if you needed help and to get some cleaning supplies so I can get the place more sanitary. Right now, it's anything but that."

"I'm doing fine. You go take care of your office. It's been closed for a while, but you'll get it in tip-top shape in no time." June sat across the table from Emma. "Before you start cleaning, would you like to take a walk around town to see what it has to offer? Maybe we could stop in a restaurant to have an early lunch. We need to find a store and buy some food so we can start cooking here."

"You're right, Mother. Let's go see what Independence offers."

June slid past her daughter. "Maybe that nice young Dr. Fletcher will be in town."

~

Douglas said hello to several people on the way to his favorite restaurant. He hoped it had not closed since he was last home. The Schmidts had opened it years before, but he knew they must be getting on in years.

"Douglas, is that you?" A lady wearing a large black hat stopped in front of him and reached for his hand.

"Mrs. Murphy, is that you?"

"It is, and I can't believe you're back in Missouri. Are

you here to stay? Did you become a veterinarian? We sure do need one in this town."

Douglas chuckled at her fast talk and rapid questions. "You haven't changed a bit."

"Oh, my, you're a sweet boy, but you must be blind. I'm old and fat and these widow weeds make me look even older."

"Widow weeds? Are you saying Mr. Murphy isn't with us anymore?"

Mrs. Murphy put her hands to her chest. "My dear Joseph passed about two months ago. I miss him dearly."

Douglas reached out and took her hands. "I'm so sorry. I didn't see him often, but my mother loved you and Mr. Murphy."

"Thank you, Douglas. Your mother is a darling. She came and sat with me for hours when she got word that Joseph had been shot."

"Shot?"

"Why, yes. Those horrible men trying to buy up land came onto our property and wouldn't leave. When they harassed me, Joseph stepped in and one of the men shot him. They rode off as fast as they could, and no one has seen them since."

A thousand questions raced through Douglas's mind. Were these the same men trying to get Lucas and their neighbors to sell? Where were they hiding out?

"Did you pass on their descriptions to the sheriff?"

"Of course, I did, but as I said no one has seen them."

He took her hand once more. "If there's anything I can do for you, please don't hesitate to send word. I'm trying to find a place in town to set up my practice. When I do, that will be the easiest way to find me, or you can get in touch with someone at Fletcher Ranch."

"You and your brother are the best. I hear he and Abigail are having another child. That's so exciting."

"Yes. I'm so glad I'll be around this time to experience

a new little niece or nephew." He gave her a big hug. "You take care of yourself."

Douglas entered the restaurant, removed his hat, and found a seat by the window.

A young waitress walked up to him with a pad in her hand, but as she looked up, she dropped the pad to her side. "Douglas Fletcher, as I live and breathe, it's you."

Douglas looked up. "If it isn't Molly Schmidt. I was so happy to see your parents still had the restaurant open."

"My parents no longer have the restaurant." She raised both of her hands and smiled a huge smile." I am now the owner, part-time cook, and sometimes waitress. They wanted to move back East by my brother, so I took over about a year ago."

"I'm so proud of you. That's a big endeavor, but you've always loved this restaurant."

"Yes, I've always loved it here, but I did find out running a restaurant is a big job. I think I now have things under control." She crossed her arms in front of her body. "I saw Lucas not too long ago and he said you're now a veterinarian."

"I am and if you hear of a vacant building anywhere in town, let me know. I need a place to set up my practice. It doesn't have to be very big. I'd even consider one of the small houses off the main street."

Molly thought a minute. Her big blue eyes had always fascinated Douglas. Most of his female acquaintances had dark brown eyes, but Molly's family was Irish. Beautiful with thick, curly blonde hair and fair clear skin, she hadn't changed a bit.

"I hear Mrs. Lamey might be moving since she lost her husband. I could tell you where she lives, or better yet, if you wait here long enough, she always comes in for lunch about 11:30. She says she can't handle being in the kitchen and not cooking when her husband isn't here."

"That must be awful. They were married a long time. I

met Mrs. Murphy on the way in. She, too, lost her husband. I was shocked to hear he'd been shot by the men trying to take our land."

"Yes, that was awful, but no one has seen them since."

"I'm glad. Maybe they're gone for good." He pulled out his pocket watch." I'll watch for Mrs. Lamey here. It's almost 11:30. That would be wonderful if I could buy her place."

Molly lifted her pad. "Now what can I get our new town veterinarian?"

He ordered a steak with mashed potatoes and brown gravy and turnip greens. His mouth watered just thinking about the same meal Molly's mother used to fix for him.

Just as Molly walked away, the tiny bell over the door dinged, and Mrs. Lamey walked in. Molly pointed out Douglas, and the lady headed his way.

Douglas stood up. "Mrs. Lamey, you might not remember me, but I'm Douglas Fletcher."

"You're right. I don't remember you, but if you're Lucas's brother, I know your family."

"Yes, ma'am, that's my family. Please, have a seat. I'd like to talk to you about your house."

They talked. Douglas bought her lunch, and she was quite interested in selling to him. They left the restaurant and headed to the lady's house, right off the main street. He was eager to see it, but as they got closer, he realized the building sat directly behind Emma O'Hara's office and small house. He laughed and wondered if he could live and work that close to the beautiful female doctor. He decided to look at the house anyway and followed Mrs. Lamey up the front steps.

He opened the door for Mrs. Lamey, then followed her inside. They stepped into the small living room. Just glancing around the room, Douglas knew it would be suitable for a reception area.

Mrs. Lamey walked into the back room. "This is my

kitchen. Mr. Lamey loved my cooking." She sniffled. "I can't make myself cook in here anymore when I know he won't be enjoying the meals."

"I'm sorry, Mrs. Lamey. He was a lucky man to have you as his wife." Douglas remembered how his mother mourned his father and Lucas mourned Sarah, so he knew how devastating losing a partner could be. He wished he had comforting words to say to her, but instead he took her hand, squeezed it, just as he'd done for his mother.

The large kitchen had a stove tucked into the corner with several open shelves built above it and a small table with a wash basin next to it. Across the kitchen was a table with two wooden, straight-back chairs. His mind raced. If he added another table, he could make this room into an examination room.

On the wall across from the stove, he pushed aside a curtain to find a rather large bed and a small chest. *Perfect.* He could use this space for his private area when he had to stay in town. Before Mrs. Lamey said anything about this being her and Mr. Lamey's room, he quickly pulled the curtain together and headed to the back door and looked out. There, right across the wooden fence, was the small house where Emma and her mother would be living. In front of it was Emma's office.

As perfect as Mrs. Lamey's house and the location was, living next to Emma would be challenging. He had a lot to think about.

Could life get any more interesting?

CHAPTER FIVE

"**Mother, that's not** funny."

"I'm not trying to be funny, Emma. Dr. Fletcher is moving into the house right behind us. I saw him this morning cleaning the windows. I went to the fence, and we talked. He's the sweetest young man, just as I suspected."

Emma leaned against her broom for support, not sure how she felt about the good-looking man who didn't approve of her being in the medical profession. She repositioned the broom and began to sweep a little too forcefully.

"I'm glad he found a place to take care of animals, but I'm sure we will both be so busy we won't be getting in each other's way."

"Oh, I don't think you'd be in his way at all. In fact, I'm sure he would appreciate the company. Being single must be awfully lonely."

"You and I are both single, Mother, and I don't consider our lives lonely."

"That's because you've stayed busy studying day and night for the last five years. It's time for you to have some fun."

"It's time for me to start my practice and make us some money. We've used almost all our savings to get here."

"God always provides, Emma. You know that. He won't

let us starve."

"We won't starve, but I can see us not being able to afford the rent on my office. Without that, we have no income."

June wiped her dust cloth across the back of a shelf. "As I said earlier, God will make sure we have enough to survive, especially since your calling is to help people."

"Thank you. I hope you're right."

June put her hands on her hips. "You *hope* I'm right? Don't you doubt for a minute your Christian up-bringing."

"I don't, Mother. I'm simply a believer in making sure you can provide for yourself by using the talents God gave you. I don't believe in sitting around and waiting for God to give us a handout."

"Emma O'Hara, you watch your mouth. God doesn't give anyone a handout. He simply offers the way to do the right things with our lives."

"Exactly. Now we're on the same page. Let's finish cleaning this house so we can move to the office and get it clean."

Emma swept along the wall, thinking about what her mom had said. Did she really believe God shows humans the right way in life? *Where was he when I married David*? He was not a good man. Why didn't God give her a hint about the kind of man he was? She wanted to believe she'd married a good man, but after years of watching him, she had her doubts. He was not an honest man, but she didn't find that out until he was killed.

Then she thought about her mother and father's marriage. Emma knew her mother loved her father, but as she got older, she realized he was a mean man, especially in the way he treated her mother and her and her brother Edward. Again, how did God allow her mother to live with such a horrible man?

She hit the floor with her broom.

"Emma, you okay?"

"Oh, yes, ma'am. I wasn't paying attention to what I was doing."

She leaned against her broom. Would she ever understand the world around her?

Emma swept up her last pan of dirt and dust and headed toward the back door to empty it. Stepping out on the porch, she realized Douglas Fletcher stood in his yard bent over the well pumping water into a bucket. As much as she wanted to turn away, she couldn't. The man might be irritating with his old-fashioned attitude, but she had to admit he was as good looking as any man she'd seen in years.

She swallowed and stepped to the edge of the stoop to empty her pan.

He looked up. "Hello, Miss O'Hara. It seems we are going to be neighbors."

Emma stopped. "I see that. Mother said you were making that house into your office."

"Yes. I couldn't find anything on the main street, but this is perfect. I'll be on the road most of my days visiting ranches and farms around here to tend to their animals. I really don't need a lot of visibility. You, on the other hand, have found the perfect location. You need to be in a place where it's convenient for your patients. Of course, you'll find some of your patients will be away from town as well."

Emma frowned, but did not question his statement.

He put his bucket down and headed to the fence. "Your mother and I visited earlier. She certainly is a lovely lady."

"That she is. I'm so glad she was able to travel with me to Independence."

He put his hand on the fence and looked directly at her and smiled. "I see you are out of your mourning clothes."

Emma glanced down at her trousers and button-up shirt. "I'm not in mourning. I did lose my husband," she corrected herself, "but that was quite a few years ago."

"I like your attire today."

"Are you making fun of me?"

"I certainly am not. I happen to think ladies should be allowed to wear what they want, especially in their own houses. I'm sure those cumbersome dresses make it hard to maneuver around while cleaning."

She still wasn't sure the man wasn't making fun of her. Stepping to the edge of the stoop, she emptied the dirt from her pan, then looked at Douglas. "I agree. Some of our dresses are quite uncomfortable. I can do more work in these trousers." She stopped talking. Thankfully her mother couldn't hear her talk with a stranger about something as personal as clothing.

"You see, I'm not stuck in the last century as you presumed. I do have a few progressive thoughts."

"But not about women getting an education in the medical field."

"I told you on the stage I hadn't had the opportunity to meet any females in the field. It's a concept I'll have to get used to."

"I hope you change your mind. I'm a good doctor, and I'm sure this town could use one." She turned to the door, then back to him. "Have a good day, Mr. Fletcher."

"Thank you, same to you, *Miss* O'Hara."

Emma swallowed a laugh that tickled her throat. One day she would make sure he called her doctor, but obviously not today. She'd work on calling him Dr. Fletcher. It would be as hard for her as it would be for him.

Maybe it could be fun getting a handsome single man to appreciate her medical expertise. June certainly would be happy.

~

Douglas picked up his bucket and started pumping water into it once more. Mrs. Lamey had moved out as soon as he'd paid for the house. He took the opportunity to immediately get it ready for his office.

Things were falling into place for him here in Independence. He couldn't wait to get back home to tell his family. He wasn't sure his brother Lucas thought he'd actually stick with the hard work and studies to become a vet, or maybe he did. Sometimes he had a hard time reading his brother. Lucas spoke very little at times, always keeping his thoughts to himself. He was glad Abigail came into his life. After losing his first wife Sarah, Lucas withdrew even more than usual, but now remarried, he smiled more and more.

He picked up the full bucket of water and headed toward the back door of the office, but not before looking in the direction of Emma O'Hara's office. He hoped she'd make a good doctor. Independence desperately needed one. He still wasn't sure he liked the idea of going to a female doctor. One day maybe he could call her doctor, but she'd have to prove she was worthy of the title. He smiled. Right now, he enjoyed bantering with her.

He put the bucket on the floor of the kitchen area, but looked up when the front door slammed. He walked to the front area. Two men, each with a thick bushy beard, stood inside the front door, both dressed in muddy work clothes.

Douglas grabbed a cloth from a table and wiped his hands. "Can I help you?"

"You the town vet?"

"I am." He took a couple of steps and stuck out his hand, hoping these burly guys were here for his services and not to rob him, not that he had anything to take. "I'm Doctor Fletcher."

One of the guys shook his hand. The other simply nodded.

Douglas didn't get a good feeling about these two, but this was his new business. He'd be as courteous as he could be. "What can I do for you? I haven't officially opened, but I don't need an office if you have an animal that needs help."

"We have an ox that doesn't look right." The taller man spoke.

"Are you joining one of the wagon trains?"

Both of the men nodded.

"Where is your animal and what makes you think something is wrong?"

"We just bought it, got it with the other oxen we bought and now it won't get up. That big thing hit the ground and refuses to move."

"If you'll give me a couple minutes, I'll follow you. Is the animal far?"

"Just around the corner behind the saloon."

Douglas didn't want to follow these two men, but if an animal needed help, he couldn't let it suffer. He washed his hands, then grabbed a small black bag. "I'll follow you."

They headed down the street in front of the O'Hara office. She and her mother opened the door just as the men passed. He waved and both ladies waved back. Mrs. O'Hara smiled. He liked Emma's mother even on the stagecoach and hoped they could be good neighbors, possibly even friends with both ladies.

That thought sent a warm streak through him. It had been about six months since he'd been dumped by Lily in New York. He pushed thoughts of her from his mind. He nodded to Emma then moved down the sidewalk. She was just a neighbor, a beautiful neighbor, but after having his heart broken, he wasn't looking for another romance.

"This way," one of the big guys turned into an ally beside the saloon.

Douglas hesitated, but followed anyway. At the back of the building, several wagons stood with three oxen tied to them.

"This way," the other guy said. He stepped closer to the building, then backed up so Douglas could get near the huge ox lying on its side. "The big thing won't get up. We paid lots of money for it. It better not die. We can't buy another one."

Douglas knelt down by the animal whose eyes were huge. Big gulps of air shot out from the animal's mouth.

Douglas ran his hand down its side and immediately realized the animal was a female and was in the process of giving birth.

"There's nothing wrong with this ox. She's about to give you a second ox for the price you paid for this one."

"You mean she's gonna have a baby ox?"

"Yep, I'll hang around to make sure she doesn't have any problems. Usually they stand, but lying down doesn't mean she'll have problems. Usually their births are easy." Douglas moved to the rear of the ox and realized the birth was about to happen. "That a girl." He rubbed his hand over her tight belly. "You're doing fine." As he said the words, he realized the calf was not in the normal position.

"What's wrong?" One of the men stepped near Douglas. "She's not going to die, is she?"

"No, she should be okay. The calf usually comes out with the front feet first and the head between the knees. This one is backwards, but we'll help her."

The ox let out a huge groan and pushed at the same time. Douglas knew what was happening. He stood behind the animal, grabbed two hind legs as it appeared and gently helped the baby's birth.

The mother threw her head back and let out a huge, wet breath, then she raised her body slightly and nudged the baby.

After a few minutes the mother struggled to get on her feet. Douglas carefully helped the baby stand as well. Shaky and still wet, the little one worked to stand as the mother licked her.

Both men had stepped back. "We've never seen such. That was amazing."

Douglas stood up. "That's nature. These animals have been around a lot longer than we have. They usually don't have any trouble giving birth. They don't need us humans."

"We're glad you came. We wouldn't have known what to do."

"Are you getting ready to move out with the next wagon train?"

"We are. We're going to California. Gold is calling."

"Gold has called many there. I hope you have luck in finding a huge claim."

Both men laughed. "We know we will." The guy looked at the calf. "So, what do we do with that baby?"

"You don't have to do anything. That mother looks like she knows what she's doing. She'll be a good momma. I'd watch to make sure the mother and the baby can keep up with the wagon train. You might have to carry the baby a little bit if it starts to fall behind."

"We can do that." One of the guys stuck out his hand and shook Douglas's. "Do we owe you anything?"

"No. I didn't do anything. That lady did it all." He patted the head of the ox, then turned back to the men. "Nice meeting you two, and good luck to you."

Douglas walked away, hoping these two men would make it across the states. It was obvious they didn't have a lot of experience with animals, and animals were an important part of the wagon train journey.

God, watch over these men and those who will travel with them in the hopes of finding a new life for whatever reason.

He knew what it was like to want to move on to find new surroundings in search of a better life, but he also knew what it was like to want to return to what he knew and loved. Becoming a veterinarian had been his dream for years, but for years he dared not talk about it to his family, especially after Lucas lost his wife and left to fight in the Mexican-American War. He was needed on the ranch, and he had resolved himself to that life forever. It certainly wouldn't have been a bad life.

Lucky for him, after Lucas found Abigail, he was free to pursue his dream.

God had been good to him. Now he wanted to thank him

by becoming the best veterinarian he could be and taking care of the needs of the animals in town.

Who's to say he wouldn't find his love along the way as Lucas had found his.

CHAPTER SIX

Emma sat at the desk in her reception area, her hands in her lap, refusing to allow the tears to surface. She'd been in the office for six hours, alone. She and her mother had written out notices of her office being open and hung them around town. Still, no one came for her services.

Around noon she'd walked to her house for lunch and caught a glimpse of several people going into Douglas's office. None of them had animals with them. Surely, they were not there for their own medical needs. Having no one come into the clinic all day was bad enough, but having them go to a veterinarian was hurtful—if that's what they were doing. To make herself feel good, she told herself they were there for animals at their farms.

After a nice lunch with her mother, she returned to the office. Picking up her dust cloth, she passed it over several pieces of furniture. She'd done it so much today, there couldn't be a speck of dust still in this room, but what else was she to do? With no patients, she was completely lost.

Tossing the cloth in a drawer, she headed for the door to get a breath of fresh air. Several people passed. She smiled and waved. They waved, but put their heads down and walked on. Disheartened, she sat on the step.

"Taking a break from doctoring?" Douglas walked around the corner and stood at the bottom of the small front porch.

"I wish that were the case. I haven't had one patient all day."

Douglas frowned, then walked right up to her and sat down on the same step. "Maybe you moved to a healthy town. That would be a good thing, wouldn't it?"

"It would be, I guess, but I don't think that's the case."

"Really? And, what do you think is the reason our good citizens of Independence aren't coming in to see the new doctor in town?"

"Maybe for the same reason you don't call me Dr. O'Hara."

Douglas stretched his legs in front of him. "That could be. And, it might not be any of my business, but why are you still O'Hara when you'd been married?"

"You're right. It's none of your business, but I will tell you it was not a good marriage, and I didn't think twice about changing my name back after he died." As soon as the words came out of her mouth, she regretted having shared that fact with him.

Douglas nodded. "I see."

He didn't say any more, but she could tell he was contemplating what she'd said. He didn't ask for any explanations, and she wasn't going to elaborate on her horrible marriage. She had said enough, much more than she should have. Douglas Fletcher was an acquaintance, not a good friend to share personal information with.

She changed the subject before he asked any more. "Why are you away from your office? People haven't stopped going in and out all morning. Please tell me you are not treating humans?"

"And if I do have a few human patients?"

"You're a veterinarian, not a medical doctor. You can harm those people."

"I won't hurt anyone. I know my limitations. What they're coming in for are simple things. I sewed up one guy who got his hand caught in barbed wire. It looked worse than it was. A few stitches and he was fine. I looked at a few with stomach aches or bad muscle aches, but I didn't do anything to them. I told them they needed to see you."

She blinked. "That was kind of you and very smart. Stomach problems or muscle aches, or for that matter, all sorts of minor sounding problems can turn into something awful if not treated properly."

"And I guess you know the proper cure for all those aches and pains."

His sarcastic remark was exactly what she'd expect him to say. She refused to let her irritation show. "No, Mr. Fletcher, I do not have all the answers, but I'm sure to have more than you do."

Douglas held up both hands. "Truce. Neither of us are miracle workers. Let's move on. We're neighbors."

Emma pulled up all the willpower she had. This man knew exactly how to push her buttons, but she refused to show her annoyance with him.

"You're right. Did you get to visit your family on the ranch?"

"Yes, it was wonderful to see everyone. I got to meet my new nephew, William. He's three. He was born shortly after I left. He's a cutie, and now he's going to have a new brother or sister soon."

"That's wonderful. Does the mother have a doctor near the ranch?"

"I never asked. I assume one of the Mexican ladies who've been with us since I was a child will deliver the baby. They have brought quite a few babies into the world. They're family to us and have our best interest at heart. We put a lot of trust in them."

"I'm sure having them close by is wonderful, but would you tell your sister-in-law I'm in town and would love to take a look at her. I certainly would try to get to her when she goes into labor—that is, if she feels the need."

Douglas nodded. "I can do that. So far, I think she's doing quite well and is happy with the ladies on the ranch tending to her."

"That's great to hear. Giving birth is a wonderful experience."

"So, do you have any children?"

Douglas's question caught her off-guard. She cleared her throat. "No, sir. We were never fortunate enough to have a healthy birth. I've lost two babies." Again, she bit her lip. She never told people about her babies. Why was she telling him?

Douglas sat up straight, then took her hand. "I'm so sorry. I shouldn't have asked such a personal question."

As if he realized he'd taken her hand, he dropped it and scooted toward the edge of the step.

"It's okay." She nodded. He looked so sincere. "Helping mothers bring babies into the world is a wonderful experience and was my favorite part of training. Having lost two I know what they're going through and how it is so important to have a healthy birth."

"The new mothers in town will be honored to have someone like you to help with their deliveries. I'll certainly tell Abigail about you."

"Thank you. I'd love to ride out and examine her in the near future if she'd like." She crossed her arms in front of her chest. "It doesn't appear the good people of Independence will miss me here since they have an animal doctor to visit."

"Emma, give the town some time. Most of these citizens have never been near a progressive city like the ones in the East. They'll come around and one day will be thrilled you're part of their town."

"How about you, Mr. Fletcher? Will you come around?"

Douglas leaned against the stair railing and smiled. "Yes,

one day I'll surprise you and come knocking at your office door with a medical problem, but I have to warn you, I'm healthy as a horse. I've never needed a doctor."

"That's a wonderful thing. I hope you never have the need, but if you do, I'm at your service." She tilted her head and squinted trying to see the side of his face. "Your bump looks as if it's healing nicely."

He rubbed a hand on the side of his face. "I'll be glad when the discoloration goes away. I'm tired of explaining how I got it. Thank you for your concern."

He hit his knees with both of his hands, then stood up. "And if you have a pet or a horse that needs medical attention, I'm at *your* service."

She smiled and lifted her hand in farewell. Maybe Douglas Fletcher, veterinarian, wasn't such a bad guy after all.

~

Douglas said hello to several people on the street as he headed to the restaurant for lunch. He had a small wood stove in his house, but he didn't want to cook. He could do okay with a hunk of beef on an open fire, but trying to pull together a meal on a stove wasn't his forte.

He wondered if Emma cooked. She probably had servants all her life to cook and clean for her, and now she had her mother living with her. She wouldn't have to worry about eating at a restaurant every day.

He walked up the two steps into the restaurant. No one else was seated so he took a seat near the window and waited for Molly.

Immediately, she walked through the swinging doors of the kitchen. "Douglas, I'm so glad you're here."

"Thanks, Molly. I'm surprised to see the place is empty."

"The lunch crowd was big, but it's two o'clock and everyone is back at work."

He pulled out his pocket watch. "You're right. I didn't realize it was so late. I've been so busy at the office, the time slipped by."

"That's a good thing if your business is already moving."

"It is, but I seem to have a lot of human patients. Right now, the town's good citizens don't want to go to see our new female doctor."

"I heard she moved to town and is a woman. I've seen two new ladies in here. One may have been her, but I was always too busy to stop by their table to say hello. The younger lady is quite attractive." She raised an eyebrow.

"That she is. Her mother is a nice-looking lady as well. I think Emma will be a good doctor for this town if everyone will give her a chance." Douglas almost laughed, knowing he was one of the ones who didn't believe in female doctors.

"So, you've already met her and are on a first name basis?"

"We rode the stagecoach into town together. I slept most of the time, but we did get to meet."

"And now I hear your office is right behind hers. Convenient, I'd say."

Douglas grinned. "I guess it will be convenient if I come down with a horrible disease."

Molly laughed, but Douglas could tell she wasn't thrilled with the idea of the location of his office. He wasn't sure why, but he knew better than to ask.

"So what can I get for you today, *Dr.* Fletcher."

"I'll take your special."

Molly grimaced. "All sold out, but I'll whip you up something really nice."

"I know you will."

Molly blushed and smiled.

Douglas watched her sashay into the kitchen and hoped he hadn't given her the wrong impression. Molly had always been a good friend, but he wasn't sure he wanted anything other than friendship from her.

As children he had kissed her behind the schoolhouse and some of the boys found out. He never lived that down.

They were ten years old when that happened, and now they were adults with pasts. She had even been engaged to one of their friends from school, but the guy decided to leave Independence without her. As far as he knew she had not gotten involved with anyone else since.

She was definitely a pretty girl. Maybe he'd find little time to spend with her. Who knows? Something could come of it. He doubted it, but he certainly would keep an open mind.

Maybe his former love, Lily, ruined him of ever looking at someone else as anything but friends. Of course, as his mother so dutifully pointed out, it was time for him to settle down.

"Yeah, right." He spoke out loud, then looked around to make sure he was still alone. He didn't want to embarrass himself the first week he was in town.

He got up and walked to the counter and picked up a one-page town newspaper and took it back to his table. He read with interest stories about new businesses in town, who'd been thrown in jail for starting fights at the local saloons on Saturday night, and several stories about horses or cattle that had gone missing. His thoughts turned to the men trying to take land for the future railroad, but nothing about that problem had been printed in this edition of the paper. Maybe he'd stop in at the newspaper office to look at some old papers. He needed as much information as possible to help Lucas and the other ranchers.

He looked up. Molly backed through the swinging doors carrying two plates filled with food.

"Wow, girl, I'm hungry but I'm only one man. You'll have me rolling down the streets of Independence if I eat like this every day."

"You deserve to have a good, decent meal. You can't take care of all those poor sick animals if you're starving." She placed the dishes on the table overflowing with mashed potatoes and gravy, thick pieces of ham, beans, and a huge piece of bread. "You enjoy and call me if you need anything. I have fresh apple pie for dessert."

"After all this, I'm sure I won't need dessert, but I might buy a slice to eat after I get home."

Molly smiled. "Since you're living alone, you can come over here after work for dessert and to visit. I know how lonesome it is to live alone."

"Thank you, Molly, I appreciate the offer."

She walked to the counter.

He glanced at her as he ate and realized she'd been looking at him. Obviously not embarrassed at being caught watching him, she smiled again.

He concentrated on his food for the remainder of his time in the restaurant. As good a friend as Molly was, he wasn't comfortable having her flirt with him.

After his meal, he pulled out money to pay.

"No, this is on the house. I couldn't take your money."

"No, I insist or I won't come back in. This is your business. You can't give food away, no matter how long we've known each other."

"Okay, but I hate to take money from a dear friend."

He took her hand. "And I do consider us dear, old friends."

She looked down at his hand and smiled, but he could tell it wasn't sincere. He had a feeling she sensed he was content with their friendship, but maybe she wasn't.

He dropped her hand. "Would you do me a favor? Would you pass around some good words about Dr. O'Hara. The town needs a full-time doctor. I'd hate to see her move on because the town didn't accept her. We need to give her a chance."

"I guess I can do that, but would you really go to a woman doctor?"

"That's not the point. Her services are needed here." He put money on the counter. "I'll probably see you tomorrow."

"So you'll be in town for the rest of the week?"

"I think so. On Friday I'm riding out toward the ranch and will stop at the Welch's. They have a mare about to give birth, and then I'll go to the Shafer's. They sent word they'd like me to look at a new colt."

"I'm so glad you're in town. You'll save a lot of the animals around here."

"Thanks, Molly. I appreciate your saying that." He stretched. "I guess I'd better get back to the office. I'm still getting things in order, but I've had so many people come in it's hard to get anything done."

"Are these people coming in with animals or people needing to see a doctor for themselves?"

"Unfortunately, I've had both animal and human patients. I've persuaded them to go see Dr. O'Hara, but it will take some time."

"We'll see." Molly pulled the money toward her. "Thanks, Douglas. I, for one, am glad you're back in Independence." She stopped, took a deep breath, then speared him with her big blue eyes.

He could tell she wanted to say more.

Do I see fear in her eyes?

"I would like us to spend more time together." Her words, jumbled and fast, were hard to catch.

Aaah, now he understood. A thousand thoughts raced through Douglas's mind. He didn't want to hurt her feelings, but he didn't want to give her the wrong impression. He groped for the right words. "I would love to do that. You and I shared a lot of good times together before I left."

Her face broke into a huge smile. "I'd love that. I could fix a picnic lunch, and we could go to the creek like we used to do."

"That would be nice, but first let me get my practice in order. My head is spinning with so much to do. I'm not sure when we can spend some quality friend time again."

But Molly didn't get the hint. "I'll look forward to it." Her expression told him she read more into it than he intended.

Douglas waved goodbye before he said the wrong thing. Maybe spending time with Molly would be what he needed. At least she respected his profession, unlike the new doctor in town.

He wondered how an afternoon picnic with Dr. O'Hara would be. Would he ever call her "doctor" to her face? One day, but not now. He'd have to come to terms with having a female doctor in town. Even though he respected her for getting her license, he wouldn't give her the satisfaction of letting her know. At least not right now. She had to have worked hard to achieve her certification. He had.

He'd spent several years getting to where he was today. She needed to respect his profession as well.

Maybe it would be fun convincing her he was as much a doctor in his own right as she was.

CHAPTER SEVEN

Loud talking, laughing, and scraping of chairs reverberated from the walls of the town hall as Douglas stepped in.

"Guess we're in the right place." Douglas looked at his brother.

"Yep, these ranchers are here for a purpose. They mean to figure out what to do with those men causing us problems. Nothing like this has happened since we had to get together to figure out how to get rid of that house where the ladies of the night kept their trade going."

"Ladies of the night?" Douglas laughed out loud. "I haven't heard anyone use that expression in years. Did the townspeople figure out how to close down the establishment?"

"Sure did. At least it's not in the middle of town anymore. I think they moved to the south somewhere."

"Hey, Fletchers. Glad you two could make it." Harry Tindel walked up to Lucas and hit him on the back. "We don't see your face in town much."

"There's a reason for that. I don't like crowds."

"Glad you came tonight. We need all the help we can get." He turned to Douglas. "And Douglas, we're glad you've come back home. I hear you've opened up a vet practice."

"Yes, sir. I have, and I've been well received."

"Glad to hear it. We need a good vet here."

Sheriff Victor Sanchez walked up.

"Vic, how you doing tonight?" Douglas reached out and stuck out his hand. "Thanks for taking care of those three brothers who tried to rob the stage."

"They're still in the jail waiting for the judge to come through, but I'll be glad when they're gone. That Sam is driving me crazy with his demands."

Somebody in the front of the room hit a pan with a hammer. "Men, can we sit down and get to the job at hand?"

Victor shook hands with both Lucas and Douglas. "Guess we'd better sit so we can get this meeting started."

At least thirty men grabbed chairs and when those were all taken, the remaining men stood along the back and side walls. Douglas and Lucas sat together. Victor leaned against the wall.

The room got quiet. "Thank you. Now, most of you know me already, but if you're new to our town, my name is Mayor Harry Miller. You know why we're here tonight so let's get started. I think most of us here frequent the churches around here, so if you don't mind, let's take a minute to ask for God's guidance in dealing with these men who are causing our ranches so many problems. Preacher Smith, would you lead us in a short prayer?"

A tall, young man with dark hair walked to the front, nodding to several men before stepping up next to Harry. "Thank you, Mr. Miller. Let's bow our heads. Heavenly Father, you know these men in this room. They're hard-working family men. Some of these families have been on the same land for several generations. Please, tonight, help us come to some conclusions that will keep our family lands intact. We pray for this guidance in God's name, Amen."

Lucas leaned toward Douglas. "Do you remember the

preacher? He came out to our ranch one day with the intentions of courting Abigail. I credit him for me finally making a move to get to know her better."

"Aaah, a little jealous, were we?"

Lucas chuckled. "I guess. I don't think he's ever gotten married. I wish he would. He's a really good guy."

"Thank you, Preacher Smith." Harry blew out a big breath as Preacher Smith took his seat. "As our town preacher mentioned, some of us have been on land that's been in our families for generations. I want Lucas Fletcher to come up and talk with us. He and his brother Douglas are the third generation on their ranch. Lucas, you want to come up?"

Lucas leaned toward Douglas. "No, I'd rather not talk, but here goes."

"You floor us, brother."

Lucas walked up front and cleared his throat. "Most of you know me and know I'm not a big speaker, but I am here tonight like the rest of you. We need to find a solution to rid our land of these men trying to take it for their own profit."

Douglas listened to his big brother talk about coming up with a plan to protect the land. He threw out several suggestions, all of which could be done peacefully, but then he stopped on the third one.

"If our first two options don't work, we'll have to resort to protecting what is ours with their style. We'll have to arm ourselves, stake out guards each night, and, if necessary, use the weapons to run the men off or throw their butts in jail."

The room exploded with applause and shouts of approval.

A tall man with broad shoulders and a head of flaming red hair stood up. "I say we forget about the first two peaceful means because we know these men are up to no good and have no qualms shooting those that stand in their way. Look at what they did to poor Mr. Murphy. The man was unarmed, trying to protect his wife, and they shot him."

"Yes. Yes. Yes." The men shouted and clapped their hands. Some of them stood up and stomped their feet.

Douglas didn't like the response. Some of these men were new to Independence or at least new since he'd last lived here, and they were the ones making the most noise. The older men sat and simply nodded. Several shook their heads.

Lucas stepped back to allow Harry Miller to come back to the front.

"Gentlemen, please." Harry shouted above the din, then hit the pan with his hammer once again. "We won't get anything accomplished if we resort to this type of undisciplined behavior. We have to have some semblance of organization."

Slowly, the talking and shouting subsided.

"We can't guard every ranch every night. We're too spread out, but if the majority of us want to arm ourselves and stand guard, we can take turns on different days and different ranches. They won't know where we are, and eventually they'll mess up and end up in front of our guns."

Again, the men started shouting.

Douglas hated chaos. He took a deep breath, stood up and walked up to his brother. "Nothing will get done like this."

"Yeah, I know. Let's see if we can make some sense out of it." Lucas stepped forward and took the hammer from Harry. When he hit the pan, he shouted, "Men, sit down and shut up."

Douglas almost smiled at his brother. The man never said much, but when he spoke it was with authority. Surprisingly, the room got quiet, chairs scraped, and men sat down. Douglas imagined his brother leading men into battle during the Mexican-American War, where he made a name for himself as a leader. The men here tonight recognized that trait and Douglas could tell they were ready to listen.

Over an hour later, the brother walked out of the town

hall.

"You did a great job, Lucas. I think the plan makes sense and can be successful."

"I hope so, but I truly hope we don't have to resort to violence. There's been enough of that, but if we have to, we'll defend our land to the end."

Douglas hit Lucas on the back. "I hope it can be done peacefully as well. We'll pray it can."

"I'm with you, brother."

"Do you know the first guy who stood up? The one with the red hair?"

"I think his name is Franklin Shaunesey. He's been in town a few years. Has a small place just north of town, but that's all I know. I've never had a decent conversation with him. I did hear someone say he lost a lot of cattle to the fever last spring, and he's struggling to keep his place going. I'm not sure he's much of a rancher, but that's all I know about him."

Douglas nodded. "I might go out to his ranch sometimes and check on his other cattle. We can't have diseases spreading to other herds."

"That would be a good gesture, brother."

As they walked toward Douglas's office, they passed in front of Emma's. "Have you met the new doctor in town?"

Lucas looked toward the office. "I haven't met the new doctor but I heard it's a woman."

"That she is." He hesitated, not sure how Lucas would feel about what he was about to say. "In the course of our conversation, I told her Abigail would have her second child soon. She wanted to know if she could come by sometimes to check on her."

Lucas stopped walking and looked at his brother, his brows coming together.

Douglas wasn't sure if Lucas would thank him or punch him for interfering in their lives.

Finally, Lucas nodded. "I think it wouldn't hurt for her

to come by. Bonita and Carmella and their aunt have delivered all the babies on the ranch for decades, but I don't think they would be offended." He stood up straight and nodded again. "Yes, I think that is a good idea."

"Good, I'll talk with her, and I'll make sure she gets to the ranch."

The two brothers walked quietly down the street, then onto a side street where Lucas had his horse tied to the hitching post in front of Douglas's office.

Douglas turned to his brother as he opened the gate. "Sure, you don't want to stay the night here?"

"Oh no, I'd rather ride half the night just to be by Abigail."

"You're a lucky man, Lucas."

"I am." He put his foot in the stirrup and threw his leg over the horse. "I thank God all the time to have found two good women to love me in this lifetime." He saluted, then turned the horse and rode off.

Douglas watched him until he was too far down the street to see. He envied his brother. One day, he hoped he could find a woman to settle down with as well. He turned to the house he was using as an office, but stopped and looked at Emma O'Hara's house. One small light flickered in the window. He wondered what she and her mother were doing. Did she read when she was alone? Did she sew? Maybe she was making plans for her office and her practice.

He'd probably never know what the lady did at night. He did know he needed to get his rest tonight because he and Lucas were scheduled to join two other men the next night to stand guard. The task of the townsmen would not be easy. Most of the ranches took up hundreds and some thousands of acres. The plan was to focus on the fields where cattle grazed and those closest to the houses.

He'd ride out to the ranch tomorrow evening along with two other men, but tomorrow he'd work in his office and would try to see Emma. Maybe they could settle on a day to ride out to see Abigail.

With the prospect of spending a little time with Emma, the day seemed a lot better.

CHAPTER EIGHT

The next day Emma sat alone again in her office, refusing to allow depression to take over. Shortly after three o'clock as she studied the amputation process from one of her notebooks, she heard footsteps on the front porch. Surprised that someone was actually coming into her office, she shut the notebook and stood up.

The door opened and Douglas stuck his head inside.

For a brief second, disappointment settled around her. She so hoped to see a prospective patient. Quickly she recovered and felt her face break into a smile. Douglas might not be a patient, but it was nice having someone to talk with.

"Douglas, how nice of you to drop in. I hope you're not feeling ill."

Douglas stomped his boots on the small porch and pulled his hat off before stepping in. "No, I'm feeling great." He laughed. "Sorry. I don't need your medical expertise."

Emma sat. "That's a good thing if you're not sick. Please come in and visit with this lonely female doctor."

Douglas looked around the office. "Still no business today?"

"No business. Not one patient.'"

He rubbed his hand across his chin. "I'm sorry." He

cleared his throat. "My brother Lucas was in town last night for the town meeting."

"Yes, I heard about the meeting from Sheriff Vic. The situation sounds dangerous. I do agree something must be done to protect the land, but I hate to know there might be bloodshed."

Douglas pulled a chair from against the wall right up to the front of her desk and sat down.

Emma couldn't pull her gaze away from him. His eyes were hazel, but today they picked up the blue in his shirt. He wasn't tall and lanky like so many of the cowboys around town. He certainly was tall, maybe six feet with a thick chest and muscular upper arms, but that didn't keep him from having a smooth motion in almost everything he did.

She wondered how it would feel to have those muscular arms around her.

She shook her head. *Where did that come from?*

Douglas stretched his legs in front of him. "If it were up to me there never would be bloodshed, but we can't sit around and let these men take our land."

"Of course. I understand. I simply hope all the other men feel the same way as you and will try to work a peaceful solution."

"You're new to this area, Emma. There are men out here who would rather draw a weapon than to sit down to talk."

"I'm beginning to understand that, but that concept goes against everything I believe in and dedicated my life towards."

"I understand your position, but we have to do what we need to." He let out a big breath. "I didn't come in here today to discuss our differing viewpoints about keeping law and order out here. I came here to talk about my sister-in-law. I told Lucas about your interest in going out to see Abigail and he accepted the offer."

A second passed before Emma realized what he said. She wanted to jump for joy, but she put her hands together and spoke softly but professionally. "I'm glad he agreed to let me see her. I'm sure the ladies on the ranch have more experience delivering babies than I have, but if something goes wrong they might not know exactly what to do. I'd love to ride out with you." She hesitated. "Are you okay with a female doctor checking on your sister-in-law?"

Douglas reared back in his chair. "Sure, ladies deliver babies all the time around here."

She crossed her arms in front of her body, the joy of having him here vanishing. "There you go again. Yes, I am a lady, but I do more than deliver babies. I've been in the room when a baby had to be removed surgically, and that saved both the baby's and the mother's life. Not just any lady could do that."

"You're right, I guess."

"I guess?" Her voice was much too loud. She shook her head and found a calmer, quieter voice. "I can't believe you said that. Maybe I shouldn't go if you still have that attitude about female doctors."

"No, Emma, I want you to go. I want Abigail to have the best care possible. Lucas lost his first wife. He couldn't live through losing another one."

Emma felt her shoulders slump. "I'm so sorry. Was it in childbirth?"

"No, she was thrown from her horse and hit her head. He and our mother raised Caroline without her. Very sad. Now he's found love again, and we're all thrilled for him."

Feeling bad for snapping at him, she nodded. "I'd be glad to ride out with you and check on her."

"Good. Do you think you could go tomorrow?"

"Sure. I'm sure no one will miss me here."

"The townspeople will accept you one day. Give them a chance. If word gets around that I'm taking you out to Fletcher Ranch to check on Abigail, it might help to change their minds."

"You're right. Thank you."

"I have to stand guard tonight. I'll catch a little sleep at the ranch before I come back into town. I'll bring the carriage and we can head back out if neither of us have any obligations at the office. If your mother wants to go out with us, there'll be room in the carriage for her."

"That would be splendid. Thank you. I know Mother would love to see the ranch."

"It's a pleasant ride with beautiful scenery. You'll both enjoy it, I'm sure."

Emma got serious. "Please be careful standing guard tonight. I certainly wish there would be a better way to solve this issue."

"We will try our best to make it safe for everyone. No one wants trouble, but we don't have a better plan. Something has to be done."

"I guess I've seen too much bad when men clash."

He stood up. "As I said, no one wants trouble. Thank you for your concern."

Emma stood up as well. A feeling she couldn't identify tingled in her chest. For some reason she wanted Douglas to stay with her longer. "I know you don't have a lot of time, but I'd love for you to come to the house and have something to eat. Mother cooked too much for lunch. I could fix you a plate."

He raised an eyebrow. "Even though it sounds tempting, I don't have a lot of time. Can I take a rain check?"

"Certainly." Emma wanted to touch his hand, but she dared not. Instead, she clasped her hands together. "Please be careful. I'd hate to use my medical training on you."

Douglas laughed. "I would, too." He put his hat on. "I'll come here when I get back in town tomorrow. If everything goes well, we'll head back out to the ranch so you can see Abigail."

Emma slid back down in her seat. "I'll have a bag packed in the hopes we can travel to the ranch."

He tipped his hat. "Have a good evening. Miss Emma."

"Same to you, especially on guard duty tonight. Do be careful."

She stared at the closed door. Her chest tightened knowing he'd be in a dangerous situation tonight.

~

Douglas sat on his horse Major in the darkness of a huge sugar maple tree. With the full moon about to set, he dared not move out into the light of breaking dawn. He gazed along the field of a neighboring ranch. The night had been extremely quiet. Dawn was only minutes away, and the only critter he'd seen was one coyote. Normally, he'd go after the animal that terrorized his ranch hands and cattle, but not tonight. The game they hoped to catch had two legs, not four.

Behind him he heard leaves rustling as something big eased toward him. He raised his gun and waited.

"Douglas." A soft voice drifted through the night air.

He relaxed and lowered his rifle. "Over here, Lucas."

In a couple of minutes Lucas guided his horse next to him. "I guess you haven't seen anything either."

"Nope. It's been all I could do to stay awake. As far as I can see, Randolph Cummings didn't have any trouble tonight."

"Makes me wonder if that gang gave another ranch some trouble."

"If so, I hope it was one of the ranches our guys are guarding."

"We can only hope." Lucas stretched. "Are you ready to ride back to the ranch? I think we've done our part tonight."

"Yep. You don't have to ask me twice." He turned his horse and led the way out to the dirt road that led to Fletcher Ranch. Once there, he hoped to sleep a few hours and then he'd ride back into Independence to see if Emma could return with him to the ranch to see Abigail.

That thought sent a warm streak through him. He looked forward to spending most of the day with her. He wasn't sure why he'd want to spend time with the lady since they had such differing views, but whatever the draw, he'd go with it and enjoy the day.

He'd allow himself a day to be with the beautiful doctor, even though that was all it would be. After what Lily did to him, one day was all he could give her or any other female at this stage in his life.

Lucas rode in front of him. In his usual style, he sat in his saddle without saying anything. That was fine with Douglas. He never tired of watching the sun come up over the trees. New York had sun rises, of course, but nothing like these red and orange skies over the acres and acres of open land. He took a deep breath.

It's good to be home.

~

By noon, Douglas was back on the trail heading to town. With Major tied to the back of the family carriage, he eased down the well-worn, dusty trail. The month had been dry, too dry. As soon as he'd gotten out of the stagecoach almost two weeks ago, Douglas knew the area needed rain. Getting water to the herds of cattle and to the horses placed a hardship on the local ranchers, especially now that some of the branches leading from the rivers around Independence were being barricaded by those who wanted to profit from building the railroad.

Progress. Progress was important, especially bringing the railroad nearer to Independence. Being able to transport their cattle from Fletcher Ranch to a closer railhead would be so much easier and safer than driving them across open country by cattle drive.

His thoughts settled on the last cattle drive he'd ridden on before he left to attend classes in the East. Cattle drives could be dangerous and that one was no exception with Lucas being badly wounded. Never had he been so afraid of losing someone. Lucas had been his steadying post for his entire life. When Lucas had left to fight for in the American-Mexican War, Douglas remembered how he'd never allow himself to think about his brother not returning. Lucas was a fighter, a winner. He'd return. Even going down a dark path after Sarah died, Lucas never wavered, or at least if he did, he didn't allow that feeling to be shared.

During the last part of that cattle drive as Lucas lay on the trail losing blood, he realized his brother was human. He could die like everyone else. He'd felt so helpless wanting to help him, but didn't know how. He tried to stop the bleeding as he'd done many times on the ranch, but Lucas's wound was different. Blood gushed out. Maybe it was then that he'd decided to study medicine. Even a veterinarian would've known how to stop the bleeding.

Whatever the reason, he was glad he'd gone away and studied. He would be of help when called upon.

He flicked the reins. The horse pulling the rig was Sunflower, a sweet gentle mare, who understood his signal and picked up a little speed. He wanted to get to town after a boring night of guard duty.

Progress. He'd seen what it had done for the bigger cities on the east coast. Independence needed progress, but he also understood why Lucas hated it. Progress brought more people, more trouble, and more problems. Of course, along with those problems came good things like a certain female doctor. He smiled hoping their day together would be a good one.

Yes, progress was a necessary evil that couldn't be stopped, but he hoped it didn't ruin the way of life that his family and many of the other ranches enjoyed. He prayed the new strategy of the townspeople would deter those trying to take away their land and their way of life.

As much as he hated violence, he'd do whatever it took to save Fletcher Ranch and the traditions he loved so dearly.

CHAPTER NINE

Emma sat next to her mother on the back seat of the older, but well-maintained Fletcher carriage. Douglas sat on the front seat holding the reins. He'd explained the carriage had been in his family for many years and was an Eckhart Surry. Its hooded top kept the sun off of them, and the upholstered seats couldn't have been more comfortable.

The cloudless sky and slight breeze eased her mind and body, one of the few times she'd felt relaxed since she and her mother traveled to Independence. Life had been hectic trying to pack their belongings, telling their friends goodbye, and finally boarding the train and then the uncomfortable stagecoach. When Douglas had boarded the coach, she remembered thinking how nice looking he was. Immediately he'd fallen asleep, and as she watched him sleep in his wrinkled shirt and trousers, she'd wondered what his story was.

Now, she knew some of his story. Would she ever find out the rest?

"This is lovely."

Her mother's words drew her out of her reverie. She blinked. "Yes, it is."

"You ladies okay back there?" Douglas turned slightly

and flashed a beautiful smile.

"We're fine. Thank you for asking." Emma smiled back at him. "This country is beautiful, just as you said it would be. How much farther is it to Fletcher Ranch?"

"I'm glad you like it. We've been on Fletcher land for the last few miles."

Emma stared at the land surrounding the trail with a new appreciation. How could so much land be in one family? "This is amazing."

"I think the same thing every time I ride this road. I love this land."

"As you should. Having this much land is unheard where we lived."

"I didn't know that until I left here and studied in New York. I've always loved living out here, but now that I'm back, I have a better understanding and appreciation of what our family has."

As he expertly steered the carriage down the road, he talked about his family clearing the land three generations ago, working it, and building fences and buildings. As she listened, she knew he'd come from a good family. Honest, hard-working people. Not the cheating swindler type like her dead husband.

A shiver ran down her spine. For years she'd believed her husband's stories about making money. Having lots of money, buying what she needed for herself and for her mother, and attending the operas and theater whenever she wanted had been wonderful. Now she knew that money had been ill-gotten. His stories had all been lies. Guilt washed over her every time she thought about the enjoyment she'd gained from his illegal wealth.

"You have a lot to be proud of, Mr. Fletcher." Mrs. O'Hara spoke up as she threw a harsh look toward Emma.

Once again Emma pulled herself out of her deep thought. "Yes, I'm very impressed. I know your family is proud of all this."

He turned and floored her again with that gorgeous smile. Another tingle in her chest reminded her how handsome he was.

"We are very proud of this land and will do whatever is necessary to keep it in our family. We pray the plan the town came up with will work."

"We are, as well."

When the carriage reached the top of a ridge, Douglas stopped the horses. "This is the best view of the ranch we have." He explained about his great grandfather starting the first house with three rooms and then being added on as each generation lived in it. "Today, the main house is comfortable and big enough to accommodate lots of guests."

"I can't wait to see it." Emma leaned toward the side of the carriage and took in the massive piece of land, the neat well-maintained fences lining huge pastures, and several structures around the main house.

Douglas flicked the reins once more. As if she sensed she'd be in her own stable soon, the horse headed down the trail with a brisk gait. As they neared the main area of the property, workers on horseback and some on foot waved to Douglas. He waved back and called several by name.

"I don't know everyone's names. Some of them like Mason on that brown horse has been with the family for years. I'm sure you'll get to meet him. He now lives in one of the smaller houses near the bunkhouse. His wife died several years ago. They had a small place on the outskirts of our land, but after she died, he moved closer to the main house. We all consider him family. You'll like him."

"And very handsome from what I can see. I hope we do get to meet him," Mrs. O'Hara whispered. She wrapped her arms in front of her body and giggled.

Emma chuckled at her mother's contagious enthusiasm for life and wished she would find a man who would finally make her life a happy one.

Emma rested against the back of the seat and watched

the landscape ease by. "This is lovely, Mother, isn't it?"

Her mother's eyes twinkled as she scanned the land around her. "Yes, it is. I just love this. Thank you for letting me ride out with you today."

"I love having you with me." Emma smiled. *I'm the luckiest lady in these parts to have a mother like you.*

Soon, the carriage pulled through a huge arched gate with the letters FR intricately encircled over the entrance. Douglas pulled to the front of the house with a front porch running its entire width with inviting rockers lining the area.

A young man appeared immediately. "Mr. Fletcher, glad to see you made it back to the ranch so fast."

"Thanks, Matthew. Take care of Sunflower, would you? I might leave again soon to get these ladies back to town unless we can talk them into staying the night here. You can take that extra bag into the house for them." Douglas turned to them and smiled.

Emma almost giggled at the thought of spending time at this gorgeous ranch, but she knew she had to get back to her practice, even though it was nonexistent at this point. She had to be hopeful the townspeople would give her a chance. As Douglas had pointed out, maybe when word spread that she was brought out to check on Abigail, confidence in her ability would spread. She could only hope.

Douglas jumped out of the carriage, handed the reins to Matthew, then stretched.

Emma realized he must be tired from his night of standing guard, then driving into town to pick up her and her mother. Having to take them back to town so fast might be a hardship on him as well, another reason she might consider spending a night on the ranch.

He stepped toward the back of the carriage and extended his hand to her mother who took it and allowed him to help her out. Emma grabbed her medical bag, scooted to that side of the seat and offered her hand to him willingly, unlike the first time he tried to help them get out of the stagecoach.

Douglas looked up into her eyes, gave a quirky smile, then took her hand.

His grip was firm, strong.

Emma swallowed and ignored the heat that shot up her arm. She took a big step toward the ground, but had to place one of her hands on his shoulder to feel steady. Her face flushed as he placed one of his hands on her waist and lifted her down.

"Thank you, Douglas. That's a big step."

"Yes, it is." He cleared his throat and stepped back. "

The front door flew open, and a petite lady stepped out. "Douglas, you're back already. I'm so glad. Bring those ladies up here and into our home."

"That's my mother in case you hadn't guessed."

Mrs. O'Hara took the steps and offered her hand to Mrs. Fletcher. "I'm June. Thank you so much for having us."

"Come in, please. We're so glad you're here." Their greeting floated down from the porch.

"They'll get along just fine," Douglas said as he placed his hand back on Emma's waist and led her to the steps.

"I hope so. Mother needs to have someone more her age to talk with. I'd love to see them become friends."

"Mother loves having people at the ranch. She'll make your mother feel right at home."

"Douglas," his mother said as she held onto June's hand. "Bring that lovely lady up here and introduce her to me."

"See what I mean." Douglas stepped up onto the porch and introduced Emma. "Emma has come to take a look at our Abigail."

"Yes, I've heard all about you." She took Emma's hand and held it tightly. "We're so glad you're here. We want the best care for Abigail."

"Thank you, Mrs. Fletcher. I look forward to meeting her."

Douglas stepped closer to Emma. "Mother will take care of you and your mother. I should get to the barn before I join you ladies inside."

Mrs. O'Hara took Mrs. Fletcher's hand. "The land here is beautiful. Would it be rude if I stayed outside for a little while and take it all in while my Emma checks on Abigail."

"Of course not. We're very proud of our ranch and love to show it off. Douglas will show you around."

"Mother, I'll take our bag. Don't get in the way of the men working." She laughed.

Douglas gave his mother a quick kiss on the cheek then turned to June. "You're welcomed to follow me into the barn, then you can wander around at your leisure."

Mrs. Fletcher looked at June. "When you're ready, please come inside and rest after your tour of the ranch." Mrs. Fletcher took Emma's hand. "Let's go find Abigail."

Emma followed Mrs. Fletcher through an enormous, intricately carved door. "This is lovely." She ran her hand along the woodwork. "Such craftsmanship."

"My grandfather and my father did most of the work. They did everything from cutting down the trees, building the structures, and even making a lot of the furniture you'll see in here. They were craftsmen for sure."

"I agree one hundred percent." Emma followed Mrs. Fletcher through the wide hallway, then into a sitting room off to one side.

"I'll go get Abigail. Please have a seat. She'll be down shortly."

The large furniture, some carved as beautifully as the door, filled the room. Two large couches faced each other in the center, but she chose to sit in a red upholstered chair, worn from years of wear, but clean. The wooden arms showed their wear as well but were polished to a brilliant shine. A huge piano stood in the corner. She wondered who in the household played.

The hall door opened and a lovely lady with chestnut colored hair and sparkling blue-green eyes stepped in.

"Dr. O'Hara, so nice of you to travel all the way out here

to check on me."

Emma stood up, stepped toward the lovely lady and took her hand. "It was a wonderful drive. The scenery is breathtaking. Mother and I are from the city. This is all so new to us." She let go of Abigail's hand then clasped hers in front of her body. "How are you doing and how far along are you?" Emma could see the lady was due very soon, but she wanted to hear it from her.

"I'm hoping my little fellow or daughter will grace us soon. I've felt wonderful until the last week or so."

"I hate to hear that. Why don't we go to your room, and we can talk."

Emma followed Abigail into the hall, then started up the steps. She watched as Abigail carefully placed one swollen foot and then the other in front of her. Emma's mind spun, remembering all of her studies and what could be going on with her patient.

Lord, it's me again. Please let me know how to help Abigail and her baby.

~

Douglas followed Matthew, who led Major and the carriage horse into the barn. June walked alongside him.

"After I get Sunflower in, do you mind if I go to the bunkhouse. Mason asked me to check on the stove in there. He thinks it needs cleaning."

"You go right ahead. I'll take care of the horse."

"Thank you, sir." He rushed out.

"This is amazing," June said as eyed the animals in the stables. "All these animals. How do you keep them in such good shape? It must take a tremendous amount of manpower to keep them up."

Douglas loved the lady's enthusiasm and her appreciation of what his family had worked so hard to build. "Yes, it takes quite a few men on the ranch to tend to these animals. Matthew is in charge of these animals in this barn. We consider him part of our family. The sheriff caught him stealing food from the general store when he was about nine years old. He'd lost both of his parents in a house fire when he was a baby. The neighbor who took him in killed his wife and is now in prison. Matthew was alone so my family took him in."

"That's a wonderful thing to do, Douglas. That boy probably would've gotten in with the wrong people and ended up in jail one day."

"It's been a blessing for our family as well. He's a good worker and a good kid. We also have a supervisor, Mason. I pointed him out as we rode in today. He oversees the entire ranch hands and keeps everything in tiptop condition. He's been with us for a long time. I'd trust anything on this ranch to him."

"Yes, I remember seeing him."

June left his side and walked to the stables lining the barn. She kept her hands to herself but smiled at the different animals.

Douglas led Major and Sunflower to their stalls and began to remove their bridles. The door opened and Mason walked in.

Douglas nodded to him. "I was just talking about you. I want you to meet June O'Hara. Her daughter is the town's new doctor, and she rode out with her to check on Abigail."

Mason looked at June and pulled off his hat. "Ma'am, it's so nice to meet you. Let me know if I can help you with anything while you're on Fletcher land."

June faced Mason with a coy smile on her face. She lowered her head, then looked at Mason once again. "Douglas was just telling me what a great help you are on the ranch. I'd love for you to show me around, that is, if you have a little time."

Mason looked at Douglas. "Do you need me right now?"

Douglas looked from the lady to his supervisor. Mason had a list of things to do today. No way would he shirk his responsibilities, but the man's eyes almost begged him for a little time.

"Sure, take all the time you need. I'd love for you to show June around. I have a few things to do right now." He put the brush he'd picked up and placed it on Major, but didn't move it. He couldn't look away from Mason, a man who had devoted his life first to his former wife, then to the men and the animals on this ranch for as long as Douglas had known him. Now that he was alone after his wife passed, he rarely left the ranch except to attend church services.

Today, Douglas was amazed at the way he looked at Emma's mother, almost acting like a young boy on his first date. Mason shuffled his feet in the barn dirt and fumbled with his hat pressed against his chest.

"Thanks, Mr. Fletcher. I won't be gone long."

"No, take as long as you want. I'm hoping Mrs. O'Hara and her daughter will be here until dinner so you have several hours."

Mason smiled big and stepped toward her. "Would you like to go outside? I'll show you where we keep our prized bulls?"

"Oh my, yes. That would be amazing. I'm not sure I've ever seen a bull up close."

"Then you're in for a treat." Mason touched her elbow and led her to the back door of the barn.

Douglas pulled the brush down Major's side. "Did you see that, Major? I can't believe that's our stoic supervisor. He's acting like a young boy." He shook his head and laughed. "I think it's great. I love it."

CHAPTER TEN

Emma sat next to her mother at the huge dining room table filled with steaming bowls of potatoes and vegetables, a platter of sliced beef and ham, a serving bowl of brown gravy, a cut-glass bowl of salad and a basket of home-made bread. Her stomach growled as she inhaled the aroma of the food.

"Lucas, would you ask grace tonight?" Mrs. Fletcher smiled at her oldest son.

"Certainly." He bowed his head and began.

Emma listened to his words of thanksgiving for the food, the ladies who prepared it, and then he surprised her by including her name. "And, God, we thank you for having Dr. O'Hara ride out to our ranch to take care of Abigail and our unborn baby." He looked at her. "Thank you."

"Amen." Everyone said in unison.

Watching such a loving family sit together to enjoy a meal warmed Emma's heart. Her husband always had a reason to be away at dinnertime. For so many years she had accepted his excuses to be gone in the evenings. Eating only with her mother and her brother seemed normal, but after his death she wondered about those evenings. What had he done while he was away from their home?

Douglas handed the platter of meat to her bringing her out of her thoughts of her late husband. "Thank you. This looks wonderful."

"Our ladies in the kitchen are amazing. I'll introduce you to them when they come out again. Bonita and Carmella have been part of this family for years."

Emma took the platter, served herself, then turned to Douglas. "Your family unit is wonderful. I love the fact you've kept together for so long."

Douglas took a big bite, then a drink. "Did you not have a close family in Boston?"

"We actually lived in Cambridge before I studied in Boston, but, no, we were not close nor big. After our husbands died, it was only Mother and me most nights. Sometimes my brother would drop by, but not often."

"I can't imagine not having family surrounding me. When I studied in New York, I missed that more than anything."

"So, you plan to settle around here?"

"Certainly. That's why I came back here to set up my first practice." He took a drink. "I was thinking. Do you plan to find a carriage?"

"A carriage? No. Why would I need one?"

Douglas laughed. "To get out to your patients. Not everyone will be able to get to town to see you. People will show up at your doorstep during all hours of the night for you to get to their homes for all kinds of emergencies. You'll definitely need a means of transportation."

"Gosh, I never thought about that. I don't know how to take care of an animal to pull it nor do I know how to drive one."

"Well, then, you're in luck. I just happen to know someone who can teach you."

"You?"

"Who else?"

She laughed. "Then I'd love a lesson or two."

"After dinner I'll give you your first one? I was wondering. Can I convince you and June to stay the night? I could take you back to town right after breakfast."

Emma looked at June.

"Emma, I'd love to spend the night." Her mother looked at Mrs. Fletcher. "I'd hate to be an inconvenience though."

Mrs. Fletcher clasped her hands together. "Oh, heavens, you would not be trouble. We love having company. It doesn't happen often enough as far as I'm concern."

"Good, then it's settled." Douglas reached for his water glass. "We'll take you for a ride right after we eat, and I'll see how you do holding the reins."

Emma tingled from the excitement of learning to drive a carriage, but even more so from the anticipation of learning something new and maybe having a little fun in the process, but then she gritted her teeth. How much would a carriage and a horse cost? The move to Independence had taken most of her money, but she knew Douglas was right. Having a carriage would be a necessity.

She glanced at Douglas, who was reaching for his nephew. He picked him up and put him on his lap. Again, Emma realized how much she'd missed by being married to David. Even had they had a child together, she couldn't imagine him forming a relationship as Douglas had already done with his nephew. Douglas's smile toward the little fellow warmed her heart.

How would it feel to have someone look so lovingly at her or a child of herst? Would she ever know real love and happiness?

She shook her head. Opening her first practice here in Independence should be reason enough to be happy. *I'm sorry, God, for being so selfish. If you can hear me, please forgive me. You've shown me the way and opened doors for me and Mother, and I am grateful.*

With that silent prayer she finished her meal and looked

forward to an enjoyable evening with the Fletcher family.

After dinner, Douglas led her out the front door.

"We still have a little daylight left. Let's go hook up the carriage. You'll need to know how it's done, then we can take a ride around the house. It'll be a good start for you."

Emma followed him out the door. All of a sudden, she felt apprehensive. "Douglas, I'm not so sure I can do this. I've never had to deal with horses."

"You'll do great. I promise. It's not hard once you understand what the horse expects of you."

"He'll probably expect and hope I find a driver who can take care of things like this."

He took her hand. "You'll do fine, Miss Emma O'Hara, and there are competent handlers in town for you to use. You won't have to do everything yourself, but you do need to know how it's done. In your profession you never know when an emergency will arise and you'll have to rely on what you know."

Shocked that he held her hand, she only nodded and followed him down the steps. She tried to follow what he said, but the feel of his big hand overwhelmed her.

The carriage sat outside the barn where Matthew had left it. The horses had been taken inside. "Let's go get our horse. We'll use Sunflower this evening. She's the most gentle and knows what to do. She'll be the easiest for you to work with."

"I'll need all the help I can get."

He laughed. "You'll be fine with Sunflower."

"I like her name."

"Caroline named her when Lucas first brought the horse home. We're not sure why she chose that name since she's dark brown, but we didn't change her name."

"I think it's adorable."

"You'll like her." Finally, he let go of her hand.

She breathed easier, but then he placed his hand on her elbow to lead her into the barn.

Emma stopped inside the door. "This is massive and so clean."

"I guess it is big. Our ranch hands do a fantastic job taking care of the animals and their stables." Douglas walked over to a stable with a huge black horse. "This is my horse, Major. I missed this guy while I was away." He patted the horse's head. "Major, I want you meet Emma. She was in the carriage today, but I never introduced you two." Major looked at Emma and tilted his head. "Come over and give him a pat. He'll love you forever."

Swallowing hard, she stepped to the railing and smiled. "Hi, Major. You're a beautiful horse." She looked at Douglas and whispered. "He's so big."

Douglas took her hand and placed it on Major's head. "He won't bite you unless he thinks you're doing something you shouldn't."

He stepped away from Emma and turned to the next stable. "And this sweet girl is Sunflower. Come over here and introduce yourself to her. We'll get her hooked up to the carriage."

Emma followed Douglas, patted Sunflower's head as she'd done to Major, then she followed him outside the barn. She listened carefully as he took her step by step through the process of hooking the horse to the carriage.

"Think you can do all that?"

"I think I'll have to if I have a carriage of my own."

Emma stood as close as possible to Douglas as he named each part he picked up to fasten to the horse. "Always make sure your straps are secure. Even if someone else hooks the horse to the carriage, it is your responsibility to make sure it's ready to be used. You don't ever want to be away from town and have a problem because things were not done properly."

Again, she nodded. She'd never paid much attention to the stable hands at their home in Cambridge. David had always hired the best, and she never worried about the safety of the carriage. Now things were different. She'd have no one to help her.

"Ready to get in?"

"Yes, I think I am." She stepped closer to the carriage, looked up at Douglas, who flashed a brilliant smile her way and held out his hand.

She took his hand, relished the feeling of his other hand on her lower back, then lifted herself with his help onto the seat of the carriage.

"I've never sat in the front seat."

Douglas frowned. "Your husband never took you on rides?"

Emma thought a moment. "Yes, I guess he did, but that was long ago when we courted and then were first married. After that he always had one of our stable hands take me where I needed to go."

Douglas didn't say anything, but his expression told her he understood more than she actually said. Was it possible he knew she was in a loveless marriage? She hated to feel pitied so she plastered a huge smile on her face. "Okay, Sunflower, you need to be a good girl and get me through this lesson."

"She won't disappoint you." He handed her the reins. "Your horse will respond to the tension you put on these."

She listened carefully. Taking a deep breath, she pushed away her nervousness.

She could do this.

~

Douglas could almost feel Emma's nervousness as she flicked the reins. He put his hand on hers to help her control the motion of the reins.

"Don't be nervous, Emma. You're doing great."

"I feel so incompetent."

"Don't be. You'll get the hang of this in no time."

He wanted to help her and protect her, but he knew she had to do this on her own. Her life and the welfare of her animal depended on her knowing how to handle the rig.

He pulled his attention from Emma to the horse. "Good girl, Sunflower. You're a sweet lady." He had picked the right horse for this lesson. She was gentle and knew exactly what to do even though Emma's commands were vague. He had taught several adults and youngsters how to handle a rig, but somehow this lesson with Emma seems personal.

Emma sat next to him on the carriage seat straining to hold the reins correctly with her focus on Sunflower. She was a tough lady, ready to take on the world, but on the inside, he sensed there was more to her than she let on. The more he was with her, the more he respected her, but so many unanswered questions loomed, not just about her life and her, but about the way he felt about her.

He wanted to get to know her better, and he couldn't deny he wanted to kiss her, hold her in his arms and break through that hard shell she wrapped around herself.

He leaned against the back of the seat and thought about those words that floated through his head. He needed to remember the heartbreak Lily caused him before he let himself be open to another romance.

Romance? What am I thinking?

Glancing at her face, tense from working the horse and carriage, he realized he really did want to get to know her better, but romance? No. His life was complicated enough right now. No way would he allow himself to get involved with another female. His heart needed time to mend.

"We're almost to the back of the barn. How do I get her to turn?"

Emma's words brought him back to the present.

Reaching over, he again placed a hand on top of hers.

She raised her gaze to his, then quickly looked back at Sunflower. Did she feel something from their touch as he did? She never seemed to let on if she did.

He swallowed and drew his attention back to her lesson. "Just put a little pressure on the rein in the direction that you want the horse to turn." He moved her hand holding the rein.

"Of course. That would make sense."

He lifted his hand away.

She moved the rein toward the right, and Sunflower eased around the corner of the building. "Douglas, look at Sunflower. She's doing what I want her to do."

"You're a natural, Miss Emma." Her smile warmed his heart. "Keep going around the barn, and when we get to the other side, we'll stop for the evening. I'll show you how to take the harness off and how to stable her."

Emma's lesson was over much too fast for him. He enjoyed sitting next to her and watching her get excited when Sunflower followed her commands. He wished their time together this evening would not end.

By the time he closed the stable gate and tossed fresh hay into Sunflower's stall, the sun had gone down and the light coming into the barn had dwindled to almost nothing.

"We need to get back to the house before it gets too dark. I'd hate for you to ruin your nice shoes in the dark."

"These shoes have survived years of studying and working in Boston. They can handle walking around a dark yard."

Once more, he placed his hand on her elbow to lead her to the house. "We'll see what the rest of the family is doing. Mother likes us to gather on the front porch after dinner. They might still be out."

"I'd love to sit in one of those big rockers and enjoy this beautiful evening."

"I'd like that as well." He stopped talking, remembering that Emma was here in a professional capacity to check on Abigail and not here to spend time with him, but if she wanted to spend a little more of the evening together, he certainly could oblige.

Emma stopped walking. "Is that my mother?"

He looked to the other side of the porch where June and Mason were strolling. "I think it is, and that man she's with is Mason, my supervisor."

"Is she safe with him?"

Douglas chuckled. "Yes, Mason is the one I explained had been with my family since I was a child. He lost his wife a few years ago so I'm glad he's at least talking to another lady. Your mother is perfectly okay with him." He took another step. "Come on. Let's go try out one of those rockers."

CHAPTER ELEVEN

Emma chose a rocker with a fluffy red cushion. She snuggled into it and closed her eyes. The rest of the Fletcher family had gone inside, and her mother was out walking with Mr. Mason. Only she and Douglas occupied the porch, and if she admitted it to herself, she was glad.

"This is wonderful. So relaxing. Thank you for inviting Mother and me for the night."

Douglas stood at the top of the steps leaning on the railing. He stared out into the night, and she wondered what he thought about when he looked over the wide expanse of his family's ranch. Did he think about the years he'd spent here as a child? Did he wish he could still work on the ranch instead of being a veterinarian?

He turned to face her. "I'm glad you and your mother decided to stay. I've enjoyed your company a lot, Miss Emma."

Her heart fluttered at his words. "I've enjoyed your company as well, Mr. Fletcher."

He laughed out loud, then plopped down in a rocker next to her. "I love these chairs. My grandfather made some of them. I remember Dad and Lucas sanding the wood on some of them. I was too young to help, except to pick up the trash and haul small pieces of wood to the burn pile, but I'd always tell people I built them. Lucas would hit me when he heard me."

"Lucas must've been a great big brother."

"He was. I learned quite a lot about life from him."

As if on cue, Lucas stepped out the front door.

"Hey, big brother, come join us."

"No, I'm not staying out here long. I told Abigail I'd be back up in a few minutes." He looked at Emma. "I wanted to ask you what you found when you examined Abigail. Do you think she'll have any problems giving birth?"

"We can never predict how easy or hard a birth will be, but Abigail seems healthy and strong. My examination indicated the baby had not turned yet, but we still have a little time for that to happen naturally."

"And if it doesn't, that could be a problem, right? We've had cattle lose their babies when the calf wasn't turned right."

"Yes, I won't lie to you. It could be a problem, but the baby could turn on its own and cause no problems."

"What can we do?"

"Right now, not much. I massaged her and tried to help the baby turn but nothing happened. I can come back next week to check on her again if you'd like."

"That would be wonderful. She had a normal birth with no problems at all when William was born. We assumed this one would be normal and easy, as well."

Emma sensed Lucas's anxiety. She took his hand to reassure him even though she could not be certain what she was about to say was correct. "And this birth could be easy with no problems, too. I'll talk with Carmella and tell her what to look for and what to do to help the baby turn, but I have a feeling she already knows all that."

Lucas nodded. "Carmella has helped lots of babies on this ranch come into this world, but I appreciate your opinion and expertise. Thank you."

He said his good nights and left them alone.

Emma watched him hurry inside. "He's worried and I wish I could tell him definitely everything will be okay, but I have no way of knowing."

"We appreciate your coming out here. As I told you earlier, he lost one wife, and I don't think he could go through that again."

Emma took Douglas's hand. "Don't think the worse. Healthy babies are born every day without the help of us doctors."

"I just want the best for my brother and Abigail. Do I remember you saying you had a brother?"

"Yes, he's younger. His name is Edward."

"He didn't want to come out here with you and your mother?"

She shook her head. Talking about Edward made her sad. She loved him so much but wasn't able to help him find his way in life. She looked at Douglas. "My family didn't have the closeness I see in yours. My father made life hard for my mother, and, even though she worked hard at giving us a good life, Edward had a hard time dealing with the family dynamics. Father always found fault with whatever Edward or I did. I think that's why I married so young. I had to get away from him, but when I did, it was hard on Edward. I regret leaving him now."

"We have to do what we think is best, and if you were young, I'm sure you did the only thing you could. He's older now. I'm sure he has grown past any resentment he might have had. So, is he still in Cambridge?"

"No, he said he would meet us here. He left several weeks ahead of us, but we haven't heard from him. Mother is worried sick, but I told her he would probably show up and surprise us one day when we least expect him."

"I'm sure he's fine. Young men have a lot to do out here. He might've found a great job on one of the nearby ranches, or, who knows, maybe he met one of the rancher's daughters."

Emma smiled. "That would be nice. I'd love for him to find someone who loves him and makes him feel good about himself. He has no self-esteem at all."

"A young lady can certainly make that happen, or not." He looked out over the railing with a serious expression.

She frowned and turned to him. "Okay, you need to explain yourself. It sounds as though you're talking from experience."

Douglas squirmed in his chair, then stood up and walked to the railing with his back to Emma.

Emma stood up then walked toward him. "Douglas, I told you a little about my family. It's your turn to tell me about yourself."

"I've told you a lot about my family."

"Your family, but not about you. I sense something happened in your past that makes you not trust women?"

"Who said I don't trust women?"

"No one had to say it. I can feel you don't trust me, and I hope it's all females and not just me."

"That's a little more personal than what you told me about your father."

"No, it isn't. It's hard to admit to anyone how bad my father was. In fact, I never talk about him. It hurts."

"I'm sorry your early life was hard, but I don't open up about my relationships."

Emma stood quietly next to the railing and watched him. He put his weight on one foot and then the other before he turned to face her. Then he surprised her.

"I found someone I thought I'd spend the rest of my life with, but it turned out she was more interested in where she lived than in whom she loved."

"Ouch, that hurts."

"Yeah, I'd say it did."

"I'm sorry. Was this recent?"

He pushed himself away from the railing and sat again.

"A few months before I left, she made it clear she would never leave New York, especially to go to a place on the outskirts of civilization. She had convinced herself people walked around shooting each other in Independence. No matter what I said, she wouldn't consider moving here."

"And you wouldn't live in New York?"

He laughed. "Never. This is my home. My roots are here, and this is where I want to raise my children. I guess we were both stubborn."

She sat down and rested her head against the back of the rocker. "I think that's wonderful. I wish I felt that way about a place. I have only bad vibes when I think about my hometown."

"And is that because of your marriage?"

Emma squeezed her eyes shut. She hated talking about her bad choices in life, and David was definitely her worse choice.

He grinned. "Hey, you're the one who said we should share."

She nodded, but could she really tell him how what a terrible man her former husband was?

She started slowly. "It was not a good marriage, but I guess I was young and naïve. I thought it was a wonderful life until I realized nothing had been real." She clenched her hands.

He placed one of his hands over hers. "I'm sorry. I shouldn't have asked. I can see it upsets you."

"No, you're right. I'm the one who said we should share." Taking a deep breath, she started again. "When I think about how I wasted seven years with a man who was a crook, I feel foolish."

Douglas frowned. "A crook? Your husband was a crook."

Now that she'd said it, she had to finish. "He was a swindling, crooked man who made a fortune on other's hard times. Everything he did was just enough above the law to keep from being thrown in jail. He had a lending business, and the people who went to him had been turned down by the banks. He would give them just enough to get by and demand extraordinary payments which they could not meet. That's when he would take away their property. He had no feelings for the suffering he caused, but I was just as bad, I guess. I lived the high life while other families were in pain."

This time Douglas took her hand and held it.

She pulled it back.

"I'm sorry." He frowned. "Did I offend you?"

She looked down at her hands. "No, I'm not used to others pitying me."

"Pitying you? I don't pity you at all. I'm simply trying to understand what made you as you are today. We're all a combination of our life's experiences. We can't get away from our pasts."

She dropped her gaze and stared at the floor. "I guess you're right. I can't get away from who I was. While I was married to David, I was a frivolous, materialistic woman. In my heart I knew our marriage was not a real marriage, but I liked the rich life we lived. I get so disgusted with myself when I think about what I had become, it makes me sick."

"Don't be too hard on yourself. He led you down that path, and if you didn't share love with him, I can see where you would turn to the things he gave you."

"Mother didn't raise me that way. I knew better. She even sat me down one day and told me what others were saying about David. I didn't want to listen. I thought she simply didn't like the man I married." She stood up again and walked to the railing. "David had swindled the man who shot him. I pleaded with the sheriff not to lock that man up, but they did anyway. At that point, as I learned the things David did, I started selling our possessions and tried to make amends to those he had wronged. I even gave money to the family of the man who killed him. When I met the lady, I was horrified. They had three little boys and were living in a shack because he had lost all of his money and his home to David."

She turned to look at him.

"It was at that point that I made the decision to become a doctor so I could help people. I kept enough money to pay for my schooling and to give Mother a place to live while I was away. We sold that house when I accepted this position, but we don't have a lot of money left. More and more people showed up at my door to collect what David had taken from them. I'm not even sure they were all legit, but I paid them."

"So you should not feel bad about your life, Emma. You made amends. That means a lot."

"I hope it does because we have spent about all the money we were able to keep." She finally turned and looked at him. "I don't even know if I'll have money enough to buy a carriage and a horse. I know it is important, but some things will have to wait."

"I understand." He walked over to her, took her hand once more and squeezed it.

His big hand swallowed hers. This time she didn't pull her hand away.

He lifted her chin with one finger. "Things will work out with God's help."

Unwanted tears filled her eyes. His slight touch sent a feeling of protectiveness through her. How she would love to throw herself into his arms. Never had she felt that way with David. Slowly, she pulled her hand back. "I'm not so sure God is still in my corner."

"Why wouldn't he be? You did what you could to make things right."

"I'm trying to pray to him, but I'm not so sure he hears me."

"Oh, he hears. Don't stop praying." He turned his head toward the front lawn.

Emma followed his gaze to find her mother being escorted up the steps by the man Douglas had called his supervisor.

With Mr. Mason's help, June O'Hara stepped up onto the stairs. She turned around and thanked the man with a coy smile on her face. Finally, she looked up. "Emma, I'm so glad you're still up. I want you to meet this nice man, Mr. Mason Malone."

"How do you do, Mr. Malone? Douglas has told me some complimentary things about you."

Mason looked at Douglas and raised an eyebrow, then smiled. "I'm not so sure of this guy. He might remember only the not-so-wonderful things about me when he was younger, and I tried to get him to work around here."

"Hey, watch what you say. I was a good worker."

"Sometimes you were, but if you were complimentary, I appreciate it."

"You know me, Mason. I only speak the truth."

Mason helped June up the last step.

"Mason, I'd like you to meet my daughter, Emma."

"Miss Emma, I've heard wonderful things about you as well. I think it's amazing that you'll be the new town doctor."

"Thank you, sir. I hope you and Mother had a pleasant stroll."

June spoke up while she reached for Emma's hand. "We had a wonderful walk. Wait until I tell you all I've learned about this ranch."

"Have a seat and join us." Douglas got up and dragged a rocker for June. Mason got his own.

June took a seat next to Emma. "Where do I start?"

Emma looked at Douglas. "Looks as if Mother is about to entertain us."

She wanted to giggle from joy. She hadn't seen her mother this happy in years.

CHAPTER TWELVE

"**Absolutely not.**" **Emma** stood on the street outside her office with her arms crossed in front of her body. She looked from Douglas to the Fletcher family carriage he stood beside. "I can't take this from you."

"I'm not giving it to you. I'm only lending the horse and carriage to you until you can afford to buy your own." He tried to hand her the reins once more.

She refused to take them. "I couldn't. It's too much."

"No, it's not too much. I'm thinking about the people on the outlying ranches. When they need medical attention, you need some way to get to them. Now, if you'd rather, I can let you borrow a horse. A horse is a lot faster than a carriage, but, of course, you'll need to learn to ride."

"Douglas, I said I didn't want to be pitied, and you're right. I can't ride a horse. I don't want to use your carriage or one of the ranch horses."

He shook his head. "You are the most stubborn, aggravating woman I've ever met. I told you I don't pity you."

Again, he tried to hand her the reins, but she pulled back.

"Emma, you're going about this all wrong. You need to think about the carriage as a gift for the town, not just for you. The people who live outside of this town need you to be able to get to where the medical need is, and right now you don't have a means to do that. You said yourself you didn't have the finances at the moment to buy anything. What if Abigail has problems? How would you get to her?"

She blinked hoping to rid her eyes of unexpected and certainly unwanted tears. No one had been so thoughtful to her in years. Douglas had a way of drawing emotions from her. *Please don't cry in front of this man.* He stood in front of her with such a sincere face.

"You're a wonderful man, Douglas Fletcher." She turned her head and wiped away a tear that had escaped.

"No, not wonderful. I see a need and I have a solution. That's all."

She stood in the street and thought about what he'd said. She had not considered how she'd get to the outlying ranches. In fact, she never considered the fact that she'd have to go to her patients. In Boston most of the doctors stayed in their offices and patients went to them. Maybe he made a good point, especially with Abigail. She'd never forgive herself if his sister-in-law had problems and she couldn't get to her.

Douglas looked at her with the cutest grin. She dropped her head, then took the reins from his hand. "If you're filling a need for the town, I'll accept the loan of the carriage." Then she panicked. "Oh wait. I can't take this. How do I tend to this horse? Where will I keep it? I know nothing about horses. I barely know how to drive this."

Douglas laughed. "Slow down. I've already talked to Murry at the stables. He understands the situation and said he would take care of Sunflower for you. When you need to use the carriage, he'll do whatever he can to help."

"How much does he charge?"

"Don't worry about that. It's taken care of for the next few months."

"Oh, no. I can't. . ."

"Yes, you can, and you will. It's a done deal. When you

start bringing in revenue at the office, you can take care of the bill. Until then, don't even think about it."

Emma rubbed her fingers along the leather reins, then walked toward the carriage. "You think I can really get Sunflower to do what I ask her to do?"

"When you took your first lesson at the ranch, she did as you instructed her. I told you she's a very gentle animal, but very smart. She's been pulling this carriage for a long time. She'll know what to do."

She wasn't used to asking for favors, but today she had to. "Do you have time to give me another lesson?"

"Of course, I do. I left the office empty, and if anybody comes by they can wait a few minutes."

Emma swallowed. "If you can spare a few minutes, so can I."

Douglas smiled at her and offered his hand. "Finally, the pretty lady has come to her senses. Come on, Miss O'Hara, let's go for a ride."

His compliment did not go unnoticed. He'd called her "pretty." She swallowed. He had a way of knowing exactly what to say when she needed it.

~

Douglas helped Emma into the front seat, then walked around the front to the horse and rubbed the horse's nose. "Don't make a liar out of me, Sunflower. Please be gentle with Emma."

He looked up. Emma's strained expression told him all he needed to know. The lady was terrified to have the responsibility of this animal and carriage. He hoped he wasn't making a mistake by making her learn something she wasn't interested in doing.

He hopped into the front seat and turned to her. "You'll do fine, Emma. Nothing is hard about driving a carriage. Let's get started."

Emma sat still. "I know I need to learn to do this, but if I'm needed outside of town, I'll be in the carriage alone.

What if something happens?"

"Nothing is going to happen, and if it does, you're a smart lady. If you can become a doctor, you can drive a carriage."

"It's not the same."

"You're right. Driving the carriage is much easier than what you did for the past few years."

She bit her lip. "Where do you come up with all this stuff?"

"I tell the truth. Now, tell Sunflower to start walking. Let's see how much you remember since our lesson."

Emma gave a weak flick of the reins. The horse did nothing. "See, she doesn't like me."

He laughed. "She likes you. She probably didn't feel your command. You have to be a little more forceful."

He placed his hand on top of hers, pretended the soft feel of her skin didn't send his heart into a flutter, then showed her how to give her command. Sunflower eased into a slow walk.

Emma smiled and looked his way.

"See. Nothing to it."

"Yeah. Right." She laughed, and her shoulders seemed to relax.

Douglas chuckled, leaned back against the seat, and watched her concentrate. She focused on the dirt road in front of her, kept looking at her reins, then up again at the horse.

"You're doing great. Don't concentrate too hard. Sunflower knows what she's doing. She won't let you run into anything or end up in a ditch."

She nodded and smiled. "I think she knows what I want her to do."

"Yes, she does." Douglas wished he could say the same about her. Against his better judgment, he wanted to know how to please her, how to be her friend, or even have her as something more. How would it be to hold her in his arms and show her he was there to protect her? Little by little she allowed him to do more and more for her, but did she think about him only as a friend?

Of course, if he were honest with himself, he should look at her as only a friend. This was not the time to be involved with anyone.

"There's a wagon coming at me." She snapped her head in his direction. Her eyes were huge. "What do I do now?"

"You ease the horse to this side of the street so the man can pass. Again, Sunflower won't run into that wagon."

He placed his hand over hers and gently put pressure on the reins. Again, his heart went into double time. He inhaled deeply and hoped his expression didn't show his emotional state.

As the wagon passed, the driver raised his hand in greeting. "Nice day for a ride."

She smiled and waved, pulling the reins up.

He grabbed the reins. "Don't raise the reins. Sunflower thinks you're trying to tell her something."

"Oh, no. See. I don't know if I can do this."

Douglas eased the reins and pulled on them to stop on the side of the road. "You're doing great, Emma, but if you think you can't do this, you won't be able to."

"I'm sorry. I want to do this. I really do."

"Then do it. Maybe I ought to get out and let you do it alone."

"No. Absolutely not. Please stay. I need you here."

How he wished that were so.

"Okay, if you want." He handed her the reins. "Let's go down to where the ally runs alongside the general store. You can turn there. There's a big field at the end where you can turn the carriage around and we'll head to the stables. I want you to meet Murry. You'll like him."

He blew out a breath and prayed he was doing the right thing. What she said about being alone on calls was correct. His chest tightened. Would she be able to deal with a broken wheel or axel? And, heaven forbid, what if something spooked the horse and Sunflower started running?

He pushed those thoughts from his mind. If she was to be the town's doctor, she'd have to learn to fend for herself even though that was the last thing he wanted her to do. He wanted to be there for her, but he knew that would not always be possible.

Emma took the carriage into the open field at the end of the ally, turned it around, and headed back toward the stables. Murry met them, took the reins, and explained what he planned to do for her.

"We're glad to have you in town, Dr. O'Hara. I'm happy to be able to help you in any way I can."

Emma shook his hand. "I hope I'm not too much of a burden. I do agree with Douglas. I need this carriage so I'm quite appreciative of anything you do for me."

Pleased that she felt comfortable with Murry helping her, Douglas stood back and watched her and the stable owner talk.

After saying their goodbyes, Douglas led her into the street. "Would you like to grab a bite to eat?" He needed to return to his office and had not intended to ask her out to eat. He wasn't even sure where that question came from. He knew he was getting too involved with the new doctor in town, but he couldn't help but hope she'd accept his offer.

"I'd like that, but could we stop at the office first? I need to check on Mother."

"Certainly. She's welcomed to go with us if she'd like."

"You're very considerate, Douglas. I'd like to ask her."

He really would've liked a quiet lunch with Emma alone, but that would have to wait. There was so much he wanted to know about her, but this was not the time or the place to try to figure out the pretty doctor.

"I like your mother, Emma. She's welcomed anytime."

~

Douglas took them to a table near a window, then pulled

out chairs for both ladies. Immediately a nice-looking young lady walked up to them. Emma had seen the waitress before but had not met her.

Immediately the lady stepped next to Douglas. "Hi, Douglas, I haven't seen you in a few days. You must be busy at the office."

Douglas turned to the lady. "It's not just the office. In the evenings, we're patrolling the outlying ranches for our troublemakers. If I don't have patients, I'm usually sleeping. I haven't had time to come in, and I can tell you I've missed your good cooking."

She stepped even closer to him and placed her hand on her chest. "Patrolling must be dangerous and very tiresome."

Emma watched the waitress be a little too dramatic as she inched her way nearer toward Douglas. He didn't seem to mind.

"It is tiring, but so far it hasn't been dangerous. We haven't had any problems out on the ranches. We're hoping the men have packed up and left the area."

"That would be nice." Finally, Molly looked at Emma.

"Ladies, how are you today?"

"We're fine." June smiled up to her. "Thank you for asking."

Douglas looked from Molly to Emma. "Molly, have you met our new town doctor, Emma O'Hara and her mother June O'Hara?"

"Not formally, but I've seen them in here. Welcome, ladies. I'm glad to finally meet you."

"It's nice to meet you as well." Emma gave her a sweet smile. "I've seen you when we were here before, but you've always been busy. The other lady who waited on us was as nice as she could be."

"I'm glad to hear that."

"Molly's parents owned and ran this café since I was a child," Douglas said. "My parents or Lucas would bring me here every time we came into town. The food was great then, and Molly is following in their footsteps."

Molly tilted her head to the side and touched Douglas on the arm. "What a nice thing to say."

Emma watched the two of them. Did she detect more than friendship between the two old friends?

Douglas pulled out a chair for himself, picked up a handwritten menu, but looked up at Molly still hovering over him.

"I only speak the truth," he said. "You're doing a great job here. I know this menu by heart already, but tell us about any specials you've cooked up today."

"Raymond Smithy brought me some fresh chickens yesterday. I smothered them down in brown gravy and everyone is raving about the meal. Of course, I still have ham and pork, as well."

"That's a no-brainer for me. I want the chicken. What about you ladies?"

"I'll have the same."

June nodded. "It sounds good to me, too."

Molly walked away with their orders, but not before looking at Douglas with a grin. Emma only glanced his way but saw a slight tint of red on his cheeks. She wondered if Douglas and Molly had a past or even a present.

A twinge of jealousy washed over her, but she shook it off. Douglas had lived here all his life and so had Molly. Of course, they would've had a past, and if so, he was free to do as he wished. She straightened her shoulders.

"Mother, I have to tell you what Douglas has done for us and for the town." She went on to explain about the loan of the carriage.

"You are such a wonderful person, Douglas. Thank you for helping my daughter."

"It's not just me. Lucas is all in favor of this as well. We talked about it briefly. It didn't take long for him to agree the town needs a doctor who can get to the patients if they are unable to get to town. Mobility is a necessity."

Emma crossed her arms on the table. "Now that I'll have the carriage, how will your mother and Abigail get into town?"

"We'll work that out. On Saturdays when we know we'll attend church on Sunday, we'll send someone to get the carriage, then return it later. We also have a wagon that we could use. It's not pretty, but it's functional. It will all work out. It's much more important for the town doctor to be able to get to her patients than for us to ride into town in style."

The door to the café opened and Sheriff Vic and two other men walked in. At first Vic spoke to two families, but before he followed the other men to their table, he walked up to Douglas.

Douglas stood up and shook his hand. "Vic, nice seeing you today."

"I'm glad to see you as well. I was planning to ride out to Fletcher Ranch to talk with you so you've saved me a trip."

Douglas sat. "That doesn't sound good."

"It's not." Sheriff Vic nodded to the table. "Ladies, you both look lovely today."

"Thank you, sir. Please sit with us."

Vic looked uncomfortable.

"It's fine, Vic. Whatever you say, they can hear, unless you'd rather not."

Vic slid his body onto a chair. "Thanks. Dr. O'Hara should hear this as well." He pulled in a huge breath then started. "Those three brothers that held up your stage on the way to town are out."

Emma's breath caught in her throat remembering the terror she felt when that man stuck a gun in her face.

Douglas leaned back against his chair. "What do you mean 'out'? I thought the district judge sentenced them for years. How did that happen?"

"They were being hauled to prison, but they managed to escape."

"They must've had help. They're not smart enough to do it alone."

"You're right. They did. Two men came up from the rear. One deputy was shot. The other deputy put his hands up when he realized he was outnumbered, but they didn't harm him."

"Oh, no." Emma pushed aside her selfish fears. "Is the wounded officer okay?"

"Yes, a couple of riders passed by and found them. They untied the one deputy and took the other man to the closest town. A doctor got the bullet out."

Douglas bit his lip. "It's bad enough that any prisoner escapes, but it could be worse trouble when the men have no sense. They're the ones we need to keep watch for. No telling what they can do."

Emma sat quietly listening to Douglas and the sheriff talk about the three escaped bandits. Just thinking about that day on the stage made her insides quiver. She would've never forgiven herself had her mother been hurt.

A shiver ran down her spine.

She reached under the table and took her mother's hand. June smiled, but it didn't go to her eyes. Instead signs of worry showed across her face. She wished she could tell her something to ease her pain, but her mother was as troubled about the news as she was.

Sheriff Vic stood up. "I'm sorry to have to be the one with bad news, but I thought you needed to know. If we're lucky, those three rode out of this county as fast as they could." He looked directly at Emma. "Ladies, have a wonderful day."

"Thank you, Sheriff."

He started to walk away, then turned back. "Are patients starting to go to your office?"

"No, not yet, but I'm not giving up. Someone eventually will put their trust in me." She glared at Douglas.

He shrugged his shoulders.

The sheriff smiled at Douglas. "Yes, the townspeople will eventually come around. You hang in there. Change doesn't come easy, especially in these parts."

She nodded. "I don't give up easily, Sheriff. I'm not going anywhere."

"Good. I knew the council hired the right doctor."

Douglas reached out his hand. "Thanks for telling us about the brothers. I'll spread the word. Call me if I need to help with anything."

"Keep standing watch over the ranches. That's the only thing we can do right now." He shook Douglas's hand once more then turned. After stopping at several tables to talk, he finally sat with the men who had come in with him.

"Sheriff Victor seems like a nice person."

Douglas nodded. "He is. The Fletchers still consider him part of the family. He and Lucas married sisters and they spent quite a lot of time at our house."

Emma thought about what Douglas had said, then it dawned on her. "The wife that Lucas lost was the sister to the sheriff's wife."

"Yes, Sarah was Betty's sister. You'll get to meet her one day."

"Sarah's death must've been hard on everyone."

"Yes, Sarah was a beautiful and wonderful lady." It appeared he wanted to say more, but he looked at the menu. Emma understood the emotion he must feel.

June reached out and took his hand, squeezed it, then pulled it back.

Douglas nodded, then cleared his throat. "I'm sorry you had to hear about the brothers escaping the jail, Emma."

"I am, too, but it's best I know the men are out. We'll keep up our guard."

June, who had been sitting quietly, finally spoke. "It scares me to think those three are loose. Sheriff Vic didn't seem to think they were still around town. Do you?"

"I have no way of knowing," Douglas said. "We'll keep

our watch, but I'm hoping those three troublemakers are long gone."

"I hope so," June said. "Emma, do you think we should buy a gun?"

"Mother, you know I don't like guns. I've seen what they can do." She looked at Douglas. "You don't think we should invest in a gun, do you?"

"Do you know how to shoot? Wait. On the coach you did say you had used a gun before."

"I did but only once when David made me shoot his gun. He said I needed to know how to shoot, but then he never bought me one and he never let me practice again. That was when I was young and didn't understand the harm they can do."

"Guns can certainly cause trouble, especially when they're in the hands of the wrong people. It's good to know how to protect ourselves. Think about it. If you decide to buy one, the general store has some. I think they might even have a few from previous owners. If you'd like, I'll go over with you after we eat and take a look."

Again, the man was making himself indispensable. She hated to accept, but she was smart enough to know she needed someone to help her. It might as well be Douglas.

"We can do that," she said.

"Of course, you'll need practice if you do get one. I can certainly help with that as well if you'd like."

"Yes, I'll take you up on your offer, but we'll go by your office to make sure you're not making your patients wait too long. I feel as though I'm taking up your time."

"I'm doing exactly what I want to do. You're not taking my time."

Emma knew he was only being nice, but she'd let him help her. This move to Missouri demanded much more than she anticipated.

CHAPTER THIRTEEN

Three people stood outside of Douglas's office.

"It's a good thing we came by here. You can't leave now." An unexpected streak of disappointment hit Emma.

Douglas made a face, then smiled as he walked up to the people on his porch to see what they needed. Finally, he turned to Emma. "We might need to put this off until tomorrow morning. I could come by your office with the carriage early and we could take a ride to the river, if you'd like. I think you'd enjoy seeing the activity, then we can stop in one of the open fields so you can fire the gun."

"That'll work. I'll pack a small basket of food."

"Let me walk you back to your office."

"No, that won't be necessary. You tend to your patients. I'll see you in the morning."

They arranged a time, and she walked around the block to her office feeling good. Douglas hadn't called their outing tomorrow a date, but it did seem like one to her. She thought about the dresses she had packed, and even considered her trousers, but shook her head and decided on a simple yellow dress. With that decision, she climbed the steps to her office, peeked in to make sure no one was waiting for her, then sat on the front porch step. She'd definitely have to find a chair to put out here since she was spending more time out here than in the office with patients.

At seven the next morning, she answered the knock on her door. Douglas stood outside dressed in a dark pair of trousers and a light tan shirt. He pulled his hat off.

"Hope I'm not too early."

"Not at all. Come in. Let me get the basket we packed so we can eat along the way."

"Sounds good." He looked around the tiny living area. "This is nice."

"It's livable," she said. "We have some trunks coming in eventually with the rest of our household things."

She stepped toward the table where the basket sat just as her mother walked through the bedroom door.

"Good morning, Dr. Fletcher. It's a beautiful spring day for a ride."

Emma smiled hearing her mother calling him a doctor.

"Yes, I think it will be. I didn't mention it to Emma, but you are welcome to take a ride with us. The river is beautiful."

"Oh, no, I have things to do around here. You two have a good day."

"I would think we'd be back by early afternoon, but don't get worried if we're later. Sometimes the river area is pretty congested with the activity of the wagon trains. Every time I've gone up that way, I've always had an animal emergency to take care of."

"I won't worry. My daughter is in good hands."

Emma kissed her mother. "Have a good day, Mother."

They walked to the carriage where Douglas helped her in.

Independence Square already buzzed with activity.

Douglas waved to several wagonloads of pioneers heading for the general store. "I assume the next train is getting ready to roll. Wagons pulled by horses leave early so the horses can feed on the shorter grasses. The wagons pulled by oxen will follow."

"I didn't know that. Interesting."

"Yesterday I checked out a couple of their horses." He turned the carriage north. "The wagons leave from the Old Independence Landing, a few miles from here."

Emma sat quietly listening to bits and pieces of information about the wagon trains and what the pioneers would face along the way.

"I've never been west of here, but I hear the Santa Fe Trail is clearly marked now." He waved to the driver of another wagon. "It's a lot safer than what it used to be with the earlier trains."

She waved to wagon with a man and a woman. "Safer or not, I would not want to be heading out. How long does it take to get to California?"

"If the weather isn't too bad, they can make it in about four months."

"That's a long time to be in those wagons. It must be scary for the women and children."

"And the men," he added. "I've heard of quite a few men who back out of the journey before they get started. Reality sets in and they realize their dreams are not as easy or safe to accomplish."

"I know back home the stories in the newspapers make the adventure sound exciting, but I can see that's not always the case."

"Exciting it is, but it's not fun. It's hard and in many cases dangerous. Not everyone will make it all the way to California."

Emma looked at each wagon that passed them. Many had women and children in them. Her heart went out to them.

"What happens if someone gets sick or injured?"

"Someone on the train takes control of the medical problems."

"A doctor?"

"No, just someone who has experience taking care of

animals or maybe gunshots or broken bones." He looked at her. "You're not thinking about volunteering, are you?"

Emma's hands went to her chest. "Heavens, no. I'm perfectly content in my little empty office here. One day I'll be able to help the good citizens of Independence if they ever put their trust in me."

He turned and smiled.

Her heart flipped. His smile always made her tingle.

"The people in town will come around. Give it time."

For the next hour, they eased along the well-worn trail toward the river. Emma could hear whistles from the riverboats along the waterway.

"I love that sound. I always enjoyed listening to the boat whistles and watching the chaos around Boston's harbor."

"Don't get your hopes up. This landing is nothing fancy like you're used to. Everything is pretty primitive, muddy, and dirty, but I guess it works."

"No expectations. Promise."

The farther away from town the carriage got, the trees along the way got thicker. Douglas pointed out a few black walnut trees near the trail. "My brother and I used to pick up the walnuts and take them home for Carmella and Bonita to use in desserts. We always had fun trying to break them open. We'd have to use hammers."

"I didn't realize the outer shell was that tough."

"Yep, sometimes we had to get Mason to roll of them with the wagon."

"Your family was lucky to have someone like Mason and the ladies in the kitchen to help."

"They are more than workers. They're family to us."

Emma thought about how hard her mother worked to keep up their house and to raise her and her brother. She always prided herself in keeping their small home immaculate. After the death of her husband, Emma insisted she move in with her and David. She wanted to give her an easier life, but as she looked back, Emma realized her mother never approved of their outlandish lifestyle.

She shook away the bad memories.

Before she knew it, more wagons pulled by oxen and men on horses passed them.

"We're getting closer," Douglas said.

"Do you know anyone at the landing?"

"Years ago, I knew some of the men leading the trains, but I'm not sure any of them are still around. I might run into someone I recognize. Who knows?"

As the trees thinned and the trail turned into a wide-open space, Emma sat up straight and took in the sites around her. Reddish dirt covered huge areas along the river. Wagons congregated in several small circles along the banks and farther away from the river. Men on horseback traveled from one group of wagons to the next, many appearing to move about aimlessly.

"Oh, my gosh, I've never seen anything like this. I thought the streets in Boston and the other big cities were chaotic. This is amazing."

"You have to wonder how they get their act together and move in one unit." He stopped the carriage.

She looked at the wagons in front of her. Several people gathered around one with one man waving his arms toward Douglas.

"Do you think there's a problem?"

"I don't know, but we're about to find out. That man is heading our way."

A young man wearing boots that came to his knees, a loose pair of pants tucked into them, and a wrinkled shirt ran in their direction. "Sir. Sir. You look like you just came from town. We need help."

"What's the problem?"

"This wagon has a young child who needs a doctor. She fell and it looks like her arm is broken. We need to get her to town."

Douglas jumped down from the carriage. "You're in

luck. This lady is Doctor O'Hara and is the medical doctor in Independence."

The young man looked up at Emma. "Can you help us?"

"I can certainly try, though I don't have a medical bag with me." She looked at Douglas. "Can you help me down and go with me?"

"Certainly." He pulled the carriage near the wagon, then helped Emma out.

"I can't believe I left without my medical bag. That was not smart," she said as they hurried toward the other wagon.

Douglas reached behind the front seat. "I have a few things with me. I usually have to take care of some of their animals so I might have something you can use."

Impressed that Douglas had thought to bring supplies when she had not, she nodded. "Thank you. That was not very professional of me to leave my bag at home." She had been so excited to be with Douglas today, she forgot about everything else.

With Douglas's help, Emma climbed into the back of the covered wagon to find a little girl holding her arm and crying. Her mother looked up. She, too, had tears running down her face. "Can you help my little girl?"

Emma knelt down by the mother and took her hand. "I'm Doctor O'Hara and the man with me is Doctor Fletcher, the town's veterinarian. We'll certainly do what we can for your daughter."

Douglas opened the back flap and crawled in the wagon.

Emma smiled at him then turned her attention to the little girl.

"Hi, sweetie. We're both doctors, and we're going to try to make you feel better."

The little girl grabbed her mother's hand.

"I know you're scared, but we'll try to be gentle."

Setting an arm was never gentle, but Douglas helped her set the bone, then to wrap it in bandages from Douglas's bag.

Within thirty minutes Emma sat in the carriage, finally

allowing herself to take a deep breath. The arm had set quickly. Though painful for the child, she knew it could've been worse.

Douglas climbed in the carriage, took the reins, but instead of flicking them, he looked at Emma.

"You were amazing. I'm glad we came out here."

"Thank you for your help. I hated to hurt that little girl, but it had to be done." She looked at the father in front of the other wagon. "Do you think they'll still leave with the wagon train?"

"Yep. That man is more determined than ever to get leave. He said they got the worst behind them. I told him I hope that was true, but not to be surprised if other things happened."

"I feel bad for the mother and the little girl, but at least her break happened here with us close by."

Word got around the wagons quickly. Three men sought them out and directed them to their wagons to look at horses, an ox and a woman with fever. It was noon before they headed away from the landing.

"I'm glad I told your mother we could be late getting back. I usually have a couple animals to look at, but never this many problems."

"I'm glad we were able to help."

"Now onto our purpose today. You need to shoot a gun."

"Great."

Douglas laughed at her sarcastic tone. "Great is right. You need to learn to handle a gun."

~

Emma stood in an open field somewhere between the river and town. Silence surrounded her. Brush grass tickled her legs above her high-top shoes and several bugs buzzed around her head.

She gripped the handle of her newly bought Colt Navy Revolver hanging at her side.

"Are you ready?" Douglas stepped next to her.

"No."

He tilted his head. "Is there a problem?"

She let her arm relax and nearly dropped the gun.

Douglas grabbed it. "Emma, this gun is loaded. You have to pay attention to what you do with a loaded gun. It can be dangerous if it goes off when you're not aiming at something."

"Exactly. It can be dangerous all the time. I'm not sure I should do this." She looked at him directly in the eye. "You know I wouldn't be able to shoot anyone."

"You could if they threatened your life or your mother's life."

"I don't know."

"Just pointing a gun sometimes solves a problem. I hope you never have to use it, but the reality today is we have to defend ourselves, especially out here away from our modern cities back East. I don't like guns either. I never have, but I carry one and it certainly came in handy on the stagecoach."

"Yes, it did." She knew he was right, but being a doctor and shooting someone clashed. "Douglas, I'm still not sure. Everything I've devoted my life to by becoming a doctor goes against carrying a gun."

"Look, you already bought the gun. At least let's get a couple shots in so you know what to do with it, then you can hide it anywhere in your office or home and never look at it again. At least you will know you can use it if you need to."

Her heart raced, but she nodded. "Okay, I'll shoot this thing, but it's really heavy."

"I know it is, but it's the best one available right now." He lifted her hand with the gun and held it out in front of her, then he wrapped her fingers around the handle. Slowly, he pointed out each part of the gun, and how and where to place her fingers.

She concentrated on every word he said. He might not like guns, but he certainly knew a lot about them. Of course, he seemed to know a lot about everything she needed to know since she moved here.

"You ready?"

Inhaling a big breath, she nodded, but didn't move.

"Emma, you have to do something. Aim the gun at those bottles I set up. They're only bottles. You won't hurt them."

She laughed at his attempt to make her feel better.

"Okay, here goes." She lifted her arm and straightened her elbow. She squinted, pulled the trigger, but missed all the bottles. The force of the shot nearly took her off her feet, but she caught herself before she lost her balance.

Douglas stepped behind her. "I won't let you fall."

He stood close behind her. She felt his body next to hers. He was strong with well-formed muscles. She closed her eyes a moment to catch her breath.

How did he expect her to concentrate on the bottles and what he'd said about the gun when the closeness of his body took away her good sense?

"Emma, are you watching what you're doing? You need to concentrate. You didn't miss the bottles by much with your first shot. Let's try again."

Nodding, she made herself look at the gun then the target. "Do I pull the trigger now?"

"If you see one of the bottles in your aim, then yes, you can. I'm going to let you go. Keep your arm straight and your eyes focused and then pull the trigger."

When he stepped away from her, she closed her eyes and blew out a breath. Now maybe she could concentrate.

She moved the gun from side to side until she saw the end of the barrel line up with one of the bottles.

She bit her lip and pulled the trigger.

The gun exploded in her ear and jerked her body back against his.

He grabbed the gun with one hand. The other arm wrapped around her tightly. "You okay?"

"I think so." Almost limp in his arms, she placed her head against his chest and never wanted to move. "I'm sorry,

Douglas. I lost control of that gun. I can't believe it threw me back so hard."

"It's okay. First time shooters usually get that reaction." He turned her to face him. "You did fine."

Emma stood still, unable to move. His face was inches from hers. His breath warmed her skin. The urge to kiss him overwhelmed her. She swallowed.

Douglas stared back at her, unmoving, not saying a word. He'd stuck the gun in his waistband and now placed both his hands on her arms.

Before she knew what he was doing, he pulled her toward him and kissed her gently on the lips.

His lips were warm and firm. She closed her eyes and savored the feeling.

His hands eased up her arm and placed them on each side of her face. He rubbed his thumb on her cheek, then moved his lips to where his thumb was.

Finally, he pulled her head close to his chest and placed his hand on the back of her head.

His heart beat as fast as hers. She closed her eyes and inhaled his masculine scent.

"Emma, I didn't mean for that to happen." He held her away from him. "But, I'm glad it did. I've wanted to kiss you for a while."

The kiss still had her shaken, but she found her voice. "I think I do, too."

He chuckled. "You think?" He let her go. "Miss O'Hara, you are the most confusing lady I've ever met. This is where you're supposed to say how wonderful the kiss was and how you want me to kiss you again." He raised an eyebrow.

He was so cute, she wanted to reach up and kiss him again, but instead she tried to look serious. "I might be confusing, but you, sir, are the most aggravating, but amazing man, *I've* ever met."

He grinned. "Amazing, huh? You think I'm amazing?"

"Maybe. You do know a lot about everything, and you

seem to always be around when I need something. So, yes, amazing."

"That's good to know because I thought you didn't like me and my profession."

"I've never disliked you, Douglas. We did seem to get off on the wrong foot, but you're coming around." *And that kiss certainly helped.* She kept that thought to herself.

Again, he laughed. He still held her.

His smile left his face. He leaned close to her and kissed her again, this time a little harder.

She didn't pull away even though she knew she should.

She savored the feel of his lips on hers, but she knew she had to be sensible. She stepped back from him, looked at the ground, then up at him.

"It's been a long time since anyone kissed me."

"And?"

"And, I have to say, I enjoyed it." She felt her face heat up.

"Don't blush. You don't have anything to be embarrassed about. I'm thrilled you enjoyed the kiss and didn't slap me."

Again, he said just the right words to make her feel good.

"I would never slap you, Mr. Fletcher."

He shook his head. "Still not Dr. Fletcher. I won't give up on you."

She smiled. "One day."

"Now, let's get back to our shooting." He pulled the pistol from his waistband.

She took the gun, inhaled deeply, and tried to concentrate on her lesson, but her mind was not on shooting. She couldn't move away from the feel of his kiss. Her lips still tingled. Her heart still fluttered.

Had she ever felt this way with David? That was a simple answer. Absolutely not.

~

Two days later Emma sat on the front steps of her office

watching the wagon traffic on the main road. Douglas had told her the next wagon train was heading out in a couple days. She'd seen the chaos at the river front with the wagons and animals and prayed the men, women and children on the journey would survive the treacherous trail across the country.

She waved to a few of the people on the wagons. Several families had brought in their children with different ailments, but the family of the little girl with the broken arm did not come in. Grateful to have patients, she wished the townspeople would put their trust in her as these wagon train people did.

She glanced down the street just as Molly from the restaurant crossed carrying a basket of what looked like food. With interest she watched as she headed straight toward the road that led to Douglas's office. Before turning Molly raised her hand in greeting to Emma. Emma did the same.

Surprisingly, Molly did not go down the road, but instead turned and walked toward her.

"Hello, Molly. I see you were able to get away from the restaurant for a few minutes."

"Yes, it's not often. We finished the lunch crowd, and my kitchen helpers are cleaning so I'm taking advantage of a little free time to take some food to Dr. Fletcher."

"I see. I'm sure he will appreciate it. People have been going up and down our little street all day. He probably hasn't had a chance to eat."

"Douglas and I have been close since we were children." She smiled big. "One day we'll have to tell you about our adventures together."

"I'm sure they were lovely." Emma tried to keep the sarcasm from her voice, but she wasn't sure she succeeded.

"I'd better go. He loves his food hot. See you." Molly turned and walked down the street.

"What was that all about?" She said the words out loud,

but she knew exactly what that short visit was about. Molly made it clear she and Douglas were an item.

Emma let out a loud breath as she watched Molly wave to several men on horseback. They waved back. One stopped and talked with her. Surprisingly, they waved to her as well as they rode past the office, but, of course, they said nothing. Why would they? They knew nothing about her. Molly, on the other hand, was one of them.

Molly glanced back in her direction before she disappeared down the side street that took her to Douglas's office.

Emma got up. Maybe it was better that Douglas was involved with Molly. The pretty restaurant owner was from here and understood the life Douglas and his family had. She, on the other hand, was new to the area and didn't fit in yet with anything. Molly probably could ride a horse, drive a wagon and shoot a gun. And, she cooked.

Emma grimaced. Having servants growing up, then living with her mother, she never had to cook for herself. Even while living alone in Boston, she managed to eat at small local cafes quite a lot or to cook simple meals for herself. She considered herself a good doctor, but had to admit she was lacking in many other areas, especially those that would make her survive in this area.

She turned to go inside, but looked at the empty sidewalk where Molly had walked.

"Maybe I should've mentioned to Molly that her 'item' kissed me." Remembering that wonderful kiss, she smiled, then frowned.

Did men in these parts just kiss anyone or did it mean something to Douglas?

Shaking her head, she opened the door to her office.

I'm a professional, not a schoolgirl. Grow up.

CHAPTER FOURTEEN

Two hours before sunrise the next day Douglas sat on Major. He scanned the fields surrounding the Thomas family ranch. With his hand on his rifle, he sat unmoving. He'd heard talking in the distance, and he knew no one in his group guarding the ranch would call attention to themselves with loud talking or with any other kind of noise.

Squinting, he kept his gaze on the edge of the woods until he spotted movement. Three men on horseback eased out of the cover of the trees and headed toward the corrals.

From behind him he sensed another horse and knew it was Lucas. Motioning to him he pointed Major toward the three men now getting off their horses near the corrals. Lucas followed. When they got as close as they could under the cover of the trees, Douglas looked back at his brother. With a nod, they both raised their rifles and charged toward the men yelling to drop their guns.

Two of the men immediately dropped their rifles, but the third raised his gun and fired. Hot, burning pain ripped through Douglas's right arm. He gritted his teeth, raised his rifle and fired. The man fell to the ground.

Lucas shouted for the other men to get on the ground. They obeyed. Lucas jumped off his horse and kicked their guns aside.

Douglas held his wounded arm close to his body, jumped off Major and ran up to the man he'd shot. When he turned him over, he realized he was just a young man. Regret filled his body. He bent down to make sure he was still breathing, then shook his head, hating to see someone that young ruin his life.

Lucas kept his rifle aimed at the men. "You okay, Douglas?"

"Yeah, it's just a scratch, but this guy needs medical attention. He's breathing, but barely."

"We'll get him to town along with these other ones. I'm sure Vic and his men heard the shots. They'll be here soon."

Douglas walked over to the men on the ground. They were lying face down, but he turned the one's head so he could see. "I can't believe this. Sam, is that you and your brother?"

Sam spit at him, then turned his head.

Lucas edged up next to him, "You know these men?"

"Unfortunately, I do. They're the ones who held up the stagecoach. There were three of them, but that third guy I shot doesn't look familiar." He looked back at Sam, bent down and made him look at him.

Once more Sam spit at him. "I told you at the stagecoach you hadn't seen the last of us. You'll regret this."

Sam's brother, Cory, raised his head. "Sam, shut up. We're in enough trouble."

Douglas kept his gun pointed at Sam, but looked at Cory. "You need to quit following your brother. You ought to know by now he's trouble." He looked back at Sam. "I heard you had escaped before getting to prison."

Sam laughed. "It's not hard when you're guarded by ignorant deputies from a two-bit town."

"We'll see about this two-bit town when you're locked up again. I hear the district judge is coming back through next week. He'll make sure you get to where you can't escape." He turned at the sound of horses coming in from the road. "The sheriff and his men are here. He'll be glad to see you, Sam."

Douglas tried to help Lucas and Vic get the guys tied to their horses, but the pain from his arm radiated through his shoulder.

Vic looked his way. "Douglas, you're bleeding pretty bad. You need to take care of that arm."

Douglas nodded.

"I've sent a deputy to get a wagon to transport that wounded third guy. I suggest you wait and let them transport you."

"I'll be okay." He pulled a handkerchief out of his back pocket and tied it around his upper arm.

Victor yanked the last rope tightly around Sam. "I can't believe these two are still around here. You'd think after they escaped, they'd have enough sense to leave the area."

Douglas grunted. "It's sense they don't have, Vic."

"I believe that."

Douglas bent over the kid on the ground, then stood up. "I hope this one comes around. I'd hate myself if he dies."

Lucas stepped near the unconscious man. "I hate to see young guys get in trouble, but if he dies, it's not your fault. You didn't shoot first."

"Yeah, I know, but still it would be a waste of a young life."

"We need to get you and him to town to let Dr. O'Hara take a look at both of you."

Douglas rubbed his hand across the top of his arm and came back bloodied. "I'm okay, but I do need a better bandage. I'd hate to ruin all my shirts."

"Come here, little brother. I've wanted to do this ever since you pressed with your entire weight to stop me from bleeding on that cattle drive." He rewrapped the handkerchief and pulled it tight.

Douglas pulled away. "Watch it. That hurts."

Lucas laughed. "Pay back!"

~

Emma heard the commotion on the main road in front of her office before she saw anyone. The sun was just beginning to light the sky, but she was already drinking coffee in her house and had gotten dressed earlier.

She put the coffee cup in the dishpan and ran out the house door toward the back door of her office. Shoving it open, she then lit a lamp and carried it into the front waiting room. She put it on a table and hurried outside.

Douglas and Lucas were on horseback with Sheriff Vic and several men riding alongside. Two men were tied to their horses. In the dim morning light, she couldn't distinguish the prisoners, but they looked vaguely familiar.

Sheriff Vic spoke with Douglas and Lucas briefly, then they headed toward the jail. Douglas and Lucas got off their horses and tied them to the hitching post. She ran out the office and down the steps.

Lucas stepped forward and spoke to Emma. "We have a wagon following us with one of the men. He has a gunshot wound in the abdomen and needs your attention. They're a few minutes behind us." He turned to Douglas, then back to Emma. "You might have time to take a look at my brother first. The wounded guy coming in got a shot off first and hit Douglas."

Emma sucked in air. Her breath caught in her throat when she saw Douglas's bloody shirt. "Oh no."

"I'm okay, Emma. It's just a scratch, but it might need stitching to stop the bleeding."

"Come in, please. Let's take a look." She put her arm around his body and led him up the steps.

"I can walk. I promise." He smiled down at her. "But I like you holding onto me."

She slapped him softly. "Be a gentleman."

"Brother, you look like you're in good hands. I'm going to Vic's to help get those guys checked in. I'll be back shortly." Lucas looked up at Emma. "Take good care of him, but you don't have to be gentle."

Douglas glared at him. "Thanks, brother."

Lucas laughed then turned.

"Let's get you in and cleaned up before the other man gets here. It looks as though you've lost a lot of blood. You're not going to pass out on me, are you?"

"I hope not." He grinned.

She held him tightly. "It's not funny, Douglas. Losing blood is dangerous." Inside, she led him to the examination table. "Can you climb up? I need to take a look."

He pulled himself up and blew out a big breath. He might have joked earlier, but she could tell he was hurting and weak.

"We need to do this quickly if that other guy is in worse shape." Emma untied the bloody handkerchief from his arm and pulled it off.

Douglas grimaced.

"Let's see if we can get that shirt off without hurting you too much in spite of what Lucas said."

She smiled while she worked, but he only nodded.

She slid the shirt from his good left arm and then carefully pulled it off his wounded arm.

Again, he grimaced.

"I'm sorry. The shirt was already stuck to the skin."

"It's okay. I didn't think the bullet did anything but get the skin, but it hurts like the dickens."

"Of course, it hurts." She turned and grabbed a tray with bandages and a jar of ointment, placed it on a table near where he sat, then got a bowl of water. "We need to clean it. Why don't you lie down?"

"I'm okay sitting."

"No, you're not. You're already pale and after I wash it, you'll probably need stitches. I don't want you to fall of this table."

He didn't argue.

She placed her hand under his head and helped him

recline on the table before checking his arm. "It looks as though the bullet went through so at least we don't have to dig it out, but it might've torn your muscle. That's probably why it hurts so badly." She picked up a piece of clean cotton batting, then soaked it in carbolic acid. "This might burn, but I need to wash it out." Before he could say anything, she placed the cotton on his wound, then poured the carbolic acid over it.

Douglas squeezed his eyes, but didn't make a sound.

She kept her face emotionless. Lecture after lecture explained the necessity of not showing emotion even when she knew the patient was in pain. As long as she did what was necessary, she couldn't let empathy get in the way. It could mean life or death. Even though she knew Douglas's wound wasn't a life or death situation, he still shouldn't see how she was affected by his situation.

"You are going to need a few stitches. It's still bleeding and it's deeper than a little scratch." She grabbed a needle and thread. "I'll be quick."

He looked at her with hazel eyes that looked almost brown this morning.

She swallowed and pulled the skin together and began to stitch. "The first time I stitched anyone, I had tears running down my face. I knew I hurt the man, but I had to do it. Now I try not to think about what the patient is feeling."

Douglas stayed quiet and still, his face strained and tense.

She hated to hurt him, but the stitches had to be done. Before she finished, she heard the wagon pull up in front of the office.

"Just in time. Just one more stitch." This time she jabbed him with the needle to hurry.

He grunted.

"I'm sorry. It's over. That's the last one."

"Thanks."

"I hate to ask you to move so soon, but we'll need this

table for the next man. Can you sit over there?”

“I’m okay, Emma. Go check on that man. I hope you can save him. He’s pretty young.”

“I’m sorry either of you were wounded. You know how I hate guns.”

She helped him off the table and to the chair, then turned toward the door, but he took her hand.

“You have to believe I didn’t want to hurt that boy. He shot first.”

“As I said, I’m sorry either of you were hurt.”

She left him sitting alone as she headed for the porch. Was this the type of medical work she was here to do? Would there be men shooting each other every week? She knew this part of the world was not as civilized as back East, but she had no idea everyone carried guns and actually used them against one another.

Maybe she was naïve.

She shook her head and opened the door. Several men worked to get the wounded man from the back of the wagon. They pulled him until they could haul him out, then carried him toward the front gate.

“Be careful,” she shouted, then stepped back to allow them to carry the man inside. “Take him to the back room. I have a table cleared.”

She held the door opened, then followed the men inside. She ran ahead of the procession and waited inside.

“That’s a good sign if they’re bringing him inside.” Douglas stood and pulled a shirt over his good arm. “At least he made it here.”

“I haven’t looked at him. I hope he’s still breathing.” She stepped aside and allowed the men to slide the wounded man onto the table, but when she looked at the man, her breath caught in her throat. “Edward.”

Douglas stepped by her. “Do you know this man?”

Emma jerked her head toward him. “His name is Edward. You shot my brother.”

CHAPTER FIFTEEN

Emma bent over her brother stretched on the examining table, his arms limp over the sides, his torso bloody.

She squeezed his hand. "Edward, this is Emma. Can you hear me?" Her heart pounded.

Edward didn't respond.

Douglas placed his hand on her arm, but she couldn't look at him. Her world spun out of control. Words for him did not come. What could she say to the man who shot her brother?

She felt faint, but throwing her shoulders back, she took a deep breath and pulled herself together. There was no room for weakness. She was a doctor. Edward's doctor. She had to get her act together if she were to save his life.

The men who'd brought him in still stood behind her. She turned to them. "Thank you for getting him here."

"We can stay if you need us," one of the men spoke up.

"Thank you for offering, but I'm okay."

The three men spoke to Douglas, but their words didn't register. She saw and heard nothing but Edward's labored breathing. The men left.

Edward bled from his side. She pulled the shirt up and removed the bundle of cloth the men had used to try to stop the bleeding. As she eased it away, the blood continued to flow. Panic threatened to take over.

Douglas stepped to her side. "Let me help, Emma."

"No, you've done enough." Her voice was too loud, but she couldn't control herself. Her brother could die in front of her.

"Be reasonable, Emma. You need help and I'm here. I told you, he shot first. I barely was able to get that shot off. I'm sure he would've shot me again had I not fired."

She spun around. "Edward is not a murderer. He wouldn't have done that. I'm not even sure he owned a gun or knew how to shoot."

"You weren't there. The boy was scared. He would do anything to stay alive, as we all would."

Grabbing a fresh bundle of bandages, she pressed Edward's side. "This is why I feel as I do about firearms and violence."

"You're not in Boston anymore. Life is different here."

She knew he was right, but how could she condone what he'd done?

"Would you go get my mother? She's in our house. She can help me with Edward."

"Are you sure that's such a good idea? That's her son. Her emotions may not let her be much help. Let me assist you. Please."

Emma refused to cry, but the tears threatened to fall. She swallowed. "Please, go get Mother."

He put both hands on her arms. She wanted so badly to lean into his embrace for strength. She needed him now, but she had to remember who put the bullet in Edward.

"Emma, I'm sorry. I truly am."

She nodded.

"I'll go get your mother, but I think it's a bad move."

She listened to his footsteps as he walked through the back door and out into the yard connecting the office to their house. Then and only then, did she allow the tears to flow.

She put her head down next to Edward. "I'm with you, little brother. I'm here and I won't let you die."

She squeezed her eyes. "God, I know I don't deserve to ask you for a favor, but my brother is still so young. He's not a bad boy. Please let me know how to help him. I can't watch him die."

Bowing her head, she prayed over and over until she felt her body calm. Only then did she turn and roll a small table toward her. She'd removed a bullet twice in training, but never one in that part of the body. She visualized the sketches of the body to make sure she remembered what was under the skin. Puncturing an organ would be horrible.

"Edward, hang with me. Please stay with me. I love you. I couldn't bear to lose you. She bent down and picked up his hand to move it, but kissed it first. "Stay with me, I beg you."

She wiped the bloody area with carbolic acid, then picked up a scalpel and a pair of long tweezers, but before she could start, she heard the back door open and her mother stormed in.

"Edward. Oh, my Edward," June O'Hara cried.

"Mother, I know you're upset, but I need you to help me. Try to get control of yourself."

June reached the table where Edward lay unconscious and threw her body across his.

"Mother, I'm so sorry." Emma looked up and Douglas stood leaning against the door frame with his right arm held close to his body.

He raised an eyebrow. "I can help if you want."

Emma closed her eyes. How could this be? The man who shot my brother wants to help save his life. Maybe that was the way things were out here on this uncivilized region of the world.

She looked up and slowly nodded.

Douglas pushed himself away from the wall. The first thing he did when he got to the table was to put his arm around June. "Mrs. O'Hara, why don't you go to the other side of the table and hold your son's hand? If he wakes up, he'll need to know you're here with him."

June looked up, tears running down her face, and nodded. Slowly, with Douglas's help, she walked around the table.

When he walked back, Emma mouthed, "Thank you."

"Just tell me what to do. I want to help save Edward's life."

~

Douglas sat in a chair pushed up against the wall watching Edward on the table. He pulled out his watch. Three in the morning.

Edward had not awakened since being brought into the office. Fear gripped his chest. He closed his eyes. *Please, God, don't let this boy die. He has his whole life in front of him. Emma and June need him.*

He looked to his left. June had fallen asleep on one chair with her head propped on the arm. Emma's slumped over her desk. After working to get the bullet out of her brother, she'd sat by him for hours. Douglas convinced her to rest, promising to wake her if he gave any indication of waking up.

Her dark brown hair flowed down her back and over her face. It shone in the light of the lantern. He pushed aside a strong urge to walk over and put his arms around her. She would need someone to help her get through if Edward didn't make it. Knowing too well what a gunshot could do, he wanted to protect her from what could happen, especially since he is the one who shot him.

He threw his head back and groaned. He'd only been home for a short time and already his world was spinning out of control. Maybe Franklin and his brother had been right. Maybe he was getting too soft, but he couldn't help the way he felt.

Growing up in this area, he had seen or heard of too many men who had died from guns. He remembered them well.

Men trying to protect what was theirs. Young men drinking too much and showing off with guns. Stupid stunts. Stupid actions from too much liquor, too much ego, and not enough good sense. He understood and sympathized with the way Emma felt about guns.

The pain in his arm seemed to be worse. He felt feverish, but he dared not wake Emma. She'd need all the rest she could get.

He looked up to heaven. *Why me? Why was it me who shot Emma's brother?*

Douglas hated violence, always had, and now what he'd done to help protect the lands he'd loved so dearly could cost him any chance he might have had with Emma. A laugh nearly broke through. He must be kidding himself. Emma O'Hara would never accept him as a doctor. Now that he'd shot her brother, he could expect nothing from her, not even friendship.

And why would he think he'd want her attention and love? The kiss they'd shared had been wonderful, and he was sure Emma had enjoyed it, as well. He wanted to know her better, but Lily had bored a hole in his heart so big it nearly consumed him. It still lingered, or did it? He sat up straight. If he admitted it to himself, he hadn't thought about Lily much since he'd been back home. Maybe he was finally moving on if he wasn't thinking about her day and night. Was it possible he'd never loved her?

Women. He'd never understand them.

He turned his attention back to June and Emma, resting after a horrible night. They had come to Independence to find a new life. They didn't deserve having to face the possibility of losing a son and a brother.

Shaking his head, he looked back at Edward. *Come on, boy. You need to wake up and give these two ladies some hope.* He blew out a big breath and tried to get comfortable in the hard straight-backed chair. He tried to position his right arm to lessen the pain. It didn't work. His arm and shoulder hurt more now than before.

By the time the sun peeked through the small window, Douglas yearned to get home to lie down. He was exhausted, tired, and hurting, but he wasn't about to leave while Emma and June slept.

He looked at Edward, blinked, then jumped up from his chair. Edward moved his head from side to side. Douglas held his wounded arm and moved toward the bed.

"Edward, you can wake up. You're in Independence in your sister's medical office. Please, your sister and your mother want to see you."

Edward didn't move any more, but Douglas wasn't giving up. He took three big steps to Emma. He touched her arm. "Emma, wake up."

Emma opened her eyes, raised her head, and looked toward Douglas. As if she just realized where she was, she pushed her chair back and raced to Edward's side.

Douglas followed her. "He moved his head from side to side, but he didn't open his eyes."

"Moving is a good sign." She leaned over her brother and gave him a soft kiss on his forehead. "Edward, please wake up. Mama and I are here waiting for you."

Edward made a sound, not loud, but audible.

Emma turned to Douglas with a huge smile on her face. He nodded.

"Please, Brother, open your eyes and tell me you love me."

"I . . . love . . . you."

His whispered, halting words brought a smile to Douglas.

Emma looked at Douglas. "Would you get Mother? It might help him if he hears her voice."

Nodding, he walked to June and touched her lightly on the shoulder. "June? Edward is trying to wake up. I'm sure he wants to see you."

"Edward? Oh my, I fell asleep." She pushed her chair

back.

Douglas helped her stand and led her to the bed, then he backed away. Emma still hovered over Edward, holding his hand and talking softly to him. June grabbed Emma's hand and said something to her, but Douglas couldn't hear.

This was his time to leave. Emma's family needed their privacy.

He picked up a small satchel he'd brought in, slung it over his good shoulder, then eased out the door. He had a good feeling Edward would be okay. Now he could go home and rest.

Untying Major, he lifted his foot into the stirrup, then barely pulled up enough strength to get into the saddle. He grunted, leaned against the saddle horn then headed for his office, his home away from home.

Before he urged Major forward, he looked up into the reds and orange of the morning sky. *Thank you, God. Thank you for letting Edward O'Hara wake up. Now, please, if it's in your plan, please let him get better.*

~

Emma stayed by Edward all day, holding his hand, encouraging him to talk, making sure he was comfortable, and getting him to sip water and soup. Close to sunset Sheriff Vic knocked and walked into the back of her office.

"Dr. O'Hara, I heard your brother was doing a little better. I came to see for myself."

Emma stood up. "Yes, sir, he's been trying to come around all day, but he's very weak."

"I hate to bother you, but I do have some questions for you. Did you know Edward was in town and running with those idiots? To be so stupid, they certainly did a lot of trouble, especially on outlying ranches."

"I had no idea Edward was actually in Independence. He was supposed to meet Mother and me here but he never contacted us. As far as him being mixed up with undesirables, it would never cross my mind. He's had some trouble adjusting to adulthood, but he never did anything like this before."

Sheriff Vic walked over to the bed. "Edward, I'm Sheriff Sanchez. Can you open your eyes?"

Edward squinted.

"You're a lucky man. Douglas Fletcher is a good shot. I'm surprised that bullet didn't get you in the heart, and it probably would have if you hadn't shot him first."

Edward nodded and closed his eyes again.

"I know you can hear me so I'm just telling you that you can be in as much trouble as those three other men if Mr. Thomas files charges against you for being on his property or Douglas for being shot by you. I'll put in a good word for you, but there's only so much I can do if they want me to apply the extent of the law to you."

Emma touched the sheriff's arm. "Is that true? He could have charges filed against him?"

"Certainly. He was an accomplice, and he shot Douglas, the son of one of the most influential families in this area."

"Yes, I know who he is, but his side of the story is the only one we have right now. How do we know Douglas didn't fire first?" Emma crossed her arms in front of her body. "My brother doesn't belong in prison. He's really a good boy. Naïve, but good."

"Douglas would not have fired unless provoked." He shook his head. "As I said, I'll do what I can, but don't get your hopes up."

She nodded. "Thank you for trying."

Emma watched as Sheriff Vic walked into the reception area. When she heard the front door close, she turned to Edward. "Brother, what got into that thick head of yours? You could've been killed and now you face the possibility of prison."

Edward didn't answer, but she had a feeling he wasn't asleep. She turned and found a chair. There was nothing else she could do for him, but she wasn't about to leave his side even though she wanted to see Douglas. She had to know if he was going to press charges and to check on his arm. He appeared to be in a lot of pain while he kept watch over them last night. She watched the door, hoping her mother would return quickly.

Checking on his arm was a good excuse to talk to him about Edward and what his plans were. She wouldn't blame him for filing charges, but she'd do her best to convince him otherwise.

Thank goodness Edward was a horrible shot. Or maybe he wasn't so horrible. Maybe Douglas shot him first and Edward shot wildly after being wounded.

It certainly was a theory, but deep in her heart she knew that was not the case.

~

Emma knocked softly on Douglas's office door, then waited. Should she go in? She clenched her hands, took a deep breath, and opened the door. It was a public office. Surely, she could simply walk in.

"Douglas? It's Emma. Are you here?"

Not hearing anything, she thought about leaving, but she had to find out if he was in the back.

"Douglas?" She opened the door to his examining room and stopped. Douglas lay on a small cot pushed up into a cubby hole in the far wall. He'd taken off his shirt. She swallowed. She blinked before she demanded her gaze to settle on the bloodied bandage.

She threw back her shoulders. This, too, was a medical building in a sense, so she had every right to check on him, shirt on or not.

She walked up to his cot. "Douglas, are you awake?"

Douglas opened his eyes only halfway. "I think so."

She placed her hand on his forehead. "You have fever."

Turning, she found a small pail. "I'll be right back. I'm going to the well." She hurried out the back door and ran down the steps to where she'd seen him pumping water.

Once she got the water flowing, she stuck the pail under the water, rinsed it, then watched as it filled.

Thoughts in her head scrambled, going from what to do next with Edward's abdominal wound to getting Douglas's fever to break. Since she'd opened her practice, she sat bored, waiting and hoping for patients. Now two men's lives depended on what she did. She'd been trained to handle emergency situations, but she didn't want her first one to be her only brother and the man who. . ." she stopped her train of thought. What was Douglas? Was he just her savior from the stagecoach or was he something more? He'd kissed her and she loved it.

But then, he'd shot her brother.

What did it all mean? Could she look at him now as she'd done before?

Water overflowed from the full bucket, pulling her thoughts back to the task at hand. She turned and hurried back into Douglas's office. No matter what he was to her, he was a patient now and her job was to help him.

He had not moved. She knelt down by the cot and placed the cloth on his forehead. His skin burned. *How did this happen? I should've checked his arm last night when I saw he was still hurting.*

"Douglas, I'm going to take the bandage off so I can see what's happening."

Douglas grunted, then grinned.

She smiled. Even in pain and burning with fever, he could still grin.

She liked that.

Carefully, she unwrapped the first layer of cloth she'd tied around his arm yesterday and removed it. Before she took away the bottom bandage, she could smell the distinct odor of infection.

Her heart pounded. She was so sure she'd cleaned it properly.

"What's the problem?"

His weak voice pulled her out of her self-pity.

"Nothing's wrong, but it seems an infection is starting to develop.

He opened his eyes and looked directly into hers. "Bullets have a way of doing that. They pick up dirt and cloth and debris going into the body. That's why so many people die from being shot."

"Well, you're not going to die. I'll get it cleaned before I bandage it. I didn't bring my satchel. Do you have something I can use?"

He nodded toward a tall white shelving unit.

She walked over to it and opened three drawers before she found the right size she thought would cover his arm.

"Ointments are in the side cabinet."

Emma nodded. "Thank you."

Quite impressed with his medical supplies, she gathered what she needed then returned to his bedside and began to clean the wound. She concentrated on what she did but was aware of him looking at her.

Finally, she applied the ointment and bandaged the area. "This should help."

"How's Edward?"

"He was sleeping when I left. Mother is with him. Let's hope we can keep his infection down as well."

Douglas nodded.

Emma pulled a thin blanket over him. "I'll come back a little later to check on you. Mother made soup for Edward. I'll bring you some."

She wondered if he actually heard her. His soft steady breathing told her he slept. Without thinking, she bent over Douglas and kissed his forehead. Instantly, she stood up and crossed her arms. Why had she done that?

She knew why. The kiss he'd given her at her shooting lesson still made her heart flutter, but now things were different. He'd shot her brother. Anger filled her soul every time she thought about how her brother could have been killed, and if she were honest with herself, Edward could still die.

Squeezing her eyes shut, she wished time could be turned back. Had she known Edward had come to Independence, maybe she could have helped him.

But time could not be turned around. Edward lay with a horrible wound on his side shaking with fever just as Douglas was. Could she live in an area of the world that solved problems with fists and guns?

Before opening the door to leave, Emma looked back at Douglas. He had so many wonderful qualities, and he certainly was handsome, but could she allow herself to get close to someone who carried a gun and believed in using it. Edward lay next door struggling to stay alive. How could she think about becoming good friends—or something more— with the person who shot him?

If Edward dies, what will I do? Could I stay here in the outskirts of civilization knowing I'm the reason he came?

CHAPTER SIXTEEN

Douglas slid his sore arm into his shirt sleeve. He felt more human today than last night when the fever had taken everything out of him.

He stopped buttoning the front. Did Emma come by last night and change his bandage? He thought he'd dreamed her, but when he awoke this morning, his bloody bandage was gone and replaced by a professionally wrapped clean one. Before he did anything else, he'd go over and thank her.

Did he also remember her kissing him or had he dreamed that? Raising an eyebrow, he smiled. If Emma actually kissed him, maybe she'd forgiven him for Edward's condition.

He headed toward the front door, but it opened before he got to it.

"Dr. Fletcher, I'm so glad I caught you. I have a mare giving birth, and she's having some trouble. Can I get you to follow me out to the ranch?"

Douglas hesitated. If he waited long enough to talk with Emma, the mare might not make it.

"Sure, Jack. You're only about twenty minutes out of town, right?"

"Yes, can you follow me?"

He nodded. "Let me get my bag."

In the back room, he glanced out the window toward Emma's office. He'd have to see her later. He ran his hand over his bandaged arm, gritted his teeth, then headed out to meet the rancher waiting for him in the other room.

"I might need you to help me saddle my horse. My arm's out of commission."

Leaving town was the last thing he wanted to do at the moment, but he was a veterinarian, and it was his job. He'd manage.

After helping the mare give birth to a beautiful colt, he returned to the office to find his waiting room full. Needing to lie down, he let out a low groan but greeted those waiting with a smile. For the remainder of the day, ranchers and even the local pastor came into the office for his services.

By the time he locked the front door, he realized the sun had set hours ago. He wanted to check on Edward, but he wasn't sure Emma would appreciate him stopping by this late. At first, he headed toward his back room, but changed his mind walked out his front door toward the street. He needed to know how the boy was.

He knocked on her locked office door and waited. Fear gripped his chest. Had the worst happened to Edward for them to be gone? Surely, he would have heard if that happened. Word flew through town when anything important occurred.

He knocked again. This time he heard footsteps.

"We're closed. Is this an emergency?"

He recognized Emma's voice.

"It's me, Emma."

The latch clicked.

"Are you okay?" Emma asked before the door was fully opened.

"Yes, I'm fine, but I wanted to check on Edward and to see how you and your mother are doing?"

"Come in." She stepped back. "Edward is about the

same. He's still running a fever, and that concerns me. One of us stays with him all the time. He's not drinking anything either." She sat down in one of the straight chairs in the reception area.

Emma's pale face showed signs of stress. He sat next to her. "He does need to drink. Do you think I can help?"

She shook her head and repeated the same words she'd said last night. "No, I think you've done enough." Her words were a whisper.

Her words, soft as they were, stunned him. "Emma, I told you I had no choice. If I hadn't shot, I feel sure he would've fired again."

"You don't know that."

"No, I don't, but Edward knew the sheriff's men surrounded him. I'm sure he felt trapped, so I do believe he would've shot me again, this time someplace besides my arm."

She put her face down in her hands then slumped over her legs.

Hesitantly, he placed a hand on her arm. Her silent sobs shook her body. He took the chance, slid his chair next to hers, and put his arm around her shoulders. She leaned into him. His heart swelled.

"If I could take back that shot, I would. I would never want to hurt your brother or anyone else."

Her shoulders shook. She inhaled a jagged breath. "I know, but who else can I blame?'

He clamped his mouth. The blame was entirely on Edward, who had gotten in with guys who were no good. He didn't have to tell her that. She already knew it.

"I just want him to live. We love him and need him. I want him to finally have a good life."

"I think God knows Edward is a good man, someone who simply made a bad mistake. Our God is all forgiving if we simply ask."

She didn't say anything.

"You do believe that, don't you?"

She let out another breath and straightened up. "I'm not sure I do. I do pray to Him, but does he hear me? I don't know."

"He hears, Emma. I believe sometimes we don't get our prayers answered because we're asking for the wrong thing."

She snapped her head to face him. "Are you saying asking Him to save Edward is not the right thing to do?"

"I didn't say that." Confusion set in. Douglas didn't know how to answer her. He truly believed God heard our prayers, but he had a feeling no matter what he said Emma would not listen.

He stood. "I think it's time for me to go."

Emma closed her eyes, then stood up. "I'm sorry, Douglas. I'm in such a state I'm not sure what I believe or what I don't."

Douglas reached out and put his arms around her. "I know. You're exhausted." He pulled her close expecting her to pull away.

She didn't. Instead, she melted into his arms.

He held her tight in spite of the pain that shot up his arm and into his shoulder. He wished this moment would never end. Holding her close warmed his heart and soul. He closed his eyes and relished the feel of her body. She was too thin. The last month had been hard on her, and now having to deal with Edward was taking its toll. How he wished he could help her.

Emma finally pulled away just enough for him to look into her face.

"Thank you, Douglas. I needed your understanding and strength. I'm sorry I snapped at you."

"I'm here if you need me."

"I know, and I'm truly trying to forgive you for shooting my brother." With another huge intake of breath, she straightened her shoulders. "If you want to see Edward you can go to him."

"No, I don't need to do that. I simply wanted to hear from you that he was the same and that you were okay."

"If you haven't figured it out yet, I'm a mess. I should be stronger. I'm not."

He chuckled. "You're exactly what you're supposed to be. No one would expect any differently."

Her lips lifted in a weak smile.

His heart swelled.

She swiped her hand across her eyes. "You always say the right thing."

"Glad to hear someone thinks so." He looked around. "I really do have to go."

"How is your arm? I know you're still in pain."

He rubbed his arm. "I'm doing better. My fever broke last night. Did you come by and change my bandage?"

"I did, but you were not fully awake."

"I thought I remembered you coming in, but wasn't sure. Thank you for taking care of me. Changing that bandage probably helped the fever break." He wanted to tell her he remembered her lips on his forehead, but he dared not mention that. His befuddled mind probably dreamed it.

She nodded. "Glad I was able to help."

Reluctant to leave, Douglas shuffled his feet. "I'll be back to check on Edward tomorrow. If you need me to do anything, send someone over."

"I will. Thank you for coming by."

With one last glance her way, he walked away wishing he could spend more time with her.

The next morning, he opened the door to his office to find several men standing on his porch waiting for him.

Never a dull moment for a vet around here. He laughed. Thrilled the citizens of Independence put enough trust in him to care for their animals, he opened the door and greeted the men even though he yearned to crawl back in his bed.

By the time the sun set, and the last patient left the office, Douglas headed to the front door to lock up for the night, but stepped back when the door opened.

"Molly, this is a surprise."

"I tried to get over earlier, but the café was full all afternoon."

"That's a good thing."

"It definitely is. I'm not complaining." She held out a small basket. "I brought you some dinner. I know how busy you've been all day."

Douglas took the basket. "Thank you, Molly. This is really nice of you."

"I hope you're hungry."

"I'm starving." His good manners kicked in, even though he wanted to be alone. "Would you like to come in and sit while I eat?"

"Yes, thank you. That would be nice." She walked past him. "Where do you eat?"

He usually ate in his back room, but for some reason he didn't want her in there. "We can sit right here at the desk." He pulled out a chair and sat. She did the same.

He opened the basket and found a plate of chicken and potatoes. "This looks great." He pulled out a fork and took a big bite. "Delicious."

"Glad you like it."

Molly looked much quieter than she usually did.

"Are you okay?"

She smiled. "I am, but I'm worried about you. Word around town is you were shot on guard duty the other night. I was a little upset I had to hear it from the local gossip mill."

"I wish it were only gossip, but it's true. I did take a bullet in my arm. Just a scratch."

"That's not what I heard."

"Well, a little more than a scratch, but it's okay. Dr. O'Hara fixed me up. We're lucky to have the lady in town."

She shrugged. "I also heard you shot her brother and he's in bad shape."

Douglas put down his fork. "I guess the gossip mill is

working overtime, but unfortunately, it's correct. I did shoot Edward after he shot me. So far it looks as if he'll pull through. I hope so. I'd hate to be responsible for a young man's death."

"I'm sure what you did was the only thing you could do." She sat up straight in her chair. "Most people in town say he deserved to be shot and they don't care if he dies."

Douglas frowned. "I can't believe they're saying something like that. The boy isn't a bad guy. He just got in with the wrong men. I for one hate I'm the one who wounded him."

"I don't want to see anyone hurt any more than you do, but I hate all the trouble our ranchers are having with these men. I hear them talking when they come into the café. Maybe it will end now that those men are in custody."

"No, it won't. These men are not the ones in charge. They're just following orders. The trouble will continue. I can almost guarantee it."

Molly frowned. "I hate to hear that, but I'm glad you're doing better. I just wish you would've let me know you had been hit. I could've been over here with you."

"Things were really hectic when we all got to town. This is my first day I've had in the office."

He was about to tell her he wanted to get to bed early, but another knock told him someone else was at the door. Without thinking, he groaned.

"No matter what you say, you aren't well yet. I'll get the door." She got up and opened the door.

He didn't argue.

"Why Preacher Smith, come on in. Dr. Fletcher is here eating a little dinner I brought him."

"Thank you, Molly." He looked around Molly. "Douglas, is it okay if I come in?"

"For you, anytime." Against his better judgment, he stood up and tried not to grimace. "Please come in and sit. Is Spunky feeling okay?"

Molly smiled. "Do you have a dog named Spunky?"

"Sure do and you can only guess why I named him that. He's a little thing, but has more spunk than a dog three times his size." He looked at Douglas. "He's getting better thanks to you. I'm here to check on you. Everyone who has been in here tells me you're not doing that great."

"Gossip mill." He laughed.

"He really isn't feeling that great, Preacher. He won't admit it, but he's not."

"I wanted to check on you myself and see if I can do anything for you."

"No, you can see I have wonderful friends bringing me food, and I have a fine doctor right next door."

"I hear she took care of you and is now taking care of her brother, the man you shot."

Douglas shook his head. "You heard right. I would hope you'd drop in next door and say a prayer with Emma and her family. They all would appreciate it, I'm sure."

"I might do that."

"Have you eaten dinner, Preacher?"

"No, as a matter of fact, I was going to your café as soon as I left here. Now, I think I'll stop next door then go over."

"I'd love for you to do that. While you visit with Dr. O'Hara and her family, I'll go whip you up something special."

Douglas watched the exchange between the town's single preacher and Molly. She certainly was being accommodating. He smiled.

"Molly, I'll get your dishes back to the café tomorrow. This is delicious." He turned to Preacher Smith. "I know she'll fix you up with something just as special."

"I hope so. I'm starving." He shook Douglas's hand. "I hope you really are feeling better. I'll take a minute and drop in next door and see how Dr. O'Hara's brother is doing."

"I know she and her mother will appreciate it."

Molly bent over his chair and gave him a quick kiss on

the forehead then looked at Preacher Smith. "Douglas and I are good friends, just like brother and sister. We've known each other a long time."

Douglas let out a sigh of relief. "It's a wonderful thing to have a trusted friend. I cherish her friendship."

Preacher Smith smiled and nodded. "Good friends are hard to find. You're a lucky man, Douglas." He took Molly's arm and led her out the door. "I'll check on you again."

Douglas watched them leave. Could something be starting between the two of them? He really liked the preacher and would love to see Molly find someone to love her as she deserved because even though she insinuated she wanted to spend more time with him, he was not ready to form a relationship with her, except one of friendship.

~

Emma sat next to her brother listening to his irregular breathing. She'd done all she knew for his wound. Now she simply had to wait for his body to respond.

Her thoughts turned to God and to the words that Douglas said. Would God listen to her? She took Edward's hand and closed her eyes. "God, I want to believe. I do. I know you're watching over my family. Maybe the hard times we've had were a test. If it is, I hope we've learned from them. My prayer is for my brother, not me. I don't deserve your blessings after the materialistic life I led, but my brother has not had a good life. Please watch over him, and if it is in your plan, please help him recover."

Realizing she was speaking out loud, she looked around the room, then back to Edward whose eyes were open.

His lip lifted into a small smile. "That was nice, sister. Thank you." His words were weak, but she heard him.

"You weren't supposed to hear that, but I'm glad you did. I love you and want the best for you. Rest now. You'll be fine. We're here with you." Hearing him speak lightened the weight on her shoulders.

She closed her eyes. *Thank you, God. Thank you.*

By the end of the day, her mother came in with bowls of soup and hunks of homemade bread.

"You sit and eat, Emma. I'll try to get Edward to take a sip."

"He was awake a little earlier. Maybe he'll wake up again for you." Emma sat at her small table and spooned her soup. "Hmmm. This really is good."

Before she finished, she heard the front door open and close. Hoping it was Douglas, she left her soup and headed into the reception area. To her disbelief, a nice-looking man stood at the door.

"Ma'am, I'm Preacher Smith. I'd love to come in to talk with you and to pray with you and your brother."

Emma's hand went to her chest. "I'm so touched you'd do this. I thought everyone in town thought bad about my brother."

"No, not everyone. God still loves him no matter what he does."

"Please, come in. My mother is with Edward. She'll be thrilled to see you."

They walked to the back with Emma saying a silent prayer of thanks.

Preacher Smith didn't stay long, but the little time he was there raised Emma's and her mother's spirits.

She walked him to the door to find a young lady with a baby on the front porch.

"May I help you?"

"I hope so. My baby can't keep any food down. I'm worried. Dr. Fletcher sent me over here. Can you look at him?"

Thankful Douglas sent this baby to her, she nodded. "Certainly." Excitement raced through her veins.

Preacher Smith touched the little baby. "Dr. O'Hara, I'll leave you to take care of this beautiful baby."

"From the bottom of my heart, I thank you for coming, Preacher."

"I hope to see the three of you in church when Edward is up and about."

She nodded, then turned her attention to the young mother. "I have a patient in the other room, but if you don't mind, we can use my desk here for me to examine your baby."

The lady looked scared, but she nodded.

"I'll be back in a second. I need my bag." She raced to the back room with a huge smile on her faced "Mother, I have a patient out front."

June smiled big. "I knew words would get around that you knew what you were doing. Go. Take care of your other patient. I'll stay here with Edward."

Maybe God does listen to me even though I don't deserve it.

CHAPTER SEVENTEEN

The hammer banged against the metal pan three times. Loud talking and chaos filled the room. Harry Miller hit the pan again. This time the men got quieter.

Douglas sat on the third row of the town hall hoping the meeting wouldn't drag on forever. Most of the men tonight were from town. Ranchers from the outlying areas sent word they did not want to leave their families. He had hoped Lucas would join them tonight, but he had not. Even though there were men on the ranch who could protect his family, he wasn't comfortable, especially with Abigail getting closer to her due date.

Even after Sam, Cory, and Edward had been captured on the Thomas ranch, everyone knew they were not the main men responsible for the trouble. Sam and Cory refused to talk or swore they knew nothing about plans for the railroad and the land grab. Edward had not awakened long enough to question, but Douglas had a feeling the boy knew only the two goons he ran with that night.

"I say we threaten to hang those three guys. Maybe they'll start squealing and tell us who they're taking orders from," the guy sitting behind Douglas shouted out his suggestion.

"Why threaten them? Just hang the lot of them." Franklin

Shaunessey stood against the wall shouting. His younger brother wasn't with him, but someone else was. Douglas assumed it was his father whose hair had turned grey, but still had streaks of red running through it.

Douglas pulled his gaze away from the Shaunesseys, then turned and spoke to the rancher behind him, but loud enough for the room to hear. "And what if they don't know who's giving the orders. Do we hang them anyway?"

"Yeah, we're tired of having our ranches attacked. My cattle are dying of thirst, that is, the ones that haven't wandered off through torn down fences. Hang them all." The guy shouted louder. About three or four others in the room repeated his words. "Hang them all."

Douglas bit his lip and refrained from saying more as the mayor banged the hammer. These ranchers and small farmers had reached their limit. Frustration replaced common sense. Douglas hoped Mayor Miller could talk some sense into them.

Miller banged the hammer twice more. "Quiet in here. If you want to talk or have a question, raise your hand. I'll give you the floor. None of us want to be here any longer than we have to."

Douglas sympathized with everyone in the room. Fletcher ranch had lost cattle and had fences torn down just as everyone else had, but if they decided to hang the men, Edward would be part of it. He couldn't allow Emma's brother to hang. He might be young and stupid, but he shouldn't be given a death sentence.

Douglas looked around the room at the outraged men. If they decided to drag the men out and hang them, could they be stopped? How could this have happened in his hometown?

He worried about Edward. The boy might've gotten himself in trouble, but he believed Emma when she said he wasn't a criminal. Douglas wondered if he'd be able to convince these men of that.

Miller lifted the hammer and hit the table this time. "Douglas, is Lucas joining us?"

"No, he didn't want to leave the ranch and his expecting wife."

"I understand, but that's a shame. Lucas has sense and we need some of that tonight."

Several men agreed with the mayor, but the room then broke out in another round of loud talking.

Mayor Miller banged the hammer once more. Finally, the men got quiet.

Douglas stretched his legs out in front of him. This was going to be a long night. He was not happy.

An hour and a half later, Douglas stomped out the front door along with all the other men. Nothing had been accomplished.

"Douglas, hold up."

He turned around to find the mayor extending his hand to him.

"Thanks for coming tonight. I hate we didn't get anything done. These men are furious and are ready to take it out on anyone caught causing troubles at the ranches."

"Yeah, that's what I'm afraid of." Douglas said goodbye to several men passing him, then turned his attention back to Miller." Nothing good can happen if they get out of control. I hate the other ranchers couldn't get here tonight. Most of these men at the meeting are the young, irresponsible ones ready to cause more trouble."

"I know." The mayor shook his head. "I thought Sheriff Sanchez would show up, but I guess he was called out. We all should've been out on guard duty rather than letting off steam in here. I hope none of the ranches had trouble tonight."

"I hope not either. If it wasn't so late, I'd ride out to see if Fletcher Ranch is okay."

"I wouldn't advise it, Douglas. Riding alone at night isn't safe anytime, but especially now." Miller started to walk away then turned back to Douglas. "How's the arm? I heard it was more than just a scratch."

Unconsciously, he rubbed a hand across the upper arm. "It's doing okay. Our new doc took care of me."

"Glad you're healing. I hear the doc's brother isn't doing well. He probably needs to be behind bars, especially with these men threatening to hang those guys." He shook his head. "I can't believe our little town has come into this mess. When you see Lucas, tell him we missed him tonight, but I understand. If my wife were on the verge of giving birth, I wouldn't leave her either, but I really needed his voice of reason tonight."

Douglas agreed. "I'll do that, but don't expect him to be coming into town anytime soon. Abigail might have that baby early and he won't leave her side. She's lucky if she can run him to the stables."

"After all he's been through, I certainly understand how he feels. Give him and Abigail my best."

Douglas headed to the sheriff's office. This late he was sure the doors would be locked, but he had to try. Vic, too, was a voice of reason, and right now he needed to listen to someone talk with some sense.

Sure enough, the sheriff's office was in total darkness. He didn't even bother to shake the door handle, but turned around and walked back toward his room in his office. Before he got a block away, two men from the meeting approached him.

"Fletcher, stop a minute. We want a word."

Douglas groaned. He turned to see Shaunessay and his father, the last men he wanted to see tonight. He blew out a big breath, then plastered a smile on his face. According to gossip he'd heard since returning, the father ran the family with an iron hand, but he had given the farm to the sons to run. Now that the boys had to deal with the death of half his herd, Lucas commented he was surprised they could survive.

Douglas stopped and turned. "What can I do for you?"

"We have a couple of questions. We know Fletcher Ranch has had trouble with these guys. Why are you protecting them?"

"I'm not protecting them. I'm the one who shot the guy lying in Dr. O'Hara's office."

"You should've killed that man. Maybe the other two would fess up to who they're working for. We need to get the hangman's noose ready."

"Killing any of them won't solve our problems."

"Yeah, well, what will?" Franklin spoke up. "We're tired of this. Your family might be able to handle losing a few cattle and fences, but most of us around here don't have the resources that the Fletchers have. We're small. Losing just one cow hurts."

"I understand," he answered. "If I had answers for you, I'd be the first to act on them, but I don't. The only thing I know is hanging those three won't get us the information we need."

"We're not so sure. I've heard they're pretty stupid. Maybe seeing one hang would make the other ones talk."

"Maybe, but we don't know that. They may not know anything."

"Again, you're protecting them. Whether they talk or not, they deserve to be hanged. They're troublemakers." The son turned to his father. "Come on. Let's go. Douglas isn't like us anymore. He went off to the East and came back peace-minded and weak. He'd probably vomit if he saw someone hanging from a tree."

Douglas didn't answer.

He watched those two walk away, not sure how he felt about them. Why wasn't the father leading his sons away from danger, not into it? If they hung the three men and later found out they did not know who the top man was, they'd all be in trouble. Even if not, they would have to live with the fact they'd killed men for nothing but causing some ranchers headaches.

Their words stayed with him.

Maybe he *had* come back a different man. Living in a more civilized area certainly would change the way a person looked at the world, especially seeing someone hang.

CHAPTER EIGHTEEN

The day after the town meeting, Douglas helped deliver two calves and a litter of puppies. Without his assistance all the mothers or the babies would not have survived. Exhausted, he left the ranch where he'd helped the last cow give birth and headed toward Fletcher Ranch. He'd been in town for a week ever since he'd been shot. It was time to spend a couple days at the ranch and help Lucas with the livestock.

As if Major knew he was close to home, he threw his head back and jerked on the reins.

"You want to run, boy?" He flicked the reins and held on. Major took off. Douglas laughed. With the wind blowing in his face, he could almost feel his exhaustion flying away with the wind. "Have at it, Major."

By the time he passed through the ranch gates, he felt refreshed, but Major was thoroughly wet. He'd need a good cooling down and a brushing before being put up. Taking care of his horse and doing ranch work would feel good after his week in town. Lying around giving his arm time to heal did not suit him well.

Lucas stepped out of the barn wiping his hands on a rag. "Would you look at this? My brother finally shows his face."

"That's me and glad to be home."

Lucas held Major while Douglas got off. "How's the arm? You had us worried. We had several people from town stop by and tell us you were feverish. Looks as though you're doing okay now."

"I am. It's still sore, but our new town doctor took care of me."

"From the smile on your face, it sounds as though you enjoyed having her tend to you." Lucas laughed.

"Don't read anything into that. She's a nice-looking, brilliant lady, but that's all. She's a doctor. She had to take care of me."

"Sure, she did." He chuckled again as he led Major around the corral. "Did you go to the meeting last night?"

"Yes, and be happy you didn't bother riding into town for it. Nothing was accomplished. Most of the older ranchers stayed home with their families so we had a room full of younger, hotheaded men ready to hang the men we found at Thomas ranch."

"Glad I didn't leave Abigail for that."

"I am, too, but your presence would've helped Miller. He couldn't keep control of the meeting. I'm afraid there's going to be trouble in town if we don't get to the bottom of who is causing all this trouble. We all agree it's not the brothers in jail and definitely not Edward, Dr. O'Hara's brother."

"I'm sorry I didn't go, but I'm not leaving Abigail at this stage in her pregnancy."

Douglas put his hands on Lucas's arms. "You don't need to apologize. You did exactly what you needed to do."

"Thanks. I'm probably being paranoid about her health and the baby's, but I can't help it."

"You're not paranoid. Just a worried husband and expectant father."

"Again, I thank you for understanding." He rubbed Major's head. "Why don't you go tell Mother hello? I'll get

Major started for you. From the way he's sweating, you must've raced him all the way here."

"He's been cooped up all week. I let him have as much rein as he wanted." This time, Douglas laughed. "And that I did enjoy."

"I'll bet you did. Racing across these lands can cure anything."

Douglas left the barn with a smile on his face. Even though Lucas was worried about Abigail, Douglas thought he looked calmer and happier. The man had been through a lot, but with a beautiful family and a new baby on its way, he had found happiness once again.

As he walked toward the house, a feeling of contentment swept over him. He'd always loved this ranch and his family, but today seemed special. Maybe being shot makes a man appreciate what he has. The wound wasn't bad, but had the bullet gone a little more to the left he could've been dead. He'd thought about that as he lay in bed with fever. He was a lucky man, and he thanked God over and over for still being on this earth.

His stomach growled as he headed to the house knowing he'd get a good home-cooked meal. He stomped up the back steps and stuck his head in the kitchen. "Mother? You in here?"

No one was in the kitchen so he rummaged through the pie cupboard to see what food had been stored from the last meal. He found two biscuits, ham, and a bowl of smothered potatoes. "Perfect" He sat down and had devoured half of it when the door from the dining room swung open.

Carmella walked through carrying a bowl and a glass. "Mr. Douglas, we didn't know you had gotten home." She looked down at his plate. "No, no. I can fix you something fresh."

"This is fine, Carmella. Leftover, cold food from your kitchen is three times better than fresh food in town." But then he thought about Molly's restaurant. Her food was almost as good as what he got here, but he'd never tell Carmella or Bonita that.

"Where's Mother?"

"She's upstairs with Miss Abigail. She isn't having a good day."

"I just saw Lucas at the barn. He didn't mention that."

"Miss Abigail didn't want her husband to worry. She thinks the cramping will pass."

"Cramping? That doesn't sound good. Maybe he should be told."

"That's not for me to say, sir."

"Of course, it's not. I'm just thinking out loud. I'll go up and see if the ladies will let me in."

He finished his leftovers, headed up the stairs, then knocked on Abigail's door. "Mother, it's me, Douglas."

He heard footsteps, then the door opened. Mrs. Fletcher stepped out and closed the door behind her.

She kissed her son. "How are you, Douglas. I was so worried when Lucas told me you had been shot. I wanted to get someone to take me to town to be with you, but Lucas insisted I stay here. I guess he was right. The wound must've not been bad, but I still wanted to be there with you."

"I'm fine, Mother. The bullet just grazed my arm, and Dr. O'Hara took care of me."

"That's what he said, or I would've saddled a horse myself and ridden there. He also said it was Emma's brother who shot you, but you shot him back." She shook her head. "I thought this world had gotten more civilized than men shooting men. How is that young man and how is June taking it? She and Emma must be beside themselves."

"He's still coming out of it. It was touch and go there for a couple of days, but I think he'll make it. The last time I talked with Emma, she was hopeful."

"And how does she feel about you shooting her brother?"

He raised an eyebrow. "You can guess what she feels about that." He nodded toward the door. "What's happening with Abigail? Carmella said she was cramping? Do you think it's time for the baby?"

"She thinks it's too soon, but Carmella and I disagree."

"Whoever is right, I think Lucas ought to be told."

"Probably."

"Probably? Mother, he needs to know so he can make preparations or send for help if we need it."

"That's up to Abigail."

"Maybe, but I don't agree. Is she decent? I want to talk with her."

"She's in her bedclothes, but she is covered. I'm not so sure she will want you to worry."

"That's for me to decide." Douglas knocked lightly on the door, then opened it only slightly. "Abigail, it's Douglas. May I come in?"

He heard the rustling of blankets. "Sure. Come in."

He headed straight for the bed, bent over and gave her a light kiss on the forehead. Her face was puffy and pale. "I just got here. I'm sorry to see you're not up and about. Is my niece or nephew about to make an appearance?"

Abigail swallowed. Tears filled her eyes. "It's too early. I'm scared the baby won't make it if it comes now."

"It's not my call, but I think Lucas needs to be told."

"I know, but I don't want him to worry."

"Of course, you don't, but if the baby comes early and there's trouble, he'll blame himself for not helping or sending for help. You know Dr. O'Hara said she'd be glad to come out if you need her."

"You're right, of course." She took a big breath and let it out slowly. "I was so hopeful these cramps would stop, and he wouldn't have to know they happened, but I guess that's not going to happen. Would you go down and get Lucas?" She grimaced.

Douglas grabbed her hand. "Hang in there." He held it tightly until Abigail seemed to relax. His heart pounded. "I'll be right back with Lucas, and I'll send Carmella and Mother in here."

Delivering babies for cows, horses, oxen, and anything else with four legs was something he knew about, but watching Abigail hurting made him feel as helpless as he'd ever felt before. He didn't know much about human delivery, but he wished Dr. O'Hara would be here.

He'd even call her "doctor" if she helped Abigail deliver a healthy baby.

~

Mrs. Fletcher came out of Abigail's room. Douglas and Lucas both stood up.

Lucas grabbed her hands. "Is she okay? The baby isn't coming yet, is it?"

"That little baby is ready to meet her or his daddy, but it's still not turned right."

"Dr. O'Hara said the same thing when she checked her out, but she said the baby might turn by itself. Now I'm really worried."

Douglas faced Lucas and tried to use as calming a voice as possible. "That kind of birth happens all the time in animals. A baby can be born that way as well, but it's better if it can be turned right."

"So can Carmella turn it or should we send for the doctor?"

Mrs. Fletcher stepped near Lucas and took his hand. "I think we should send one of the guys to get Dr. O'Hara. The baby might decide to be born before she gets here, but it's best to be on the safe side."

"I agree," Lucas said.

His mother kissed Lucas. "She'll be fine, son. She's asking for you. You go to her, and I'll go to the kitchen to find Carmela and maybe grab a bite to eat."

He pulled her into an embrace. "Thank you for helping."

"Unless you need me here," Douglas said. "I'll go get Dr. O'Hara."

"I can send someone else. You just rode here. You don't

need to strain your arm any more than you've already done."

"Thanks for thinking about me, but I'm fine, though I don't think I need to use Major. If you don't mind, I'll take one of the other horses. I don't think he's ready to hit the trail again."

Lucas nodded, his face strained.

Douglas stepped near Lucas and took his hand. "Abigail is going to be okay. I'll ask God to watch over her while I ride. It wouldn't hurt if you did the same."

Lucas smiled. "I started talking to him as soon as you got me from the barn."

Douglas nodded and squeezed his hand. "I'll be back as soon as I can."

He hurried into the barn. Major neighed. He walked straight to him and gave his horse a pat on the head. "Sorry, Major, not this time. You need to rest a bit." He saddled one of the other horses, then headed out. "Come on, boy. Give me all you got. My family needs you."

Douglas's overtaxed body responded to the afternoon breeze blowing around him. His long day had taken a toll on his arm, but sitting in the saddle with the air blowing from the distant Missouri River invigorated him.

Thirty minutes later, he rode through the streets of Independence, waved to a few walkers and horsemen, then headed to the doctor's office. He knocked on Emma's door, assuming she or her mother would be with Edward. When no one answered the door, he worried Edward may have taken a turn for the worst, but then he shook his head. He'd seen Emma earlier today and she said nothing about that.

He tried the knob, but it was locked. His mind flew through numerous explanations, even one that had Emma and her mother moving Edward someplace away from town to escape his punishment.

Stupid ideas from an exhausted body and brain. He pushed that thought aside.

He hurried around the building and through the gate that

led to their small house. A light shining through a window took away his worry. They were home.

He walked up onto the porch and knocked.

The door opened and Emma peeked out. Her hair flowed around her shoulders as if she'd brushed it getting ready to relax for the evening. He wished he were here to spend time with her instead of having to rush her out to help Abigail.

"Douglas, is there a problem? I thought you went back to the ranch today."

"I did and that's why I'm here. Abigail might need your help."

"It's really early for the baby to come. Is she having contractions?"

He shrugged. "She called them cramps. It might be nothing, but we'd feel better if you could go to the ranch, that is, if you can leave Edward."

"I can. His fever has broken. He's still very weak, but doing much better. We moved him out here with us today." She opened the door wider. "Come in. It won't take me long to get my things and talk to Mother and Edward."

"Is it okay if I see him?"

At first Emma hesitated, then nodded. "Of course, but please don't get him upset."

"I'll be considerate, but I have a couple questions that might help us and him if he has answers."

"Emma, is someone here?" June walked through curtains that separated the living area from their bedroom.

"Yes, Mother. Douglas rode back into town to get me. Abigail might be having some problems. Would you be able to take care of Edward if I went to the ranch with him?"

"Of course. You do what needs to be done for Abigail to bring that baby into this world. Edward and I will be fine."

"Is he awake? Douglas would like to see him."

June looked at Douglas. He could read the hesitation on her face, but like Emma, she finally nodded.

"I won't get him upset if that's what you're thinking,

Mrs. O'Hara."

She didn't say anything, but walked to her daughter. Douglas understood. He's the one who shot her son. He'd be leery as well.

He opened the curtain to find Edward lying with his eyes closed. "Edward, this is Douglas Fletcher. I'm not sure you knew who you were shooting at the Thomas ranch, but I'm the one who took your bullet and then shot you."

Edward squinted. "Emma told me."

His weak voice startled Douglas. Enough time had passed for him to be much stronger.

"I wanted to check on you and to ask you a couple of questions."

Edward closed his eyes, but Douglas knew he wasn't asleep.

"We know you and Sam and Cory were paid by someone else to do their dirty work and cause havoc on the ranches around here. I'm hoping you'll cooperate and tell us who gave you the orders."

Edward opened his eyes. They were golden like his sister's.

"I don't know. Sam didn't tell me. He only told me how much I'd get if we could get that Thomas guy or any of the other ranchers to sell."

"I believe you, but anything you tell me, if it helps, will help you when you stand before the judge."

Edward pretended to be asleep again.

"Think, Edward. You're in big trouble, but if you tell us anything helpful, you might save your hide. Did they say anything that might hint at where these men were? Were they local? Did he have to ride out to meet them someplace?"

Edward's brows wrinkled and he looked at Douglas. "I'm not sure, but it seems like they might be local. He had met with someone the night before the Thomas ranch job but he was back pretty fast."

"That's something. I'm taking your sister to my ranch to

help deliver a baby. If you think of anything else that might be helpful, get your mother to go tell the sheriff. I'll pass on what you just told me before I leave town."

Edward nodded.

"Your sister and mother love you, Edward. I'll do what I can to help you because of them."

He nodded again. "Thank you. I shouldn't have gotten in with those three guys, but I didn't know how else to make money."

Douglas turned to go then turned back to Edward. "Did you say three guys? We only caught two."

"Three brothers."

"Charlie." Douglas shook his head. "I should've guessed it."

"Yes, one of them was named Charlie."

The curtain pulled apart. "I'm ready, Douglas."

He nodded to Emma then looked back at Edward. "Thanks for the information."

Emma stepped by her brother. "I'll be back as soon as I can. Please do as Mother asks and please don't try to leave. You're in enough trouble, not to mention the fact you'd probably die on a horse. You're far from being healed."

He nodded, then closed his eyes.

They stepped out of the bed area. Emma took her mother's hand. "Please don't let him try to leave. He's not strong enough to be moved again, and trying to leave the town would only make things worse for him."

"I guess," June said and dropped her head.

"Mother, there's no guessing. The best way for us to save him is to help the sheriff catch the other guys. That means Edward has to stay here."

"I know you're right." She wrung her hands. "Go on. Don't worry about us. We'll be here when you return."

Emma kissed June, then looked up at Douglas. "I'm ready."

"I'll go get the carriage from the stables and meet you in

front of the office. I need to stop by Victor's office on the way out."

Douglas hoped June and Edward would stick to their word and not try to get Edward out of town. He'd have to mention it to Victor to keep an eye on them.

The stable was empty when he walked up. He called out to Murry, but no one answered. He didn't have time to search for the owner, but he'd tell Victor to pass on the message that he had the carriage. He grabbed the reins and straps and got the carriage ready himself. "Come on Sunflower. You'll be glad to see your old stables."

He, on the other hand, wasn't eager to face the possibility of Abigail having a hard delivery. After tying his horse to the back of the carriage, he climbed up and headed out. As he got into the clear afternoon light, he looked up to heaven.

Watch over Lucas's family, God. Please.

CHAPTER NINETEEN

Emma's thoughts spun uncontrollably, bouncing from one lesson she'd studied to the next and to the childbirths in which she'd assisted or delivered. The beautiful moment of a baby being born could quickly turn into a tragedy. Twice she'd witnessed her doctors surgically remove a baby when the mothers could not give birth naturally. One was successful. The other was not.

If Abigail had problems, would she be able to save her life and the baby's? Her chest tightened. Lucas had already lost a wife. She would never forgive herself if something went wrong and Abigail died.

She shoved those thoughts away. She was a good doctor. Even though she had not delivered a baby surgically, she'd done numerous other kinds of surgeries, all with spectacular results. If she had to surgically remove the baby, this one too would be successful, but she'd pray the baby would be born naturally. All of her worry might be for nothing. Abigail may have already given birth by the time the two of them arrived at the ranch.

As if Douglas knew she was worried, he took her hand. "Everything will be okay."

"Thank you for showing confidence in me, but I'll feel better when I'm with Abigail. We can hope she has had the baby on her own."

"That would be my hope as well, but we weren't taking any chances. Your presence will make all of us more confident that the baby and Abigail will be okay."

"How much farther?"

"Not far. We're making good time even with the horse tied to the back. Of course, that weather heading straight for us from the north might slow us down a bit."

Emma looked around Douglas to see black clouds heading their way. "Oh my, the day's been a little overcast, but nothing like that. That looks dangerous."

"I don't think we can outrun it. I had Sunflower moving a little faster than normal, but she can't go much faster."

Thunder rumbled and lightning lit the sky.

Emma pulled a shawl close around her body. Bad weather terrified her.

"It's been cloudy, but I was hoping it would turn." As soon as his words got out, the wind picked up and big drops of rain hit the top of the carriage. "So much for outrunning the rain."

"Is it safe to be out here with this lightning?" She tried to keep her voice calm.

"Probably not. There's an old shed right over that hill. We can take cover in there. I hate taking longer to get to Abigail, but we have to be safe." Douglas flicked the reins harder. "Hold on. Sunflower, give us all you got."

Lightning lit the sky once more. The horse tied to the back of the carriage pulled at his reins.

Emma scrunched down closer to the seat and pulled her shawl up over her head. She held on with both hands as Douglas pushed Sunflower faster and faster toward the shed. Rain came down in sheets and even though it was the middle of the afternoon the day had turned dark.

"Can you see where we're heading?"

Douglas shook his head. "Not really," he yelled over the wind and the rain, "but I know where we are. There. There's the shed in that clump of trees."

Sunflower cooperated as Douglas guided her as close to the shed as possible. He jumped out and tied the carriage to a tree alongside the shed.

"Get your bag." He shouted. "I'll help you in."

Emma grabbed her bag of medical supplies and a few pieces of clothing she'd thrown in. As she stood up, thunder crashed again and both horses jerked at their ropes. She held on tightly and squeezed her eyes. Cold rain pelted her in the face. Wind blew her shawl from her head.

Douglas put one foot up on the carriage floor and grabbed her around the waist. "Hold on to me."

She reached around his neck as he pulled her out of the carriage. No longer under the half-protection of the carriage top, rain pounded her body. As she hit the ground, she threw her arms around his waist, and he wrapped his arms around her shoulders. Together they stumbled toward the shed. A small eave over the shed door offered a slight amount of protection as Douglas tried to get the door opened. Finally, he threw his body against it and it flew open. They nearly fell into the dark interior of the shed.

Even with the musty, dank odor of the structure, Emma felt safer.

"Stay here. I need to make sure the horses are tied and safe."

Before she could answer, he disappeared into the torrential rain.

Still holding her bag, she wrapped her arms around her trembling body. Was she shaking from the cold or from fear? Not sure what was inside the building, she dared not move. Thunder and lightning continued. She held herself tighter.

Outside, she heard Douglas moving the horses while he talked to them, probably trying to calm them. She wanted to help, but knowing nothing about horses, she'd be in the way.

Finally, the door flew open, and Douglas stomped inside and closed the door. In two steps she went to him, dropped the bag on the floor and threw her body against his.

"It's okay, Emma. The horses are okay. We're inside and this storm will pass fast. I could tell the sky looked a little lighter to the north." His arms pressed her against his body. "You're trembling." He held her closer. "I'm sorry I don't have anything dry."

"I'm okay." She wanted to say more, but her words were shaky.

Another clap of thunder made her bury her face in his wet shirt. Through the dampness he smelled like the outdoors, and she savored the feel of security his body offered.

Finally, she pulled away. "I'm so sorry. I've always been terrified of bad weather. I know it's silly, but there's nothing I can do about it."

He put his hands on each side of her arms. "It's okay. You don't have to apologize. We're all afraid of something in the world."

She couldn't imagine Douglas Fletcher being afraid of anything. She pulled in a big breath to get control of herself. "I think it's already starting to calm down outside."

Without taking his gaze from her face, he nodded. "I think it is. We'll be able to leave in a little while. I just wish we had some dry clothes. I can't have our doctor getting sick."

"I brought a gown to sleep in tonight, but I think I'd like to stay in these clothes if we're close to the house. That way I'll have something dry for tonight."

"Do whatever makes you comfortable." As if he realized he was still holding her, he dropped his hands and stepped back.

Rain still came down hard, but a brighter sky told her the storm was passing.

He looked around the building.

She followed his gaze. Cobwebs hung from the ceiling, but other than that, the room wasn't in bad condition. Straps and ropes and a few tools hung on the wall. "Why is this shed in the middle of nowhere?"

"I know it seems as though it's in the middle of nowhere, but it's next to one of our pastures. It's easier and faster for our men to come here for certain problems than to ride back to the main ranch."

"So we are pretty close."

He nodded, then pulled off his hat and hit it against his leg to shake the water off. "We'll give it a few more minutes and then head out again. My main concern with us being out there was having Sunflower get spooked. This carriage is sturdy, but it's old. I'm not sure how it would hold up if she decided to take off through the woods."

Another clap of distant thunder made her shiver and grimace.

Douglas stepped next to her and put his arms around her again.

She melted against him and wrapped her arms around his body.

"You're still trembling." He rubbed his hand up and down her back.

She felt so foolish acting like a scared child, but she couldn't help it. She buried her face against his shirt once more and wished she could feel this protected always, but that wasn't possible. She stepped away. Embarrassed, she looked down at the floor. "I'm sorry. I truly am. I feel I should explain."

He put his hand on her arm. "No, you don't have to explain anything to me unless it will make you feel better."

She thought a minute. "Maybe it will." She took another step away from him. It would be easier to confess her insecurities when she wasn't standing so close.

"When I was a child, maybe seven or eight, my mother went to visit her sister. Edward and I were alone with our father. Mother never left us with him. He drank a lot and sometimes he got mad at me for just being in the same room with him so I stayed in my room a lot. I was outside that day and the sky turned dark, the wind blew as hard as it did today, the thunder was horribly loud, and lightning lit the sky. Father was outside as well tending the horse. I started crying. He screamed at me to shut up, but I guess I was frightened of both the weather and him. He left the horse and grabbed my arm and dragged me to a run-down shed behind the house, threw me in it and locked the door."

Emma squeezed her eyes. "I can still remember him laughing when I started screaming to get out. It was dark. I heard something scurrying across the floor. The storm got worse. The rain and thunder went on and on. The trees around the house started losing limbs. One fell and hit the shed ripping off one side of the roof. I wasn't hurt, but I was terrified. I know I kept screaming and crying, then Edward, who wasn't more than five or six, unlocked the door. Father had only stuck a stick to hold the door shut. I didn't know that. Edward opened the door. He was crying, too. He grabbed me and we ran and got under the front porch and hid until Mother got home. Ever since then I'm terrified of bad weather."

Douglas held out his hands. "Come here." He pulled her into his arms and kissed the top of her head. "No child should have gone through that. I can see why you are so scared of bad weather and why you and your brother are so close."

"We were close while we lived at the house, but I took the easy way out. I married the first man that asked me just to get out of that situation. I look back now and realize I had left my little brother to fend for himself. He never was the same."

"Emma, being young and afraid would make anyone try to save themselves. What your father did to you was unthinkable. Everyone has something they're afraid of, but you have more than most."

"I can't imagine you being scared of anything."

Still holding her close, he chuckled. "I'm scared of

stupid men having guns."

She stood up straight. "You weren't scared when you made Charlie put down his gun on the stagecoach."

"Who said I wasn't scared? He wasn't a smart bandit and that scares me. They're the ones who shoot before they think. So, yes, I was scared for you and your mother and for me."

"I'm not sure I believe you, but thanks for telling me that. I do feel better."

"Look, I can see light in the crack of the door. The storm has passed."

Emma reached up and placed a soft kiss on his cheek. "Thank you for keeping me safe and thank you for listening."

He only nodded. "Let's get back on the road. We have a baby to deliver."

Douglas concentrated on keeping the carriage on the road and not talking. That was fine with her. He probably decided she came from a strange, dysfunctional family and he wanted no part of it. Maybe that was best. He would never understand her view of the world since his life on the ranch seemed idealistic.

Finally, he looked at her. "How many babies have you delivered?"

"Aaah, are you questioning my ability?" She used a lilting tone to lighten the question, but deep inside she wondered how much confidence he had in her.

He laughed. "Not at all. Just making conversation."

"Good, because I do know what I'm doing. I'm not sure how many births I've done. I assisted in numerous births and delivered alone in quite a few. I've never had a problem."

"Great. Between your medical knowledge and Carmella's delivery experience my sister-in-law will have the best." He flicked the reins. "There's the ranch ahead of us. We should be there in about ten minutes. I know you're cold. I think we can find some of Abigail's dresses to fit you and get you into something dry."

"I'm okay until we get there."

Emma made herself enjoy the spectacular view surrounding the Fletcher Ranch. The spring rains had washed the fields and refreshed the grasses. Taking in the thousands of acres of cleared pastures, many with herds of grazing cattle, eased her mind. The idea of owning so much land still seemed unreal, but she reminded herself she was in Independence, not Massachusetts.

Life was different here. Would she change as well?

~

Douglas sat in the hallway in the dim light outside Abigail's room. He wasn't sure what time it was, but the sun had gone down hours ago. Lucas sat next to him some of the time, but mostly he paced the hall.

Caroline came out of her room and leaned against the wall next to Lucas. "I'm so scared."

"I know. We all are, but Abigail is in good hands. Dr. O'Hara, your grandmother, Carmella and God are all watching over her."

"I hope they know what they're doing. I never want to have a baby if this is how it is."

"Don't say that. Bringing a baby into the world is a wonderful experience, and usually there aren't problems. You'll have your own little baby one day and make me the happiest grandfather in the world."

"I've been in my room praying for Abigail."

He stood up and put his arms around his daughter. "Thank you. I love you for that."

The exchange between father and daughter warmed Douglas. "How about we all go down to the kitchen and see what kind of food we can find?" He stood and hoped his brother and Caroline would join him.

Lucas passed a hand across his chin. "Why don't you and Caroline go down and bring back something for me? I can't leave."

"I understand the way you feel, but sitting here won't

make the baby come any faster." Douglas looked at Caroline. "You go down and find us something to nibble on. I'll be down in a second."

Caroline looked from her father to Douglas. He was sure she understood the men needed to talk alone.

"Sure, Uncle Douglas."

When she was halfway down the stairs, Lucas crossed his arms in front of his chest. "It shouldn't take this long. William's birth was so quick Carmella thought she wouldn't get here in time. I don't understand why this one is different."

"I don't have any answers, but I do know you have the best help possible for your wife. Between Dr. O'Hara and Carmella, she has the best of both worlds."

Lucas plopped down on one of the chairs and threw his head back. "I hate not being able to help. I want to be in there with Abigail."

Douglas sat next to him. "I can imagine, but you'd probably get in the way."

"I can't stand to hear cries. I could at least hold her hand. She's got to be in so much pain." Lucas put his head in his hands then raised it up. "It's been too long, Douglas. Something is wrong."

Douglas didn't answer though he'd thought the same thing. He had delivered many four-legged babies and had only lost two. Most animals were capable of delivering their babies without the help of a veterinarian. By the time he was called, a problem existed. He remembered listening to discussions about animal births and many times the men correlated the experience to that of a human birth, but he had never assisted in any himself. Now he wished he knew more about the process.

As he tried to think of something uplifting to help Lucas, the door opened. Both he and Lucas jumped up.

Emma stepped out. The worried look on her face sent Douglas's heart into overtime.

Lucas grabbed her hand. "What's happening?"

"Abigail is fine but very weak. The baby is still in the breech position, and I don't think Abigail will be able to give birth unless it is turned."

Lucas swallowed. "Can you do that?"

"We've tried everything. Nothing is working."

Douglas took her hand. "So what are you saying?"

"Carmella agrees with me that we need to do something else if we want to give the baby and Abigail a chance."

Douglas glanced at his brother. He'd turned pale.

"Surgery?" Douglas asked.

Emma nodded.

Lucas grabbed her hands. "Have you ever done that before?"

"No, but I have assisted in two. I have done many surgeries, though, just not a Cesarean Surgery, but I do understand the concept and know the procedure."

"I don't know. I've never known that to be done around here."

Douglas took a step to the side, then back again. "Can you do that outside of a hospital?"

"If necessary, yes. Of course, we'd have to take extreme precautions to make sure she doesn't get an infection."

"What about anesthesia?" Douglas had a lot of questions, but he didn't want to upset Lucas more than he already was.

"I brought chloroform with me. It would work." She looked up at Lucas. "I've spent many hours talking with other doctors and studying the use of chloroform. If administered correctly, it is safe and effective."

Lucas sat again and once more dropped his head into his hands. "I can't lose my wife."

Emma sat next to him and took his hands. "Lucas, we understand and will do everything possible to have this baby born healthy and Abigail okay." She looked up at Douglas, then back again at Lucas. "Do I have your permission to operate if nothing positive happens soon?"

Lucas raised his head and looked at Douglas. "What do you think?"

"I don't think she would suggest surgery unless it's necessary."

"Would you help her?"

His question took Douglas off guard.

Lucas stood up and stepped near him. "You've had experience with surgeries. You could assist. I'd feel better." He looked up at Emma. "It's not that I don't think you are capable. I don't understand about cutting people open and at least Douglas has done it on animals."

Douglas watched Emma's face as she thought about Lucas's request. Would she allow an animal doctor to help her?

Finally, she placed a hand on Lucas's arm. "If it comes to the point that we think surgery is the only way to save her and the baby, I'll welcome Douglas's help."

Relief spread through Douglas to know Emma trusted him enough to help, but alongside the relief, a case of nerves crept in. He had studied human anatomy, but not as extensively as a medical doctor. Would he actually be an asset to Emma?

He nodded to Emma. "If you need me, I'll be glad to assist you."

CHAPTER TWENTY

Douglas washed the tabletop in the kitchen as Emma had asked. The whole situation seemed surreal. Thirty minutes ago, he and Caroline sat at this table and ate a piece of apple pie that Bonita had made. In a few minutes the same table would be used as an operating table. Nothing seemed right, but he knew it had to be done.

He stood back and looked at the wooden table made by his grandfather years ago. So many wonderful memories had been created around it. Dinners for the entire family were celebrated in the big, more formal dining room, but this was the table of choice when someone needed to have a quiet place to talk over a cup of coffee, or to sneak down in the middle of the night to find leftovers.

His grandfather would be amazed to know what he'd built could be used to save two lives. It was the closest thing to a surgery table in the house. Now that the table was cleaned, he hoped he and Lucas could get Abigail down the stairs and on the table without hurting her too much.

When he felt the table was as clean as he could possibly get it, he dried it with a cloth, then sat down. He was comfortable and confident operating on animals, but could he be a help if the patient was Abigail? He bent his head and prayed for strength to help Emma with the surgery and for

Abigail and the baby to be safe and healthy when it was all over.

The door opened and Emma walked in. "I wanted to check the room to see if anything else needs to be done to make it safer for Abigail." She walked around examining the table and the surrounding area. She nodded to see water on the stove. "I'm glad you started the water boiling."

"I washed down the table with lye and then rinsed it well. I sent Carmella to find sheets to cover it and to bring down something to place under her head that isn't too big."

"Perfect." Emma looked at him. "Are you okay assisting me? I need someone to help and you, at least, understand the process of some surgeries."

Douglas nodded. "I've never done a human surgery. I did remove a bullet once, but that's it."

"Have you studied human anatomy at all?"

"Somewhat, but not extensively. I'll expect you to be clear in your instructions if you want me to do anything."

"Certainly."

She looked around again. "I don't like doing this in here, but nowhere else is more suitable."

"You'll administer the anesthesia, right?"

"Definitely. I've studied that part quite a lot. I'm confident in using the chloroform."

Carmella opened the kitchen door carrying several sheets and towels. "Mr. Douglas, they want you upstairs to help move Mrs. Abigail."

"Thank you, Carmella. We'll both go."

"I'll have the table covered when she gets down here."

Douglas and Emma walked side by side up the stairs, not talking. Douglas had never realized how many steps there were in this staircase, but now he counted each one, hoping that Abigail could be carried down safely.

Lucas met them at the door. "She's so weak. We'll have to carry her."

Douglas took his brother's hands. "We can do that. I

think we're ready downstairs." He looked at Emma.

For a second, he thought he saw hesitation on Emma's part, but just as quickly she smiled confidently. "We are. Let's see if she's ready." Emma walked to the bed, bent over Abigail and talked softly to her. Finally, she turned around. "We'll have to carry her. We'll use a blanket as a sling to keep her from being jostled too much, and we'll drape her arms around your shoulders. I'll be right behind her holding her head."

Quickly, Mrs. Fletcher helped Emma position the blanket under her, then everyone took a position around the bed.

Emma nodded. "On the count of three, lift. One. Two. Three."

Abigail kept her eyes closed but bit her lip.

"Baby, hang on." Lucas whispered to her. "We'll be downstairs before you know it. I love you."

"I love you, too." Her words were barely audible.

Douglas hadn't had a case of nerves as he experienced now. Even when he knew he'd been shot, he kept his senses. Now his body trembled at the thought of what could happen to his brother's family. He tried to pray but thoughts jumbled in his head. Now he knew he was terrified for his brother's family.

He eased his side of the sling toward the stairs then one step at a time they made their way halfway down before Abigail threw her head back and cried. Everyone stopped.

"Abigail, breathe hard. The contraction will pass in a second." Emma tried to give her confidence. "We have you. You're okay."

Douglas wanted to do something to help Abigail, but holding his side of the sling was the best he could do. His chest constricted every time she cried out. He looked at his brother and could imagine how he felt not being able to help his wife.

Two more times before they reached the kitchen, Abigail

suffered contractions. Her face contorted in pain. Perspiration soaked her bedclothes.

Douglas tried to hurry to get her to the table, but Lucas had the opposite side of the sling and he kept talking to his wife.

"Lucas, we're almost there. Keep moving."

Finally, they were near enough for them to lift her and place her on the table as gently as possible.

Lucas collapsed over her and held her. "You're going to be okay. I love you. I love you."

Emma placed a hand on his back. "Lucas, I need you to step outside the kitchen with your mother. I promise we'll take care of Abigail and will keep you informed." She looked at Carmella. "Would you stay in here?"

Carmella's eyes were huge, but she nodded.

"Good." Emma gave Carmella an encouraging smile. "You'll do fine."

Lucas and his mother held onto each other as they eased to the door. Lucas looked back and threw a kiss to Abigail.

As soon as the door closed, Emma lifted the blankets from Abigail, draped her with sheets, then cleaned her abdomen as well as possible. She walked by her head. "Abigail, I'm going to put this cloth on your face and dribble some medication. You'll feel lightheaded, then you'll go into blessed sleep. When you wake, you'll have a new little Fletcher to hold."

Douglas prayed that was so.

Abigail tried to smile, but Douglas could tell she was scared. He took her hand. She looked at him and mouthed, "Thank you."

When Abigail was deep in sleep, Emma explained to Douglas step by step what she would do and how he could help. He pulled up every iota of strength from within to be able to help Emma.

If he couldn't do as Emma asked, Abigail's life could be at stake.

~

With the cool night air surrounding her, Emma sat on the back steps by herself. Never had she been so terrified to do anything since she'd started medical school, but delivering that baby by surgery had to be done. Without the procedure, Abigail or the baby would not have made it. Tonight, though, Lucas and Abigail had a beautiful baby girl with dark hair like her father. Abigail still had not awakened from the anesthesia. That had her worried, but as soon as she could grab a breath of air, she'd go back in to watch her.

Carmella and Douglas had been a tremendous help. Carmella immediately took the newborn girl and cleaned her while Emma stitched the incision. Douglas handed her instruments throughout the procedure, helped control the bleeding, and held open the incision as she reached for the baby. He never flinched and never questioned what she asked him to do. He was a veterinarian, but she now understood he was as much a medical professional as she was. She would find the right time to tell him.

Maybe it was the fact that she knew Abigail and her family personally, but the birth was the most emotional experience she had ever been through. She'd been strong throughout the procedure, but after the baby was born and the stitches tied, she had to come get a breath of air.

The back door opened, and Douglas stepped out.

"Mind if I sit by you?"

Emma had come outside for some quiet time, but when she saw Douglas, she was thrilled to have him with her. "Yes, please."

He sat on the step next to her and stretched out his legs. He rolled his head on his shoulders. "That was quite an experience. I've helped a lot of four-legged babies into this world, but what I saw in there was amazing. I learned a lot watching you, Emma."

"Thank you for saying that. I'm glad you were there to help. I couldn't have done it alone."

"I don't know about that. You seemed to know exactly what to do and did it with amazing grace and precision." He looked at her. "Are you okay?"

His question caught her off guard. "I think so. Thank you for asking. I had to get a breath of air."

He stretched his arms and took a huge breath. "I totally understand. That's why I'm out here."

"Douglas, I really mean it when I say I appreciate all you did."

"Thanks, but not as much as my family appreciates what you did, Emma, or should I say Dr. O'Hara. You saved the life of my sister-in-law and my niece." He grinned and took her hand. "You also saved my brother. I don't know if he could've lived had he lost another woman he loved."

"And they do love each other. I could sit and watch the two of them all night." She leaned against the railing. "Did I hear you right? Did you call me Dr. O'Hara?"

Douglas rubbed his hand across his chin. "Did I say that?"

"I think you did, and you can't take it back." Happiness and contentment flowed through Emma. At this moment everything seemed right with her life, that is, except the fact that her brother could go to prison for his part in the scheme to get ranches to sell. She wouldn't let that fact ruin the night. As soon as she could leave Abigail and the baby, she'd turn her attention back to helping Edward.

"I like your big smile." Douglas grinned.

"I have a lot to smile about."

"Yes, you do, and so does my family."

~

The next afternoon Emma checked Abigail's incision and changed her bandage. "You're doing great, Abigail." She pulled the blanket back over her. "I've talked with Bonita and Carmella and explained to them what had to be done to keep the wound clean. I feel confident they'll be able to keep you healthy until I can come back in a few days.

Abigail smiled. "I'm still nauseated."

"I know you are and it's normal with the chloroform. I think you'll be better by tomorrow morning. Carmella has made chicken soup. If you can get the liquid down, it will help your stomach."

"I'll try. Where's my little girl?"

"Mrs. Fletcher has her. When I leave here, I'll find her and tell her you want the baby with you."

"I hope I don't have trouble feeding her."

"Carmella says she'll help you. You did fine yesterday. I'm sure you won't have problems, but Carmella knows all about and will help you. She said you did great with little William when he was born."

Again, Abigail smiled. "He was the sweetest baby."

"And this one will be as well." Emma checked the medications she had lined up on the nightstand. "I've explained to Carmella when and how much to give you. Don't be afraid to ask for something if you start to hurt. It will be normal for you to experience pain at the incision site."

"Thank you, Dr. O'Hara. I owe my life and the life of my baby to you."

"That's why I'm here. Thank you for letting me help you bring that beautiful baby into the world. By the way, have you and Lucas picked out a name?"

"We thought about naming her after his mother, but now we're leaning toward the name Emma, if that would be okay with you."

Emma inhaled and placed her hands on her chest. "You want to name your baby after me? I'm honored and thrilled beyond words."

"Without you, my baby and I might not have made it."

Emma swallowed and choked back tears that flooded her eyes. "No one has ever done anything so nice for me."

"You deserve it, Dr. O'Hara."

CHAPTER TWENTY-ONE

The next afternoon Emma sat alone on the front seat of the carriage. Matthew stood by Sunflower holding her reins and waiting for Emma to leave. Douglas rode out at daybreak to get back to town, but she didn't feel comfortable leaving Abigail. She assured him she could handle the carriage alone. Now she wasn't so sure she'd made the right choice.

"Dr. O'Hara, do you need anything else?"

She looked at Matthew, plastered a smile on her face, and told a little fib. "No, I'm fine. I'm thinking about my medical supplies I packed to come here. I have to make sure I have it all with me now."

"Yes, ma'am, you'd hate to turn around and come back for something you left." He handed her the reins, then stood with his hands in his pocket and shuffled his feet. "If you don't need me here, I have to get to the back pasture. Mr. Mason is waiting for me."

"You go back to your work, Matthew. Thank you for getting Sunflower and the carriage ready."

The young man jumped on his horse and with one last wave headed around the barn to the open pastures. Having been taken in by the Fletchers years ago when his adoptive father killed his wife, Matthew knew his place in the world. Even with his terrible background, he fit into the Fletcher family. Emma knew the man was now in prison, but Matthew kept up with his news through Sheriff Sanchez.

Emma wished she knew her place. Her life was getting better, especially now with the birth of little Emma, but too many other things still made life confusing. Watching the Fletcher family stick together made her realize how disjointed her life was. Her brother nearly died from a gunshot wound from the one man she thought she could get close to. Now Edward might face prison time or even hanging. How did their lives get so out of control?

She'd spent years working to become a doctor and now the town did not accept her. Should she and her mother go back to the East where people were more accepting of new ideas? Where would they go? How would they live with no money to get them there and no money to live and to set up a practice?

In the distance Matthew raced across the fields. How would that feel to sit on a horse and have the wind blow through your hair? Would she ever have that invigorating feeling?

With a last glance to the front door of the Fletcher home, she bit her lip. "Okay, it's now or never. Can't sit here forever." She flicked the reins. "Let's go, Sunflower. You need to help me get back to town."

As if she understood her command, Sunflower headed toward the gate. "So far so good. Yes!"

Feeling confident about giving Sunflower the right command, she waved to several workmen in the fields. Still, she wished Douglas sat alongside of her on the front seat of the carriage, but she refused to let fear take over. She could drive the carriage alone as long as she didn't have any major problems with it. Flicking the reins a little harder, Sunflower responded. Pleased with herself, she relaxed and tried to enjoy the ride.

Things went smoothly for the first half of the trail, but halfway into town she heard hooves behind her. Turning, she saw a group of riders coming directly at her. "Slow down, Sunflower. Let's give them space to pass us." She eased the carriage to the side of the trail.

The horses rushed toward her with tremendous speed. She squeezed her eyes and held the reins tightly. "Please, Sunflower, don't get spooked."

As the riders approached an inkling of fear inched up her spine. What if these men were bandits? Did they mean to do her harm? Now she wished she had her gun, but then what would she do with it? No way could she shoot someone.

Six riders approached from the back of the carriage. She held the reins tightly. The pounding of hooves on the hard trail was deafening. She scrunched down in her seat.

Two horses flew by her. One of the men glanced in her direction, but kept going. The other man never looked her way. Four other riders flew past her. With their hats pulled down low on their foreheads, they looked ominous and on a mission. Several had longer dark hair sticking out from under their hats. One had red hair, but she couldn't see any other distinguishing traits.

Who were these men and where were they going in such a hurry? Their galloping horses left a cloud of dust as they flew past her. She pulled her scarf over her mouth, closed her eyes against the thick air, and held the reins as tightly as she could.

When the sound of the hooves moved away from her carriage, she looked at the empty trail and wiped her hand across her eyes. Dust crusted her lips and teeth. She reached for the canteen of water under her seat and took a sip.

Sunflower shook her head and stomped her feet. She didn't know what that meant specifically, but she assumed the horse was as miserable as she was. She climbed down out of the carriage with the canteen.

"Thank you for not running away with the wagon, girl."

She poured a little water in her hand and let the horse slurp. "I'm sorry it's not more, but this is all I can do for now."

Taking a ragged breath, she climbed back into the carriage and eased Sunflower back on the trail. She'd been gone for only about twenty-four hours, but she was ready to get back to check on Edward and her mother. Now that the cloud of dust ahead of her was nearly gone, she'd try to enjoy the ride back home, but she knew it would be hard to shake the fear from the sight of those riders.

She flicked the reins. "Come on, girl. Let's go home."

As she pulled into town, two ladies on the sidewalk by the general store waved to her and called her Dr. O'Hara.

She waved back and smiled big. "That's different. I didn't think anyone bothered to find out my name." She waved again. Maybe word had gotten out about her helping bring the Fletcher baby into the world. Would she now get patients and the confidence of the town?

Waving to several other people, she headed to the stable.

Mr. Murry met her at the stable door. "Dr. O'Hara, come on in. Hi, Sunflower, how are you doing, girl?" He took the reins and helped Emma down. "I hear you're a celebrity today. Everyone is talking about how you helped Lucas Fletcher's wife give birth to their little girl. I hear it was done with surgery." He shook his head. "That's new to me. I guess all this modern medicine is leaving me behind."

"Medical procedures have come a long way. It's amazing what doctors are learning about and doing in the surgery arena."

"I hear Mrs. Fletcher and baby would not have been here had it not been for you."

"I had lots of help from Dr. Fletcher. Douglas was right alongside of me and assisted. We have to make sure he gets the credit as well."

"I'll certainly spread that piece of information. He's the one spreading the news, but I don't think he mentioned helping." He reached into the carriage. "I'll get your bag to your office."

"No, no. It's not heavy. I can carry it, but thank you for your offer."

He pulled the bag out of the carriage and handed it to her. "You have a good day, Dr. O'Hara."

She headed toward her house and office, but before she got in that block, Douglas passed her on Major. Her heart fluttered seeing him and knowing he was safely in town.

He stopped and got off.

"Emma, you got the carriage home safe and sound, I see. I knew you could do it."

"I did."

"You didn't have any trouble?"

"No, my only tense moment was when a group of men raced past me in a cloud of dust. They sure were in a hurry and not very friendly."

Douglas frowned. "That's strange. People around here speak to each other on the roads. Did you recognize any of them?"

She shook her head. "I think I saw red hair under one of the guy's hats, but that was all."

Douglas passed a hand across the back of his neck.

"I tried to see them but their hats were pulled down low and they were riding really fast. Does the red hair ring a bell?"

"I know of only one red-haired man around here. It could've been him. Hope not. He's a troublemaker." He took her bag. "Come on. I'll walk you to your office."

"Thank you." The tension she'd felt all day slid away as she walked alongside Douglas. "I'm sure you're as tired as I am after all we've been through."

"You got that right, but what a wonderful accomplishment, right?" His smile was priceless.

"A baby's birth is always amazing, but this one was truly wonderful." She smiled. "I hear you've passed word around about the surgery. I've had several nice greetings because of it. Thank you. That means a lot to me."

"What you did deserves recognition."

"I was doing my job, and I seem to have had a lot of help."

"I'm glad I could lend a hand." They reached the front porch of her office. "Here we are. Do you want this bag in here or in the house?"

"Here would be fine."

"I'd like to know how Edward is. I haven't had a chance to see him today. I've been swamped with sick animals. In fact, I was on my way to an outlying ranch when I saw you just now." He stepped up on the porch and opened the door.

"I'll put my medical bag in here, then am heading out to the house if you have time to follow."

He looked around, but eventually shook his head. "I have to get to this next ranch before sundown. If I get back early enough, I'll drop in. Tell Edward I hope he's doing okay. I'll be by to see him tomorrow."

Both stood perfectly still. She looked into his eyes and knew if it were not still daylight and they were not on the main street, he would have kissed her. Her heart raced thinking about his last kiss.

He took her hand. "I'm glad you made it safely. I worried all day and wished I hadn't left you to fend for yourself."

"I had to do it one day. Today was as good as any."

Still, they didn't move. He squeezed her hand, leaned down and gave her a quick kiss on the cheek.

It's not what she wanted, but it would have to do.

"And, Douglas, be careful riding out to that ranch and coming back into town. It's my turn to worry."

He gave her a crooked grin. "Then I'll make sure I get back safely. Maybe I can get a better kiss from you later."

She bit her lip, then smiled. "That would be nice."

They said their goodbyes. Effortlessly, he threw his leg over the saddle and sat up straight. He tipped his hat and rode off. She watched him until she lost sight of him.

She pulled the front door to the office shut and carried her bag to the back room before going out the back door and into the house. "Mom, Edward, I'm home." She dropped her bag on a chair and headed to the back room.

"Emma, we're in here."

Emma hugged her mom. "Well, look at you, little brother. You're sitting up in a chair."

"Miracles do happen, Sister."

"Yes, they do." She bent over and kissed him on the forehead. "I witnessed a miracle yesterday with the birth of the Fletcher baby."

"We heard all about it, Emma. I went to the general store this morning, and everyone is talking about it," June said. "You did a wonderful thing."

"I did what any doctor would've done. I helped a baby come into the world."

"But I heard you had to perform surgery."

"It's called a Caesarean Section. Doctors have done them for years, but for quite a long time the surgery was risky. Now we're able to save more of the mothers and the babies."

"Sis, do you think you can help me to the bed? Mother is brutal when it comes to my recovery. She doesn't want me in the bed."

Emma looked at June. "How long has he been in the chair?"

"I'll answer that." Edward raised a hand. "She's had me here since lunch, and I really need to lie down."

"Mother was following my suggestions." Emma laughed. "But, we'll get you to the bed. You've been up enough."

As they helped him to the bed, Emma looked at June. "Has Sheriff Vic been by?"

"He has. He wanted to make sure Edward was doing okay."

Edward squirmed trying to find a comfortable position. "Mother, he was making sure I was still in town, that's all."

His tone told Emma he was reverting to his bad attitude. June popped him lightly on his arm.

"Ouch, that hurts."

"No, it doesn't," she said, "but I can show you something that does."

Emma smiled, then fluffed a pillow behind his head and pulled a blanket over him.

"Thanks, Sis. I'm not sure Mother understands I have a hole in my side."

"Oh, I understand. I also understand why you have it there."

Edward shook his head, grimaced, then eased onto the pillow.

"We'll let you rest." Emma tucked the blanket, then turned to June. "I need to get my bag unpacked, then I might lie down for the rest of the afternoon. I think I'll go into the office and lie out there."

"I'll get your bag. You go rest."

Emma smiled. "Thank you, Mother, and thank you for taking care of Edward while I was gone."

She left the house and walked toward the office. Once inside she stretched out on the examining table and closed her eyes. "God, if you had anything to do with the birth of that baby and my helping it, thank you." She frowned. "Maybe that's not the right way to put it." She tried again. "Thank you for letting that baby and mother be alive today."

She smiled and eased off to sleep.

CHAPTER TWENTY-TWO

Douglas carefully slid his shirt sleeve off his right arm. He couldn't wait to lie down and rest. Going out to the Walker ranch took longer than he thought. He rode back into town in the dark but didn't have any problems. Now his entire body ached for rest.

The last few days had been stressful, but thank goodness his little niece had come into the world healthy. Before getting into bed, he slid the curtain back and looked at Emma's house. He wanted to check on Edward, but mostly he wanted to see her. The little kiss he'd given her this afternoon only made him want to be with her more, and she seemed receptive. All the way to the Walker's ranch and back he thought about her.

He wasn't sure how or when it had happened, but he cherished the time he spent with her. He loved watching her walk, listening to her talk and watching her smile brighten when she saw something new. She amazed him with her medical knowledge and with her eagerness to learn.

The lights in her house were out. He assumed everyone was asleep, or at least he hoped they were. Surely, they would not have tried to get the boy out of town. Naturally, they were worried about him, but helping him escape would only make matters worse for him.

He dropped the curtain and stretched. His bed invited him for some much needed sleep, but sleep was not in the cards tonight. As soon as he pulled his covers up, someone knocked on his office door.

Groaning, he dragged himself out of bed and pulled on his pants, lit a lantern, then went into the reception area. He expected to see a man with an animal standing on his porch, but as soon as he cracked open the door, someone jammed a gun barrel inches in his face.

"Get back in and close the door and you won't get hurt."

Douglas raised his hands and stepped inside. "Doing what you said." He tried to see the face behind the gun but the glare of the lantern obstructed his view. He moved back into the reception area and held the lantern out in front of him. His intruder wore a mask, but something about him looked familiar.

"This is a veterinarian's office. I don't keep a lot of money in here, but you can have it."

The man kicked the door closed. "I'm not interested in your money."

"Then what?"

"Shut up. Sit down."

Douglas did as the guy said and placed the lantern on the desk next to him.

The man stood in front of him shifting his weight from one foot to the other. He was nervous, the most dangerous kind of intruder.

Douglas held his hands up again. "Tell me what you want. Maybe I can help you."

"You can help alright." He pulled his mask off.

"Charlie? Is that you?"

"It's me, and I don't want trouble. I need your help."

Douglas relaxed for the first time. He put his hands down. "Tell me what you need, and I'll try my best to do it."

"I need you to save my brothers. I've been moving around town doing odd jobs here and there. No one remembers me. I've heard rumors that they plan to hang Sam and Cory and that other guy who joined us at the Thomas ranch."

"Yes, I heard you were there."

He pointed the gun back at Douglas. "Who told you I was at the ranch with them? Nobody knows I was there. Nobody saw me."

"I heard it in town. Who knows where they heard it. Maybe they just assumed you were there with your brothers. Now, tell me what happened that night."

He seemed to relax. "Sam and Cory had sent me ahead to make sure everything was clear. I was in the barn when you and that other man came flying in on your horses."

"Charlie, I know you love your brothers, but surely you realize they put your life at risk by sending you in first to keep them safe."

Charlie frowned and pointed the gun at him again. "You're wrong. My brothers love me."

"They might love you, but they love themselves more. Why didn't they send the new boy in?"

Charlie thought a minute. "They told me I was smarter than he was and older."

Douglas shook his head. "Go on. Tell me what you remember."

"I slipped around the house and peeked in the windows. Everything was quiet so I went into the barn. When I saw the two of you with your rifles drawn, I ran out the back of the barn and watched from the woods. I saw you shoot that kid."

"Yeah, I shot him after he shot me."

"I heard he's still alive."

Douglas nodded, his thoughts spinning in his head as he tried to figure out what Charlie thought he could do for his brothers. "Yes, you heard right. That boy is still alive. Now, tell me what you want me to do. I can't break your brothers out of jail if that's your no-brain scheme."

Charlie lowered the gun again. "They're keeping the jail

pretty well guarded. I guess they know my brothers are smart and would break out again so I know I can't get them out. That's why I want you to save them."

"I don't understand. I can't and I won't try to break them out."

Charlie raised his gun again and pointed it right in Douglas's face.

Douglas let out a big breath. "Would you put that gun down? I'm not going to hurt you."

Charlie nodded and lowered the gun. "You're not listening to me. I don't want you to break them out. The men in town want to know who hired us. I can tell you if you promise to use the information to keep them from hanging Sam and Cory. I don't care about that other kid."

"You might have a good plan." Douglas thought a minute. "I can try to help them. That's all I can do, but if you know the person behind all this trouble, you need to tell me."

"They'll hang me, too, if you turn me in."

"Not if you tell me who your bosses are. You would be invaluable in breaking this case."

Sweat rolled down Charlie's face. His lips quivered.

"Charlie, I don't want your brothers to hang either. I don't understand why they won't tell us who hired the three of you."

"They're scared. The man who hired us told Sam he'd find us and shoot us himself if we told anyone his name. If I tell you, you have to protect me, too."

Douglas blew out a big breath. "You're asking a lot, but I can do my best. I think the main issue here is finding the men or man behind this mess. Your brothers and you are not the ones who the men in town and on the ranches want."

As if Charlie gave up, his shoulders slumped, his arms relaxed, and the gun wobbled in his hand.

Douglas wanted to grab the gun, but he didn't move for fear he'd upset him again. "I know you're scared. I would be as well. The ranchers are up in arms because they're losing their livelihood. Were your brothers involved in the damning of the streams?"

"No, two ranchers did that."

"Ranchers? You mean landowners from here were damning the water and tearing down fences? I can't believe that."

Charlie stiffened up again and aimed the gun at Douglas's face. "I'm not lying." His voice was hoarse and loud. "I wouldn't lie about something like that. I heard him say we were too stupid to damn the streams."

Douglas didn't respond immediately even though he had a million questions. He waited for Charlie to settle down once more. When the boy seemed to relax again, Douglas took a chance.

"Did you see this man who called you stupid? Is he one of the ranchers?"

Charlie swallowed and nodded.

"Do you know his name?"

"Only his first name. I think it was Frank or Frankie."

"Could it have been Franklin?"

Charlie twisted his lips. "Yes. He was a big fellow with red hair."

"I know exactly who you're talking about. He's the one trying to get the townsmen to hang your brothers. I guess he thinks hanging them will guarantee they won't talk."

Charlie let the gun drop by his side. "Will you help my brothers and me?"

"Yes, I will. Now that I have this information, I can talk on your behalf and get the sheriff and his deputies to go out to Franklin's ranch and arrest him."

"And get my brothers out of jail?"

Douglas stood up.

Charlie grabbed his gun tighter.

Douglas held up his hands. "Wait. I said I'd help, and I will, but you and your brothers can't get off Scot free. I know you're not the ones in charge but you did a lot of damage recently and, let me refresh your memory, you held up the stagecoach."

"But we didn't get anything."

Douglas chuckled. "Only because we took you down before you got away. You and your brothers will be held accountable for those things as well as escaping from the escort deputies a couple weeks ago. I can almost guarantee the punishment won't be harsh since you're being cooperative."

Charlie walked in circles. He looked confused. "How do you know the town won't take us and hang us anyway?"

"Why would they do that? If you're cooperating, it's bound to keep them satisfied, especially if Franklin is behind bars. He's the one keeping everyone up in arms against your brothers."

Douglas gave him a moment to think about what he'd said.

"I know the sheriff is standing guard over the prisoners right now. Why don't we walk down to the office and talk with him."

Charlie aimed the gun at Douglas's head. "You must think I'm really stupid. I'm not going near that jail."

Douglas raised his hands. "Okay, I understand how you feel." He gave Charlie a moment to calm down. "Do you want me to go to the jail alone? I know what you want me to tell him. You could stay here or hide somewhere else until you see me come back."

Charlie's hands shook. The boy was scared to death. Douglas wanted to feel sorry for him, but he had to remind himself the trouble he and his brothers caused over the past few months. In fact, had it not been for their involvement with Franklin, Edward would not have been shot. Knowing he could've killed Emma's brother sent a wave of anger through him.

He pushed aside his feelings and tried again with Charlie. "I swear I'll protect you from the crowd of men wanting to hang somebody, but the sheriff has to be involved. I can't do it alone."

Finally, Charlie lowered the gun. "You go talk with the sheriff. I'll be close by." He raised the gun again. "Don't try anything sneaky. I have to know he'll help my brothers before I talk with him."

"I understand." He nodded toward the back room. "I need to get a shirt."

Charlie looked toward the back.

Douglas could almost hear the wheels turning in his head as he tried to decide. Finally, he nodded. "Get it, but I'm following and watching you. Don't you get a gun or I'll shoot first."

"I understand." Douglas headed toward his bed area, grabbed a shirt and slipped it on. His gun lay next to the bed. For a second, he considered reaching down and grabbing it, but then if Charlie shot him, there would be a good chance the brothers and Edward would hang, and Franklin would never be held accountable for his involvement.

After he buttoned the shirt, he raised his hands again. "I'm heading out the door. I'll be back as soon as I get the sheriff on board with your plan."

Charlie frowned. He gripped his gun. "I'll be someplace watching. You won't see me, but I'll be watching."

"I know you will. I'll come down the center of the street so you'll see me."

Charlie followed him to the door with his rifle stuck to his back.

When he got to the porch, Douglas turned to him. "Don't do anything stupid while I'm gone. You leave that other boy in the doc's office alone." Douglas swallowed and dug up a lie. "He'll probably die soon so you won't have to worry about being charged with his death."

"Good. I didn't like him anyway."

Douglas headed toward the street, not asking why he didn't like Edward. He had no idea how Charlie's plan would work out, but he'd try his best to get Vic to listen. Of course, he had a feeling Victor was going to laugh when he heard what he was about to tell him.

~

"You've got to be kidding." Victor pushed his chair back and stood up. "That boy must think we're all as stupid as his brothers." He looked at the cells.

Sam and Cory each had a cell. They appeared to be asleep.

"I understand exactly how you feel." Douglas kept his voice down. "I feel the same as you do. The only merit here is Charlie wants to help us catch the head men."

"Sure, he does if that information saves the lives of him and his brothers."

Douglas nodded. "Yes, but his testimony will help us put away Franklin and the bunch he has behind him. There's no telling what they're up to right now." Earlier he had told Victor about the men passing Emma on the road, and they both agreed Franklin and his cronies were probably in town.

"If they're here they might be planning to break out these boys and hang them. I guess I can go along with Charlie, but I'll need you to find my two deputies. Tell them to round up some help and then to get back over here. I don't know if you and I could hold off a gang of these men alone."

"I agree, but what about Charlie?"

"After you inform my guys, go back and talk with him. Tell him we need him to testify, and it will look good for him with the judge. I'll try to protect him, but I can't if he's out on the street alone."

"And Edward?"

"I think we can get the judge to be easy on him, but we need to get him locked up in here for his protection. Think you can get him over here by yourself?"

"I can try. I'll see what I can do." Douglas hated doing something that wasn't well planned, but at the moment he didn't have anything else to offer. "You'd better keep these doors locked and your guns loaded."

"No need to tell me that." He was already heading to the gun rack.

Douglas used the back door and hurried toward one of the deputy's home. After making him aware of what was going on, he hurried toward the main street to make sure Charlie saw him going back to his own office. His mind spun. Nothing about this plan seemed right. If Franklin and his men were actually in town, it would be difficult getting Charlie and Edward into the jail for their protection. He tried to devise several plans if Franklin surprised them before Vic and his men were ready, but nothing he came up with sounded reasonable.

As he turned down the alley, Charlie jumped out from behind a shrub.

"Charlie, it's a good thing my gun wasn't in my hand or you would've been dead."

"What did the sheriff say?"

"He agreed what you know will help you and your brothers, but he also said you need to come into the jail for your own protection. Those men running with Franklin are near town and there's no telling what they'll do. Your safety can't be guaranteed if you're on the street alone."

"He'll lock me up."

"Yes, for your protection."

Charlie put the gun down by his side, shaking his head. Douglas waited for the right moment. When Charlie turned his back to him, Douglas jumped him, yanked his hands behind his back, and took the gun away. He pushed him against a fence with the gun in his chest. "You're going to jail whether you want to or not. I can shoot you or you can walk, but one way or the other you're going."

Charlie's shoulders shook. He nodded as he turned and headed down the main street. Douglas followed close behind hoping Franklin and his men wouldn't show themselves before they made it to the jail. As soon as he got Charlie behind bars, he had to get Edward out of Emma's house for his safety as well.

But the big question remained: Would Emma and June let him take Edward to jail?

CHAPTER TWENTY-THREE

"No, Douglas, no." Emma stepped away from the door. "I can't allow you to put my brother in jail. Not now. He's still in pain and is very weak." Her heart raced.

"Exactly, Emma. If those men come to this house, there is no way you and June can keep him safe. They'd drag him out into the street before you knew what was happening."

Emma sat down. "I want to protect him, but not in jail."

Douglas put his hands on both of her arms. "Right now, jail is the safest place for him, not here."

June walked through the door. "I heard what you said, Dr. Fletcher. We can't allow you to drag our boy to jail."

Emma's heart went out to her mother. She went to her. "I know you want to protect him. I do, too, but we need to listen to Douglas."

Douglas walked up to the ladies. "Would you rather a gang of unruly men drag him to the nearest tree and hang him? That's what they'll do. The man leading the bunch wants Edward and the three brothers all dead because he's the one damning up streams and wanting the railroad to be diverted to his land. He's getting scared and he knows those men can point fingers at him."

"You know who it is?"

He nodded. "We feel sure it's Franklin, the guy with the red hair you saw on the road. Right now, Victor can't go out and arrest him. He has to protect the brothers in jail and Edward, and he doesn't have enough men to do both." He looked at Emma.

Emma's thoughts scattered in her head. Her face felt clammy. "Had they known I was the doctor and had Edward in my office, they might have done something to me."

"You're lucky they didn't know who you were."

"I don't want my brother in jail, but I want to protect him." She looked at June. "Mother, those men looked mean. We don't want to deal with them."

Douglas faced June. "Then let me take him to the jail where he'll be safer than here."

June sat down. Tears ran down her face.

Douglas took her hand. "June, please believe me when I say we want to protect Edward."

June nodded. "Promise me you won't let them hurt him."

"Ma'am, I'll do my best, but we really need to hurry."

Emma hated what she was about to say, but she knew Douglas was right. No way could she and her mother protect her brother here. "How can we help?"

"Convince your brother to go peacefully."

"We'll try. Come on, Mother. Edward knows you have his best interest at heart."

June wiped away the tears. Emma's heart broke for her, but she needed her help. "Please come help us." She offered her hand.

June finally took it. "I know God will help us do what's right."

"He will." Douglas smiled and helped her get up. "Your boy is not a bad man. God knows that."

Edward met them at the door. Bent over and holding his side, he stared at Douglas. "I'm not deaf. I heard everything."

"Then you know what has to be done. The jail is safer

for you than here."

Edward nodded. "I don't want to hang."

"If we can keep you out of the hands of the crowd, we can protect you, but as I told Emma and June, we can't do that in this house."

Edward took Emma's hand and pulled his mother into his arms. "I'm so sorry I've got the family in this mess."

Emma kissed his forehead. "We know, and we'll do our best to get you out of it, but right now we have to follow Douglas." She turned to her mother. "Would you help Edward get on some clothes? I'll be there in a minute."

June took Edward's arm and helped him into the room.

Emma turned to Douglas. "I'm putting my brother's life in your hands, but I trust you."

Douglas put his arms around her. She leaned into him and put her head on his chest. Closing her eyes, she wished they were alone somewhere other than here where her brother was being prepared to go to jail. "I don't want this to be happening. It's like a bad dream."

Douglas put his hand on her head and pressed her to him. "I know, and if I could change things, I would." He held her a few inches away from him and looked into her eyes. "You know that, don't you?"

"I do. I trust you with all my heart."

He bent down and kissed her on the lips. The kiss was warm and sweet. She returned the kiss and clung to him never wanting to leave the shelter of his arms.

He pulled away. "Thank you for trusting me."

June opened the door. "I need your help, Emma."

"I'm coming, Mother."

"I'll help." Douglas kissed her once more then stepped back. "We need to hurry."

~

Douglas struggled to keep Edward upright as they made their way down the sidewalk toward Victor's office. Emma helped as much as she could, but the boy could hardly walk.

"We're almost there, Edward." Douglas had his good arm around Edward, but the strain still pulled his right arm. "You need to keep moving."

"I'm trying." Edward's words were weak.

Douglas looked over Edward to Emma and smiled to give her hope, but he was afraid his gesture lacked encouragement. June kept up with them holding onto Emma's arm. He was glad they had convinced her not to stay in the house alone.

The streets of the town were empty. It was only a little after nine so most nights would have had quiet streets by now, but not this empty. An ominous feeling of impending danger swept over him. Nothing moved but the four of them on the sidewalk.

Douglas tried to stay in the darkness of the buildings, but he knew they were visible. He hoped he and Victor had gotten the situation wrong. Maybe Franklin and his men had gone someplace else, possibly harassing another ranch and were not in town. He could only hope.

They crossed a small alley and stepped up onto the sidewalk leading to the jail. Douglas heard loud talking coming from the saloon on the other side of the main street. He didn't like it. His gut told him to hurry.

Emma heard it, too, and without comment they each coaxed Edward to pick up speed.

Even though the shades were pulled in the sheriff's office, a thin ray of light shone through the side cracks. "Looks like Victor is up and waiting."

They dragged Edward to the front of the office. Douglas banged on the door. "Victor, it's Douglas. I've got Edward."

He heard footsteps on the wooden floor, but before the door opened, someone in the next block fired a shot.

The door flew open. "Hurry. Get him in."

Douglas shoved Edward inside the door into Victor's arms, then grabbed Emma and pushed her and her mother in. He slammed the door behind them.

Vic's deputy slid the locks.

Sam and Cory were now together in one cell. Charlie stood alone in the other.

"Step back, Charlie."

Charlie cooperated.

Victor, still holding Edward upright, got the key and unlocked the cell door, then dragged Edward toward the cot in the cell.

Footsteps and loud talking could be heard on the sidewalk.

Douglas made sure he had bullets in his gun. Victor and the deputy did the same.

Victor turned the main lantern off, then peeked out the side of the shade. "Franklin's in the middle of the crowd. That coward won't even lead the group."

"I think we need to talk with these men, Vic. Most of them are newcomers and have no idea what's going on. Franklin has only a few men working for him and causing damage. I'm not sure we can fight off that many."

"You're right. I had a feeling something bad was going to happen so I sent my other deputy to get a few men in town to help us. They're positioned on rooftops, I hope."

"I hope so, too!"

"I'll go and talk with these men. They need to know what Franklin's up to."

Douglas touched his arm. "You don't need to go. I can do this. You're the sheriff. The town needs you."

"You're not going out there alone."

Douglas nodded. "Then, we'll go together."

Emma stepped alongside Douglas. She put her hand on his arm, but didn't say anything.

He looked down at her. "I'll be okay. Most of these men are followers, not murderers."

"But it only takes one."

"I know." He kissed her on the forehead, not caring if anyone else saw his display of emotions.

He looked at Victor. "Come on, brother-in-law."

As soon as they opened the door, the crowd exploded in shouts.

Victor stepped out first.

Douglas followed, his heart racing. His hands gripped a rifle.

Victor held up his rifle over his head. Douglas kept his aimed into the crowd as Victor tried to get the crowd quiet.

Finally, he was able to be heard. "I know you ranchers and farmers have had problems with the men in my jail."

Shouts erupted again.

Victor held up his hands. "We want to end this nonsense as much as you do, but you have to listen to me and Douglas." Victor looked at Douglas.

"We've lost cattle on Fletcher ranch just as you have, but killing these men won't stop the problems."

Victor stepped up again. "We need to take down the head of these guys, not the little guy, and whether you'll believe me or not, we have evidence that he's standing in the midst of you."

All the men jerked their heads and stared at men standing by them, some aiming their guns in a circle.

Victor shouted. "Franklin Shaunessey is the man you want."

Douglas watched Franklin. As soon as Victor said his name, Franklin raised his gun and pointed at him, but Douglas was faster. He fired a shot, making sure he only grazed him.

Franklin fell to the ground. Douglas pushed his way into the crowd and grabbed Franklin's gun.

The crowd hushed.

Victor stepped forward. "Franklin has men who helped. You know who they are. I want to lock them up. We'll make sure they answer for what they've done."

The crowd turned on four men who immediately threw down their guns.

One man stepped forward. "What about the others in your jail?"

"They, too, will answer, but they are not the ones you have to worry about."

Douglas stood up. "This has gone too far. We want the trouble stopped. The railroad will come through here just as planned even though these men wanted to divert the route through land they wanted to take illegally. It won't happen." He hoped to hear agreement, but most of the men stood silent. "Believe me, the men you're holding along with Franklin are the ones you want and they'll pay for what they've done."

Several men shouted their agreement, then the rest joined in.

Douglas let out a huge breath. Relief washed over him. He looked down at Franklin. "You'll pay. I promise." He looked around. "Can I get someone to help drag this guy to the jail? The doctor is inside. She needs to tend to him."

Franklin screamed when they tried to move him, but Douglas knew his bullet had only grazed his right arm. He'd be okay. He could've easily hit him in the heart, but he had no intention of killing him. He didn't like violence, but that didn't mean he couldn't do what needed to be done if necessary. Disabling Franklin was enough.

As the men dragged Franklin and his men into the jail, Douglas looked up to heaven. *Thank you, God, for letting this end as it did.*

Had things happened differently, the night could've ended in a blood bath.

CHAPTER TWENTY-FOUR

Emma stood in the center of the jail listening to the din around her. The men in the overcrowded cells complained about their discomfort with Sam and Cory egging them on.

Franklin sat in one of the cots propped against the wall. The bullet had come out easily, but Franklin screamed as Emma dug for the bullet that sat just under the skin.

Since Charlie and Edward had each given them information about the men in the cells, Sheriff Vic took precautions and had Edward taken back to Emma's house and had let Charlie out on his word he would not leave town.

"I'm sure you're ready to get back to your house and get some sleep." Sheriff Vic walked up to Emma. "I want to thank you for helping out tonight and for agreeing to watch Edward at your house once again. I couldn't guarantee his safety here now that we have our cells full."

"He's my brother, Sheriff. I'll do anything to help him."

"I realize that, and I'm going to talk to the judge when he comes through town next week to see what we can do for him. Douglas said he'd put in a good word for him as well."

Emma blinked. "Douglas said that?"

"Yes ma'am. Even though the boy shot him, he said he believed he's a good kid."

"He is. He's had a hard life and got in with the wrong crowd. I'll thank Douglas for trying to help him."

She left the office. The morning sun had just spread its pinkish rays over the streets. She realized she'd been up all night and was exhausted, but in her heart she wanted to see Douglas. He'd left earlier to help get Edward out, and she assumed he'd be sound asleep by now.

As she neared her office, a smile broke out on her face. Douglas sat on her steps with his head leaning against the railing. He appeared asleep.

She tiptoed up the steps and sat next to him.

Douglas opened his eyes. "Am I dreaming or do I have a beautiful dark-haired lady sitting by me?"

"Not a dream, but after last night this lady looks a little ragged."

Douglas sat up and stretched.

How she'd love to rub his aching muscles. She dared not.

"Edward is back in your house. He's a little worse for wear so you need to check on him. I'm scared we opened that wound dragging him down the street last night."

"I hope not, but I'll certainly check on him." She needed to go in to examine her brother, but she didn't want to leave Douglas. She clasped her hands in her lap. "Thank you for all you did last night. I had horrible visions of men being shot and men hanging. You defused the situation. I was deathly afraid for Edward."

"I helped Sheriff Vic, that's all, but I'm certain he could've done it by himself."

"I'm not so sure about that. You're quite a calming, yet demanding figure when you want to be. Those men listened when you spoke."

"They were afraid of the gun, not me."

"Whatever it was, it worked." She looked at his strained, bloodshot eyes. "I also want to thank you for thinking about putting in a good word for Edward."

"I told you before. I tell the truth, and as far as I know

he's a good guy who needs a little guidance."

"He shot you."

"And I shot him back." He laughed. "I think we're even."

"I'm more grateful than you'll ever know for trying to help him."

A wagon rattled down the road. She pulled her gaze from Douglas and watched it pass. They both waved.

"That man is an early bird," she said.

"He has a farm not far from town. He'll do his business and be out by the time most of us are eating breakfast."

"Speaking of which, I'm sure you're hungry. Please let me fix you breakfast."

He sat up straight and smiled. "Best offer I've had in quite a while." He stood up then held out his hand to her.

She took it and stood up. "I'd like to go through the office so I can pick up some more bandages. I used the ones I brought on Franklin."

She opened the door, and they entered the dark room. She reached for the lantern, but he took her hand and turned her into him. Her breath caught in her throat.

"We don't need a light." His arms encircled her and she melted into his chest. His lips touched hers.

She kissed him back and heard herself groan.

He pulled away. "I've wanted to give you a proper kiss since last night in the sheriff's office. That little kiss made me think twice about going out to face that crowd."

"I was terrified for you. I'm not sure what I would've done had you been hurt."

He laughed once more. "You would've patched me up again."

"Yes, I would have, but it would not have been anything I wanted to do. You've been hurt enough, and we've had too many others hurt as well."

"You're right about that." He rubbed his hand along her arm. "Maybe things will settle down now that Franklin and his men are in jail."

"I hope so, but I'll feel much better after the judge comes through and they are in prison some place."

"We all will feel better when that happens, but right now I don't want to talk about Franklin. I'd rather kiss you."

"Hmmm, that sounds nice." She raised her face and relished the kiss he gave her. She heard herself sigh, then snuggled against his body. "I love being in your arms, Dr. Fletcher."

"Aah, I'm Dr. Fletcher now."

She could see his big smile from the thin ray of light coming in from the window. "I think maybe you earned that title."

"Maybe?"

"I might have to have you help me with more surgeries to make sure though."

"Does that mean you might stay in Independence?"

She tilted her head and smiled. "Oh yes."

~

Two weeks later on a Sunday morning Emma chose a dark brown dress with white lace around the sleeves and neck. The rest of the trunks from Boston finally arrived the day before, and she and June spent Saturday going through them. When she found this dress at the bottom of one of the trunks, she was glad she had not given it away as she'd done with most of her clothes bought with ill-gotten money. Now she was glad she had something nice to wear. The Fletcher family was coming into town to attend church and she wanted to look her best.

June came out of the bedroom area dressed in a different dress as well.

"Oh, Mother, you look so beautiful. Blue suits you."

"I'll take your compliment, but I haven't been beautiful for decades." June looked at the floor.

"Mother, are you blushing?"

June grinned. "I wanted to look nice for the Fletchers."

"I understand. I do, as well." Emma thought about June's

blushing. "Mother, do you think just the family will be coming in, or maybe some of their ranch hands?"

"I have no way of knowing until they get here."

"Of course, you wouldn't." She bit her lip to keep from smiling. "It would be nice if Mason came in with the family. The way Douglas talks about him, he's part of their family so there might be a good chance."

Again, June looked down at the floor and smiled.

"Nice man that Mr. Mason. I didn't get to talk with him a lot when I was at the ranch, so I hope he comes along today. I'd like to get to know him better."

Emma smiled and hoped Mason came into town for her mother. Sunday would be wonderful having Mason for her mother and Douglas coming in with the family. With all her heart she hoped they invited her and her mother to sit with them. When was the last time she had someone special sit by her in church?

If she were honest with herself, it was never.

David went with her to church a few times at the beginning of their marriage, but after that she went with her mother and Edward. Even her father would not go regularly, and when he did, Emma always felt he was being hypocritical.

Today might be different.

"Let's hurry, Mother, but let's not forget the pudding you made for the picnic afterwards. My stomach is growling just thinking about it."

June stepped next to her. Tears filled her eyes. "Emma, this move has been wonderful. I haven't felt as safe and as loved as I do here. I can't wait to see some of the ladies at church. I've made some good friends."

Emma gave her a hug. "I'm glad we moved here as well." She swallowed and pushed back unexpected tears. "Let's go see if Edward needs help dressing."

"I'm glad he can go with us. It's time for him to talk to God about his life. Like Douglas said, he's a good boy. He just needs a little help right now."

Emma knew that the town of Independence would be the place for Edward to turn his life around. She hoped he would not have to go to prison.

Before they walked into the bedroom, someone knocked at the front door.

"I'll get it. You go help Edward."

She hurried to the door, excited that Douglas would probably be standing on the porch. The past two weeks had been busy for both her and Douglas, and they had very little time to spend together. Today she looked forward to being with him.

When she opened the door, her breath caught in her throat. Douglas stood on the porch wearing a white shirt and a light brown jacket. She held onto the door. "Come in, Douglas. We're almost ready. Mother is helping Edward right now."

He took off his hat and held it in front of his body. "You look beautiful." He looked as if he wanted to say more, but didn't.

"You don't look so bad yourself." She regained her composure and laughed. "Please, come in."

As he stepped through the doorway, he reached out and took her hand, squeezed it, then quickly let it go.

She took a deep breath. She wanted to go to church with him and his family, but how she'd love to sit here all day and hold his hand and taste his sweet kisses.

Straightening her shoulders, she walked next to him and led him to the back. "I'm thrilled Edward is able to go with us. He has truly gotten stronger this past week."

"That's great." He grinned. "He had a good doctor."

June opened the door as Emma reached for the knob. "Good morning, Dr. Fletcher. We're all ready, Emma." She looked back into the bedroom. "Edward, let's not hold up the Fletcher family."

"Mrs. O'Hara, you look lovely today. I don't think I've

ever seen the dresses you and Emma are wearing."

"Our other trunks arrived, and we've had such a wonderful time unpacking."

"The other ladies at church will be envious of your seamstress back on the east coast."

Edward stepped to the door and nodded to Douglas.

"Glad to see you up, Edward."

Edward stood but still stooped over slightly. "Not as much as I am. I'm tired of being in that bed."

"I have the carriage so you won't have to walk."

"I appreciate that." He hesitated. "Do you think the townspeople will accept me at church since I worked with Franklin's men?"

Emma had wondered the same thing though she hadn't spoken it.

Douglas nodded. "The people who go to this church are good people. They believe in giving everyone a second chance. I've seen them do it many times. We won't know how they'll treat you until you show up, but by joining them in worship, I think they'll understand you're ready to mend your ways." He shrugged his shoulders. "That's only my opinion, of course, but they've welcomed Emma and June so I think they'll welcome you."

"I hope so."

Douglas stepped back so Edward could pass into the front room. Emma was glad the two men could be cordial, even though they'd shot each other. That concept still made her head spin when she thought about what could have happened. Now she was ready to see how the townspeople treated her brother.

Emma grabbed a shawl, and Douglas stepped next to her and helped drape it over her shoulders. She looked back and smiled.

Douglas followed June and Edward out the front door and around the office, then helped them into the back seat of the carriage. Emma carried the bowl of pudding, placed it on the floor of the carriage, then waited for Douglas to help her into the front seat.

Sitting next to Douglas on a beautiful Sunday morning heading to church made her feel as she'd never felt before. Except for sharing kisses, Douglas had never said anything about how he felt about her. How she would love to know if he had feelings for her because if she were true to herself, she knew she had strong feelings for him.

He sat quietly on his side of the seat leading Sunflower slowly toward the church. What was he thinking? His face showed no emotion except for nodding to several people walking toward the church. She hoped he wasn't sorry he'd asked her and her family to attend services with his family. If the fellow church goers refused to accept Edward, would it reflect on the Fletcher family? Could he be considering the consequences of his befriending Edward? She pulled in a big breath and hoped her brother was accepted.

As they pulled to the side of the church, Douglas finally turned and smiled at her. "Let me help June and Edward down, then I'll help you."

She watched him be the gentleman he normally was. He took June's arm and led her and Edward toward the small crowd in front of the church. Abigail, holding William's hand and Lucas, holding baby Emma, walked toward them. Mason followed behind them.

Emma smiled. Her day would be complete having Mason with her mother. Several people walked up to them, one lady giving June a hug, then extended her hand to Edward.

Relief washed over her. *Thank you, God. Thank you.*

Douglas walked back to the carriage. "Your turn." He stood by her side of the carriage and held out his hand.

"Should we leave the food for the luncheon here in the carriage?"

He nodded. "That will work. It's cool today so nothing will spoil."

She clasped her small purse and reached for his hand. "Thank you," she said as she leaned into his body. He held her for a brief moment and looked directly into her eyes. She had the feeling he wanted to kiss her. Her knees went weak.

"Be careful," he said as he lifted her to the ground and broke the mood.

He helped her get her balance, then stepped back, his face serious. "We'd better get into church before we have to stand in the back."

His mood changed so rapidly she was startled. She blinked. "Certainly."

Maybe she'd read him wrong. Maybe he didn't want to kiss her. Could it be he didn't want to be here with her at all?

She smiled at different people as she passed them going into the church. Lucas nodded to them from his pew. They took their seats next to them. Caroline and Matthew sat in the pew behind them. She sat next to Abigail, gave her a hug, then they whispered about the baby.

Douglas sat on the end of the pew, spoke to several people, but mostly he was quiet.

Again, Emma worried she had done something or said something that made him act differently today. Maybe he had reservations about bringing Edward here. He had said the congregation believed in giving second chances. Did he really believe that or was he trying to make her family feel good?

Preacher Smith talked about the importance of families and how everyone here was part of the town's family. She hoped he was right. How she wanted the town to accept Edward as part of them. She listened, but glanced at Douglas periodically. His mind seemed miles away.

After service she followed everyone out to the tables lined under three trees. Luckily the weather cooperated so everyone could enjoy the outdoors. She hoped she could push aside the trepidation she felt and could enjoy the luncheon.

Young boys immediately ran into an open field to play ball. Little girls took their dolls in the grove of trees behind the tables. Toddlers sat on blankets with their families as they ate. Some curled up on the blankets and slept.

Emma loved the atmosphere and relished being part of this small community. A sense of belonging washed over her.

Preacher Smith walked around the group talking to each family. Emma was thrilled to see Molly walking alongside him. They made a nice-looking couple, and she wished them both well.

She helped the ladies uncover food and place the platters and bowls along the table. Everyone brought their own plates and utensils so she helped Abigail and Mrs. Fletcher set theirs out for their family. Finally, Preacher Smith asked everyone to stand for the food to be blessed.

Emma stood next to Abigail and held her hand. Douglas ran up at the last moment and held Matthew's hand at the very end of the table. She wished he would've gotten to the table earlier so she could hold his hand, but that didn't happen.

Maybe he'd planned it that way.

The way he'd been acting since they'd gotten in the wagon, she thought maybe the latter option was right.

She took a big breath, closed her eyes and listened to Preacher Smith bless the food. Afterwards, she joined the Fletcher family as they walked along the tables sampling the dishes, then sat with them to enjoy the food. She spoke to Preacher Smith and Molly, then realized Douglas was not among the family members. She refused to be sad on this gorgeous Sunday morning, but if she were honest with herself, she knew she'd rather be home in her house alone so she could shed tears.

Was she already losing Douglas? She squeezed her eyes. They actually did not have a relationship. They had shared kisses many times, but obviously he had not put as much meaning in them as she had. It had been a long time since she had been courted. Maybe men today kissed all the girls with no meaning behind the gesture.

"Can we sit here?" Mason had walked up to her area of the blanket with June close at his side.

"Certainly. I'd love to sit by you two." She scooted over a little to allow them both to sit. "Tell me what's happening at the ranch, Mason."

Mason talked about the ranch getting the cattle ready for the summer months, but as he talked, he was attentive to June. He held her plate as she sat on the blanket, then kept looking at her to make sure she had everything she needed.

Emma loved the way he took care of her mother. It would be a perfect day had Douglas not acted differently and then disappeared. For the entire dinner she forced a smile for her mother's sake. She ate, but didn't taste the food. How could she? Her beautiful Sunday had not turned into anything she had expected.

Douglas stayed away from the family for the entire time they ate. Afterwards, she helped scrape the food from the plates into a big tin that someone took for the dogs in town, then she took the stack to the stream along with the other women.

By the time everyone had packed their belongings back into carriages and wagons, some families left, others lay on blankets and rested before heading out.

Still Douglas did not show.

Finally, she gathered her things and told her mother she thought Edward needed to be home so he could rest.

"Oh, Emma, please stay. It's such a beautiful day."

"I know. I want you and Mason to enjoy it. I think Edward has been up enough. He needs to lie down."

"Don't blame your misery on me," said Edward as he walked to her side. "I know why you're miserable and it's not my fault."

Emma gave him a soft hit on the arm. "You know

nothing, little brother."

"I know more than you think, but come on, I'll play the invalid and let you lead me to my bed." He laughed.

They made their way down the street, talking to several people who also headed to their homes. By the time they stepped up on the porch steps, Edward leaned on her.

"I guess you knew what you were talking about. I do need to lie down. I'm whooped."

"I'm proud of you, Edward. That's the longest you've been out of bed since you've been wounded."

"And I feel it, but I'm glad I went. No one made me feel unwelcomed even though I'm sure they knew why I was wounded."

"I think being with Douglas helped. If he could forgive you, they should as well."

He stopped walking and took her hand. "Emma, give Douglas a chance. I'm not sure what's going on between you two, but I'd like to see it work out."

"Thank you." She looked down at the floor. "I really thought we were getting along great, but today, he wasn't himself. I'm not sure what's going on, but if he wants me to know I'm sure he'll tell me. If not. . ." She just shrugged.

She helped him into bed, kissed him on the forehead, and smiled as he closed his eyes and seemed to be asleep immediately.

She closed the bedroom door, then walked out onto her tiny porch and sat on the top step. Closing her eyes, she inhaled the warm spring air and leaned against the railing.

"Can I join you?" Douglas walked around the corner of the office.

Startled, she sat up straight. "Yes, please." She couldn't believe he was actually at her house after not being with the family after church. What should she expect from him? Would he still be in his standoff mood?

He placed one foot on the bottom step. "I'm so sorry I missed the luncheon. I know the food must've been fabulous. It always is."

"It was very good." She looked down. "I wondered why you weren't there."

"I had to take care of some business."

"On a Sunday?" The words came out much too sharp, but she didn't apologize.

"Yes, even on this Sunday."

She swallowed, not knowing how to respond.

He pushed away from the post and stepped right up to her. "The stage brought me a package yesterday, but I wasn't in town to get it. I had to find someone from the post office to open up, and we dug through the boxes in the back to find it."

"That couldn't wait until tomorrow?"

He chuckled. "Yes, I guess it could have, but I didn't want to wait." He reached inside his jacket and pulled out a small box. "I ordered this, and I wanted you to have it today." He stumbled over his words. "I'm hoping you'll take it."

Her hand went to her chest. "You ordered a gift for me?" Now she felt terrible questioning him and sounding like a shrew.

He nodded. "I hope you'll accept it." He shuffled his feet.

Why was he nervous? "I'm confused. Why wouldn't I accept a gift from you?"

He pushed out a huge breath. "It's not just a little trinket." He stood up straight and swallowed. "I'm trying to ask you to marry me, Emma O'Hara." He flipped open the box that held a beautiful ring sitting on pink fabric. "This may not be the most romantic way of doing this, but I didn't know how else to do it."

Emma's breath caught in her throat. "You want to marry me?"

"Of course, I do."

She stared at the ring, then up at him. "I'm shocked. You don't really know me, Douglas."

He shook his head. "Of course, I know you. You're the most interesting woman I've ever met. You're brilliant. You're caring, gentle, and selfless."

She smiled. "You called me aggravating and confusing not too long ago."

Douglas laughed. "That, too." He took her hands. "I've come to care a lot about you. I love you, Emma. I do. I'm not sure when it happened, but somewhere between our arguing, disagreeing and aggravating each other, I realized I wanted to be with you always. When I wasn't with you, I couldn't stop thinking about you. I don't think I've ever felt this way before."

She still hadn't taken the ring or given him an answer. Her insides tingled. "Not even with Lily?"

Douglas grew pensive. "I've thought about that a lot lately. I loved being with her. Maybe I just needed someone to be close to me and help me get through my time away." He knelt down by her side. He still held the ring in one hand, but he took one of her hands with the other one. "I never had feelings for Lily like I have for you. I know we've never talked about the way we feel. I hope I haven't read more into our time together than you have." He squeezed her hand gently. "You'll make me the happiest man in the world if you'll tell me you want to be my wife."

Tears flooded Emma's eyes. She nodded. "I do love you, Douglas. I do." She still didn't take the ring or hold out her hand for him to put it on her finger.

"I sense a 'but' coming."

"I do love you, but I'm scared."

Douglas let out a big breath. "I'm not David, nor your father. I won't make your life miserable as the other men in your past did. There won't be any shady dealings going on in our lives. Everything will be out in the open. You're a doctor. I'm a veterinarian. We could have a good life here in Independence for our practices, and we could build a nice home on our family land. I want you in that family."

Finally, she touched the ring. "It's beautiful."
"Will you wear it, and one day be my wife?"
She nodded.
Douglas blinked. "Really?"
Now in spite of the tears, Emma laughed. "Yes. Really."

CHAPTER TWENTY-FIVE

Warm summer air surrounded Emma as she sat on a swing hanging from one of the huge walnut trees facing what would be their new home. Where had the time gone? How could it be a year since she and Douglas married and a month since their baby boy had been born.

She looked at the carriage next to the swing where baby Oliver slept. Every day she thanked God for letting her have a healthy baby. After losing two babies in her former marriage, she worried constantly about having a normal birth, but with Carmella's help, she gave birth in the Fletcher home where numerous other babies had been born.

She closed her eyes and inhaled.

"Did you fall asleep?" Douglas walked up to the swing and sat next to her. "I hated to wake you, but I have good news and bad news."

Emma sat up straight. "Oh no. Give me the bad news first."

"I talked with Matthew at the house. He's leaving this afternoon to catch a stagecoach tomorrow morning in town."

"What? Where is he going?"

"He got word his adoptive father is out of prison. He's been at Jefferson City, but they've let him out because he's old and not in good health. Matthew is torn about going to see him, but he told me he's been living with hate too long. He has to see him and try to forgive him for killing the only mother he remembers."

"He's a good boy. Not many of us could do that."

"To make a decision like that tells me he's not a boy anymore. I'm going to miss him on the ranch. He's been an asset since he's been here with the family."

"We'll pray his father has changed and will accept Matthew."

"Yes, we will." He took a deep breath. "Now I'm excited to show you the good news. Do you feel like walking up to the house with me?"

"Always."

Douglas started to get up, but she touched his arm. "Do you know how happy I am?"

He raised an eyebrow. "A lot, I hope."

She laughed. "More than 'a lot.' You've given me more than I could ever imagine."

"Even without the theaters and shopping and modern conveniences from the big city?"

"Those things don't matter. They're just things." She waved her arm in front of her. "This is what is important. This land. This new home. Our child."

"Our love?"

"Definitely our love."

He pulled her in an embrace and held her tightly. "I'm so glad you feel that way because I feel the same. I didn't know anyone could be as happy as I am right now." He leaned toward her and kissed her.

Little Oliver let out a cry.

She laughed.

"Those kisses will have to wait."

Douglas got up and lifted the baby into his arms. "What's the problem, little fellow?" The baby snuggled against his shirt. "I think we're spoiling him."

"I know. Isn't it fun?" She got up. "Let's go see our new home."

"I had the men change a few things. I hope you don't mind, but I think we needed another bedroom. This little boy needs several brothers and sisters."

Happiness spread through her body. "I like that." She placed her hand through his bent arm, and they walked toward the house. "I want a big family." She looked down the hill where Mason and her mother now lived. "I can see them running down to see their grandparents."

"And their Uncle Edward. He likes the idea of building close to here. We have enough land for everyone. He seems to be catching on about how to be a rancher. I think he'll be a good one."

She stopped walking and looked up into his eyes. "Who knew life could be so good after the rough start we had?"

Douglas chuckled. "Not me. I kept thinking of ways to avoid you in town."

"Douglas, really?"

"Yep, but then I always managed to find you."

"I'm glad you didn't stop looking, Dr. Fletcher."

"Me, too, Dr. O'Hara."

"Oh no. You have that all wrong. It's now Dr. Fletcher. Remember, you married the old Dr. O'Hara."

He laughed, then cradled the baby against him. "You're right. Best move I ever made. Let's go show little Oliver his room and where his brothers and sisters will live."

With a spring in her step and a smile on her face, she walked side by side with her husband and baby. Looking up at the clear blue sky, she sent a silent thank you.

How did she ever doubt He listened to her?

Her prayers had been answered. Her life was complete.

She squeezed Douglas's arm.

"Ouch. That hurt."

"That was a love pinch."

"Then pinch me all you want. Remind me that all this is

not a dream."

"No dream, Douglas. This is real. This is our life."

THE END

If you liked reading THE HEALING WAY, try the first book in this FLETCHER RANCH SERIES, THE WAY HOME. Abigail Cook never fit into the life of her prominent Boston family. When vicious lies surround her broken engagement, she endures a grueling stagecoach ride to Independence, Missouri, to start a new life. What she finds is nothing she expects. She accepts a job as a governess at a ranch where she meets Lucas, A handsome widower whose life is in as much turmoil as hers. After losing his first wife, Lucas turned away from God and from living. Can Abigail show him the path to accept faith once again and to open his heart to love?

The Way Home

LOOK for the third book in this series, LOVE FINDS A WAY, and follow the story of Caroline and Matthew.

ABOUT THE AUTHOR

 Fran McNabb, author of traditional, clean romances, recently moved to Louisiana with her husband of over 50 years. Even though she lived most of her life along the Mississippi Gulf Coast near the islands and the water, she feels she has come full circle since her father was born in south Louisiana. Visit her at www.FranMcNabb.com or Facebook at Fran L. McNabb or Fran McNabb, Author.

Follow me on Amazon

Other books by Fran McNabb
The Way Home
Paradise Lane
Return to Paradise
Paradise Found
Gulf Coast Romances